QUESTIONABLE ETHICS

BOOK ONE

A MEL ADDISON MYSTERY

A NOVEL

BY

ANGELA ABDERHALDEN

Seventh Wave Books, LLC

Questionable Ethics

Seventh Wave Books, LLC
2012

Seventh Wave Books, LLC
www.seventhwavebooks.com

First Paperback Edition: 2012

Questionable Ethics: a novel/ by Angela Abderhalden.

ISBN: 978-1-938852-01-5 (pbk)

Cover design by Jason Wilcox

Printed in the United States of America

ANGELA ABDERHALDEN

CHAPTER 1

I didn't want to be the next one to die. But here I was, staring down the barrel of a gun. And it was my first day at work.

"Hey! Are you listening to me?"

My eyes snapped to the face behind the gun, and I found myself thinking, *This can't happen in here in Quincy, Illinois. We're such a small town!*

"I said, I wanna talk to Rich!" The gunman repeated.

Rich? Who? My thoughts were slower than cold oatmeal. Oh yeah, my brother. I was working for him. "Rich, uh, Rich isn't here." I blinked a couple of times, trying to clear my mind.

"Call him!" The man's voice held a note of desperation. As I dialed and held the ringing phone, I decided that this was too scary and I never wanted it to happen again.

Rich's voice mail answered. "Rich, call the office now!" I set the phone down with shaky hands, wondering what the gunman was going to do.

He had barged into the office with a determined, angry stride. His eyes were wide and glassed-over, and I wondered if he was high. The gun came out before I could even open my mouth to greet him. After the gun, everything blanked out.

Now I saw that his mop of black, greasy hair looked like he hadn't combed it in days. His jeans and T-shirt were wrinkled, food-smudged and untidy. He was clearly a man who didn't want to wait for anything.

I needed to get some control over this situation. My life depended on it. "Look sir, Rich will call back any second now. I know he will. I won't do anything, I promise. I don't want to get shot."

The man nodded at me. "Okay. Don't do anythin'."

"Why don't you sit down?" He hesitated and glanced over his shoulder.

The reception area of the office was small, containing only the front desk with one chair in front of it, a couch on the side wall, and a small refrigerator. The large plate glass window looked out over the street.

I was desperately hoping that someone, anyone, passing by would see us and call the cops, but I couldn't hang all my hopes on that.

The guy took two steps backward and then sat down on the edge of the couch. The gun was still out and pointing at me.

"Who are you anyway? Where's Pam?" he asked. He licked his lips again and ran a hand through his tangled hair.

"Pam's on maternity leave. I'm just filling in until she gets back. I'm Mel Addison."

The man stopped combing his hair with his fingers and scratched his scalp. "Rich's little sister?" His tone wasn't quite as desperate.

I managed a weak smile for him. He no longer seemed quite as threatening. "That's me."

"I thought you lived in Maryland." He adjusted the grip on his gun.

"I did. I moved back." *This is good, get a rapport going.* "What's your name? So I can tell Rich when he calls."

"Eddie Baker. He knows me." Eddie relaxed a little more.

I studied the gun for the first time. It was a Hi-Power Browning nine millimeter. Single-action. The hammer needed to be cocked in order to fire the gun, if I remembered correctly, and it wasn't. Plus, the safety was on.

"Call again." Without hesitation, I did. Still no answer. Eddie tugged at his T-shirt and he licked his lips again.

A plan popped into my head. "Eddie?" I waited until his eyes rolled around and met mine. "You look thirsty. Can I get you a soda or something while we wait for Rich to call? The fridge is right there." I pointed. "I promise, I won't do anything. I don't want to get shot."

Eddie's eyes lingered on the fridge as he licked his lips again. "Okay, but go slow."

I moved to the fridge as though I was walking through water, and grabbed Rich's coke with my left hand, leaving my dominant right hand free. As I turned back, I studied Eddie's position on the couch. *I can do this.*

"See?" I held out the bottle as I approached. One more step. Eddie focused on the bottle.

I passed his outstretched hand. The bottle connected with the gun, pushing the barrel away from me. I pivoted, hooking my right arm around Eddie. My momentum threw both of us to the floor; a modified hip throw. We went down in a heap, with me on top. The gun clattered to the middle of the room.

Now that I had the upper hand, I needed to keep it. I grabbed his thumbs and slammed him into the floor again. Eddie swore as he hit.

This is not good. Eddie not only outweighed me, but I knew he could easily out-muscle me if we stayed this way for more than a couple of seconds. He struggled under me. This would be over too quickly, ending with me dead, an impulsive, stupid corpse.

I immediately switched holds on him, going for a choke hold. At this point, I didn't care if Eddie lived or died; it was him or me. He clawed at my arms around his neck, frantic. I grimaced, tightening my hold. *Come on!* His body arched beneath me in what had to be a last-ditch effort. After what seemed like hours, Eddie collapsed, a deadweight in my arms. I released my hold on him and took several deep breaths in relief. My arms ached.

As I looked at him, lying there motionless, it suddenly hit me. *What have I done? What if I had killed Eddie?* It was certainly possible. My heart seemed to stop. I felt for a pulse on his neck. *Please don't let him be dead.* I had never done anything like this before, never used any of my judo training anywhere except in the dojo. A nice, steady beat thumped under my fingers. *Thank God!*

I untwined our bodies, pushing Eddie away from me. As I sat there on the floor next to my assailant, catching my breath, I thought about what a stupid thing I had done. This feeling wasn't anything new. It was déjà vu from my teen years, but I hadn't felt this way in a long time. My life had been so routine since leaving home, until six months ago. When a careless truck driver took my only son and husband from me. Nothing was the same since. Then I felt the tears welling in my eyes. For these last six months, I had been on a roller coaster of emotions, never knowing when I would cry, get angry, or be depressed.

I narrowed my eyes even as I wiped the tears away. I stepped over Eddie, then kicked the gun under the desk as I headed for the phone to call the police. As I grabbed the receiver, it rang.

"Yeah?"

"'Yeah?' You're supposed to answer it, 'Security Investigations,' Mel. You called?"

Rich. Anger surged in me. Zero to sixty miles per hour in a nanosecond. My anger is legendary. I think it's gotten better as I've gotten older, but most people would probably disagree with me. "Yeah, I called! You leave me all alone here, this guy barges in!" I spluttered in a high-pitched voice.

"What the…?" Rich interrupted, obviously confused by my tone.

I took a deep breath to calm myself. "'Just a piece of cake', you said. 'Answer some phones, run the computer.'"

He chuckled. "Did a problem crop up?"

"You might say so. A man walked in here and pointed a gun at me. I was just calling the police."

"Are you okay? Is he still there?"

"I'm fine. His name is Eddie Baker."

"Eddie? What would he-Is he still there?"

"Yeah. He's unconscious on the floor," I said, and took a deep breath to calm myself. "Let me call you back after I call the po-"

"No. Don't call the police, Mel. Eddie's not a bad guy. I want to-Just wait on calling the cops. I'll be there in five minutes or less. Are you sure you're okay?"

I took a deep breath. I trusted Rich. I had to; he was my oldest brother. "Yeah, okay, I'll wait for you. But I have to say, this is one heck of a way to start a new job."

"Ha, ha, Mel. Are you sure he's unconscious so he can't hurt you?"

"Of course. Just get here before he wakes up or I might do permanent damage."

"If it looks like he's waking up, hightail it out of there. Got it?"

"Yeah."

"I'm on my way."

I waited for Rich to show up, staring at Eddie on the floor, my thoughts wandering. Finally, Rich scurried into the room. He took a look at Eddie, then me. Then he smiled. Brothers can be so annoying. "Are you sure that you're okay?"

"I'm fine. Who is he?" I asked. I interlaced my shaking hands to calm them, and leaned my elbows on the desk.

"He's an old informant. I have no idea what he wants. Did he say anything to you?"

"Just that he wanted to talk to you or John. He might have been on something." I shrugged. "His gun is under here." I gingerly scooted the gun out with my foot.

Rich picked it up and unloaded it. He smiled once more at me. "How'd you do it?"

I told him, a little pride sneaking in. Now that Eddie couldn't hurt me, I felt pretty good about my plan.

Rich nodded in approval. "Guess that money wasn't poorly spent like Mom used to think."

I chuckled and relaxed. Mom hadn't wanted me to take judo lessons when I was a kid or later when I was married. It just wasn't the ladylike thing to do but I never did do anything ladylike when I was younger. I was always the tomboy, unlike my older sister Teresa. "I also used the move that you taught me when I was still in high school, you know, that thumb-hold thing."

"I'm impressed that you still remembered it Mel," Rich said. "How long has he been out?"

"About five minutes. He should be coming around anytime now," I said, studying Eddie.

Rich sighed as he sat in the chair in front of Pam's desk. "Eddie used to give me information when I was still on the force. He's an okay guy. Maybe a little shady at times, does a little coke. He works at a manufacturing plant on the other side of town. I wonder why he threatened you with a gun. Why does he even have one?"

Just then, Eddie groaned, then slowly opened his eyes. He looked around and saw the two of us watching him. He slowly lifted his head.

"Hi Eddie. I see you've met Mel. I don't like my little sister being threatened. You've got some explaining to do." Rich's face was stern.

Eddie glanced at me, then back at Rich. "Sorry. Can I get up, Rich?"

"Are you going to behave?"

"Yeah." Eddie looked at me with new respect.

"Get up. Sit on the couch." Rich watched him closely. After Eddie sat, Rich pointed at him. "Talk."

Eddie stared at me for just a second, rubbing his neck, then turned his attention back to Rich. "My brother Wally was shot dead three days ago. Didja know that?" Rich nodded with a serious look on his face. "Then the next day I get a call from a man sayin' that I need to return 'it.' I hang up on him, 'cause I don't gotta clue what he's talkin' about. That night my car's windows get shot out with me in it."

Rich frowned. "Did you call the police?"

Eddie nodded. "Nothin' came of it. Then last night I get home from work, and these guys are in my house. When I walk in, they start shootin' at me. I barely got outta there alive. I head to my car and they shoot it up worse than before. So I took off runnin'. Been runnin' all night. Every time I settle down somewhere, they seem to find me. I gotta piece to protect myself. I didn't know where else to go, Rich." Finally he looked at me. "Sorry about the gun. I didn't know you and I guess I'm runnin' on low over here."

I waved that it was okay, even though I was still unnerved by the incident.

Rich was watching him. "What do you want from me?"

"Help."

"How?"

"I need to find out who these guys are and what they're after." Rich looked down at the floor. "Look, I can't really pay you, but I'll do my best to come up with somethin' and ya know I'm good for future information and stuff." Eddie sounded desperate. "I'll make payments or something. Please! I need help."

Rich looked up at him. "Okay, Eddie. We'll work something out." My brother glanced at me. "Do you want to press charges, Mel?"

I studied Eddie. "Are you going to pull a gun on me again?"

"No, ma'am," Eddie said sheepishly.

"Then no, I won't press charges." I smiled at Eddie. "Sorry about choking you."

"That's okay, Mel. I understand." Eddie smiled back, then looked at Rich.

Rich nodded. "Come on, Eddie. Come into my office and we'll see what can be done."

CHAPTER 2

As Rich and Eddie left the detective agency, I waved at them, then turned my attention back to web surfing for information on various people they were investigating. It took me the rest of the day, mostly because I was struggling with getting used to the various programs.

At the end of the day, I locked up the office after pulling the shades down and making sure everything was secure. I paused in front of the office to take in the late afternoon sunlight.

Quincy, Illinois hadn't changed much in the ten years since I called it home. Although it had grown a lot, it still had that small hometown feel to it, a sense that everyone knew everyone. Quincy was on an upswing, but it was still a podunk town in the middle of nowhere. Quincy is sometimes referred to as the belly button of Illinois. When asked about the city, I mention Hannibal, Missouri, and Mark Twain. We're upstream about fifteen miles. Nothing exciting happens here. Still, it's home. Again.

I hopped into my parent's Taurus and headed home. I was temporarily living in an apartment they owned. I hated being so dependent on them.

Dickie, my dad, is a retired cop, and he now runs a bar close to the house, the Full Moon. It's heavy on family atmosphere in the daytime. At night, half the police force can be found there. Beside my dad, two of my brothers are cops: Rich, retired due to an accident he suffered while on the job, and Mitch, currently a patrolman.

Then there are the firefighters who like to show up too. I also have a brother in that department, Cameron, and two cousins. Many nights at the bar it's a big competition between the cops and the firefighters: darts, pool, cards. One time they even had a competition for who could carry a railroad tie the farthest. It probably doesn't help that Cam is part-owner of the bar; he and Dad are always egging on the friction between the two forces.

My apartment is a small two-bedroom place above the bar. I took the outside steps up to my apartment and let myself into the relative cool. August in Illinois is a hot and very muggy affair, sort of like swimming in thick chicken soup. Dropping my purse, I looked around the kitchen for something to eat. Nothing looked good. I sniffed. A savory smell drifted into my apartment, making my mouth water. *Dad must be cooking tenderloins in the kitchen downstairs.* I smiled, realizing that was just what I wanted.

I locked up my apartment and headed downstairs to grab a sandwich. Dad probably would sucker me into waiting tables or tending bar if they were busy. Since I didn't know what I was going to do with my life, again, I had accepted the odd job here and there. First the bar and now with Rich.

I walked into the Full Moon and wandered into the back, where Dad was cooking on the grill. He smiled in greeting.

"I heard you had some excitement at Rich's today."

I nodded as I grabbed a fry that had fallen on the counter. "Tenderloins?" I pointed to the fry basket.

"Yep."

"Where's Mom?"

"Church meeting." Dad swung his head out the door to check on his patrons. "Can I get you to help here tonight until things calm down a bit?"

"Sure. I didn't have any plans anyway."

He leaned over and gave me a kiss on the cheek. "Doing okay?"

"Yeah." Tears crowded my eyes, but I refused to let them spill. I swallowed hard. "The nights are the hardest, but I'm okay."

"Have you heard from the lawyers in Maryland about your lawsuit?"

"No, not recently." I stuck my hands in my pockets as I looked at the bubbling oil in the fryer. "Look Dad, I really don't …" I glanced at him, hoping he would drop the subject.

He stopped working and looked at me, his blue eyes full of love. He gave me a quick hug, then he stared into my eyes. "Do you want to talk about it, Sweetie?"

"No." I swallowed down a lump. Dad only called me 'Sweetie' when something bad happened.

"I know you don't like to talk about emotional stuff. You're kind of like me in that respect." His smile was soft and gentle. "But that's my job."

"I know. But I'm fine. Thanks."

"Sure." There was skepticism in his voice. "If you want to talk, you know where I live."

I smiled, thankful that he'd dropped it for now. "I'll go help Cam." I grabbed an apron from the hooks near the door.

I slipped by several men and slid behind the bar. "Hey Cam, the cavalry is here. Where do you need the help?"

He turned from making change and smiled in relief. "Can you bus the tables first? Then do the waitress thing for awhile?"

9

"Sure." I exchanged greetings with a couple of regular customers and headed to the back for the square plastic bus box to gather up glasses, plates, and trash. Within minutes, the tables were cleared and I was working the room for orders.

"Hey, Mel!"

I turned to the raised voice from a far table. There were only a dozen tables in the bar and this group was a bunch of police officers. I smiled and worked my way over to them. "Yeah, Butch?"

He was an older guy with gray touches at the temples, and less than a year before mandatory retirement. "Last time I saw you, you were a blond." I grimaced. I had experimented with being blond for about two weeks over a year ago.

Butch chuckled. "Brown suits you better. Can't tell you're an Addison without the brown hair and blue eyes. Anyway, how about a refill on the pitchers, since you're playing waitress?"

I shifted the weight on my hip. "Why should I? You're one of the lousiest tippers in the whole town." Everyone at the table laughed at him.

Butch smiled and wagged his finger. "Be good, or I'll tell everyone about the time I found you in the Blairs' back yard, holding an impromptu swim party while they were on vacation."

"Everyone already knows that story, Butch. And again, let me thank you for telling my dad. I was grounded for four weeks, thanks to you." I grinned. This was an on-going joke with us. "What can I get you guys?"

A younger guy spoke up. "Bud." His face was new.

"I don't know you. Let me see some ID." The group at the table laughed even harder. They began teasing the 'rookie'. He took the ribbing with a natural grace and ease.

"What's your name?" I asked him.

"Why?" He had short brown hair and intense blue eyes. His smile was genuine as he gazed up at me.

Steve Wettle, another cop at the table, leaned over and in a mock-conspiratorial whisper said, "Hey man, she's one of us. Mel is okay, in a best-friend's-little-sister kind of way."

"Little sister?"

"Okay." Steve grinned. "More like one of the guys but softer." He lifted his eyebrows suggestively.

"You wish," I sneered. The guys at the table laughed at Steve as he stood and moved to the bar with a chuckle.

I turned my attention back to the new guy. "I don't serve anyone I don't know," I said evenly. "If I don't know you, you have to get your own beers." I gave him a mocking smile.

Steve's voice interrupted us, quieting the entire bar instantly. "Check out the news." Cam turned the TV up louder.

"Marion Williams, the Republican candidate for mayor, has announced that, should he get elected, he will raise the pay of city workers with at least a cost-of-living increase. He'd like to see an across-the-board pay raise for the police officers and firefighters who protect this town with their lives."

A cheer went up from those assembled, mostly city workers.

"Quiet!" Steve silenced the crowd.

The reporter continued, "Mayor Schnabel couldn't be reached for comment but his chief publicity agent, Tom Bressler... " I stopped listening when a picture of a man dressed sharply in a blue suit appeared on the screen.

"Tommy?" I whispered to myself, then chuckled. *Who'd have thought someone I would never have taken home to Mom and Dad would be in such a powerful position now?*

"... But the constraint of the city council put an end to the proposal put forward by Mayor Schnabel. Bressler assures us that the mayor is not going to give up his fight to fairly compensate the police, fire, and city workers. I'm Cindy Singleton. WGEM news... "

The immediate muttering around the bar was that both men were out-and-out liars. I shook my head at the thought of my old friend and his job.

"My name is Max Bauer."

I snapped my attention back down to the lopsided smile of the rookie. His blue eyes were shining bright in the fluorescent lighting of the bar. He held out his hand.

We shook and when I touched his hand, I felt a warm rush of feeling. *Weird.* His grip was light yet strong. "I'm Melissa Addison. Call me Mel."

"Addison? Are you related to Mitch?"

"She's related to everyone," Butch interjected with a chuckle.

"Mitch is my older brother," I explained. I gathered up the three empty pitchers. "Who's buying?"

In unison, they all said, "Max." I smiled and moved off to the bar. Cam was busy, so I put the three dirty pitchers in the sink, grabbed some clean ones, and drew the beer.

After I sat them back on the table, he handed me the money. "Keep the change," Max said. I could feel his eyes burning into my back as I walked away.

The night went by quickly and things started to slow down. I was just getting ready to call it a night, when I felt a body move in next to me. It was the new cop, Max.

"Hey," he said, putting the empty pitchers on the bar top. He looked at me. "We missed our waitress. I thought once you knew me, I wouldn't have to get my own beers."

I smiled. "I only do the waitress thing when Cam and Dad are busy." Dad had long ago closed down the grill and was now serving behind the bar with Cam. "So, I haven't seen you before."

Max nodded. "I'm new to the area. Just took the job. Nice town." His blue eyes lingered on mine.

"How long have you been here?"

"Three weeks."

"Where are you from?"

He gave me a startled look. "Is this some sort of interrogation, Mel?"

I shrugged. "I like to know the men in blue, in case I should ever need to call on any of you."

"California. Breakers Point on the coast." He leaned on the bar facing me.

I was puzzled. "So, what brought you to Quincy?" He shrugged. "It must be the tremendous pay rate."

He laughed. He had a really nice laugh, deep and vibrant. "Steve Wettle knew I was looking to leave the coast and sent me an email. I met Steve in college." He smiled. "Just a change of pace, for awhile."

"Well, Quincy has one of the fastest paces around," I said with sarcasm.

He laughed again. "I take it you've lived other places too."

I nodded as I drained my bottle. Dad walked by and, without a hitch in his stride, set another beer in front of me. He winked as he moved further down the bar.

With a quick twist of my wrist, the bottle cap came off. I noticed that Max was watching me. I gave him a smile and with a flick of the hand, tossed the bottle cap into the trashcan behind the bar at the end.

He chuckled. "That's an impressive distance. Do you do that a lot?"

"Practice. And it's just hand-eye coordination. I play a lot of darts." I nodded toward the three steel dartboards hanging on the wall and took another bite of my sandwich.

"Are those things any good?" He dipped his chin at it.

I nodded. "One of the good things about Quincy."

"Really?"

"Yep."

Suddenly there was a hand grabbing me around my waist, a soft voice in my ear. "Hey WT, wanna go for a ride?"

I grimaced, setting down my sandwich. I recognized that voice. It was a former date who just happened to be on the force, and it sounded like he was already two sheets to the wind. I turned slightly. "Hi, Frank. I think you've had plenty."

A drunken laugh echoed in my ear. Frank's hands squeezed my waist, then migrated upwards.

Anger burst inside of me. I grabbed his thumb and with a quick move, twisted around on the bar stool. Standing, I turned him at the same time, pushing his arm up and behind his back. Then I slammed him to the ground. He jerked a couple of times and I ground my knee into the small of his back.

The bar went silent for the second time that night. Everyone was staring at us. I was breathing hard. Anger does that to me.

"Uh, Mel," I heard my father's voice. "Calm down. Do you have a problem here?"

I took a deep breath. "No problem, Dad. Just Frank and his fast fingers. I think he's had enough and maybe someone ought to take him home or call a cab for him." I looked up to see everyone still staring at me. My eyes locked with my father's. I could see that he was assessing things and trying to defuse the situation.

"Sure, Sweetie… Uh, Mel, you want to let him up?" Everyone in the bar laughed and went back to their conversations. I released Frank, and two other cops helped him to his feet. They patted him on the back, hustling him out to one of their cars. As Frank left, he looked at me and I gave him a finger wave to show that I had no hard feelings.

I brushed my hands off. Twice in one day now I had used Rich's thumb-hold. Several men in the place called out to me good-naturedly and I smiled at them. When I turned, I found Max still leaning on the bar watching me with a very amused look on his face.

Dad was moving down the bar toward me. His eyes were, however, watching the path taken by Frank. He moved nearer to us as I sat down again. "Maybe I should have a talk with Frank tomorrow."

"Dad, you know Frank. Let it go."

Dad shook his head.

"Let it go. He probably won't remember in the morning anyway. It's history. No harm done."

Dad just stared at me. I knew that look. I'd gotten it lots of times in my youth. It was the 'You needed to be more careful' look. "But-" he began.

"Don't go there."

He held up his hands, resignation on his face. This was not a new thing for us. "Okay, okay. You can take care of yourself. It's history." Dad walked away shaking his head, as usual. He muttered to himself.

Max looked between my dad and me, perplexed. However, when his gaze returned to me, he smiled. "Good move on Frank, Mel." I laughed softly, taking a drink of my beer. "I take it you know him." Max's blue eyes were shining with amusement.

"Yeah, I dated Frank for awhile a long time ago. When he drinks, he forgets that it was a long time ago. I think some of the guys egg him on just to see how fast I can knock him to the floor. It's happened before."

Max laughed. "Where did you learn that move?" He held up his thumb and wiggled it.

"From Rich, my oldest brother. He used to be on the force until about two years ago. Took a bullet in the line of duty. Now he runs a detective agency here in town."

He just looked at me, his eyes burning into my soul. "You got fast moves."

"Judo. I took lessons as a kid. Then before I moved back to Quincy, I got my black belt." I lowered my voice and looked at the beer bottle on the bar. Sometimes life was just so hard.

Max touched my arm. "I'm sorry. I didn't mean to stir up any bad memories."

I nodded, not really looking at him. I could feel my emotional roller coaster starting again. *I need to get out of here.* "Not a problem." I swigged down most of the rest of the bottle. "I gotta be going anyway."

Cameron walked by just then.

"Cam, get one to go?" I handed him the nearly empty bottle and he replaced it with a cold one.

My little brother smiled. "Thanks for the help, Mel."

I winked and stood up from the stool.

Max caught my arm, giving me a strange look. "He shouldn't let you go with it. You can't drive with an open beer."

"I'm not driving." I pointed up to the ceiling. "I live upstairs. Nice to meet you, Max." I walked out the door to the back of the building.

After locking my door, I stripped off my clothes and cranked up the air conditioning. I hopped in the shower, and when I emerged, I found that the temperature had only slightly cooled in the apartment. I rummaged around in a box for a pair of shorts, located a T-shirt in another one, and sat on the bed looking at the room.

The bedroom was cluttered with unpacked boxes from the move. I really needed to get a dresser from somewhere. I didn't know where to start unpacking, so I went to the kitchen.

The kitchen was somewhat organized. There were no boxes in there, and it looked like I had actually moved in. I walked back out to the living room and looked over the vast number of eclectic CDs crowded in a box. The only thing set up in here was the stereo system.

What did I feel like? I ran my finger over the CDs and finally decided on a somber classical piece. A dark Dvorak symphony keyed up as I walked into the small second bedroom. This one was packed floor-to-ceiling with boxes. I leaned against the door frame. I knew I had to go through them, but I couldn't move as the music washed over me.

After a couple of tracks, I reluctantly pushed myself away from the frame, picked up the nearest box and headed to the living room. I set it on the coffee table.

A smell wafted up and hit me. Craig's cologne. Tears swelled in my eyes and I quickly closed the box; I hadn't expected this. As the tears flowed down my face, I slowly opened it up again. I had to do this-I had to figure out where everything was. My family had packed my entire house for me, and now I felt lost, confused. I didn't know where anything but the essentials were.

This box contained legal documents and file folders, probably from Craig's desk at home, judging by the bottle of cologne and the necktie that had been thrown on top. I quickly scanned through the files and placed them on the coffee table to go through later when I was a bit more coherent. Under the files, I found his business-card holder. I picked up one of his business cards. Craig Blakemore of 'Landry, Blakemore, and Brooks'.

Why Craig? You never did answer me. What were you thinking, you rat bastard? I crumpled the card and threw it against the wall. My eyes drifted down to the box again, hoping to find something else I could throw, something that I could destroy, but instead my eyes lit upon a small frame with a drawing in it.

I gently picked it up and tears slid down my face unchecked. Robbie had drawn this for Craig on my husband's birthday, four months before the accident. I hugged the frame to my chest, heaving out sobs. Leaning back on the couch, I cried for my son, and cradled the picture until I could cry no more.

Setting it on the couch next to me, I wiped at my tears again, replaced the files and card holder, and closed the box. I grabbed the black marker on the table and wrote, 'Craig's office stuff.'. Then I walked it over to the other boxes in the room and set it on the pile.

Time for bed. I lay down and prayed for sleep tonight. I couldn't cry anymore, but the ache in my heart was an open, festering sore. I curled my hands around the frame, and finally, at some point, fell asleep.

CHAPTER 3

I hit the alarm clock with an angry swat. *How could it already be seven o'clock?* I breathed out a huge sigh and flung the sheet off me. As I stood, my right leg gave a twinge before almost dumping me to the floor. I grabbed the bed and held on until the leg was ready for some weight.

It was getting better as I exercised it, but I still couldn't count on it yet, a constant reminder of the car accident. After I could walk, I dressed, grabbed a bagel, and headed down to Security Investigations, the private detective agency my brother Rich owned with John Huddleston.

John was hard to pin down. In contrast to Rich, who was of average size at best, John still had the cut and build from his Army Rangers Special Forces training. He also still had the quiet, 'don't mess with me' attitude. I had met him several times at family gatherings, and liked him, but he was away on business and I hadn't seen him since I moved back.

As I neared the office in downtown Quincy, I saw a large number of flashing lights. Hurriedly I parked near the office and ran down to see what the commotion was all about. Since my younger days, I've always been a siren chaser. I guess it comes from having so many family members in emergency services. And I'm morbidly curious, I have to admit.

I got nearer and realized that the commotion was from Rich's office. I hurriedly pushed my way through the crowd and saw that there were four squad cars, along with two fire trucks lined up in front of the office. The firefighters were going in and out of the building. I ducked under the tape placed on the sidewalk, and looked around to pick out the cop in charge of the scene. It was Butch.

"Hey, Butch, what's going on?"

He turned and grimaced. "Hi Mel. Where's Rich?"

I shrugged. "He told me to open the office this morning." I looked though the front window. Someone had not only trashed the place, but had apparently tried to set it on fire. "What happened?"

"We got a call from one of the neighbors who was walking by. Looks like they broke in the front door here." Butch pointed at the mangled lock on the door. "Jeremy, the fire marshal, is inside determining what was used to set it. I tried Rich at home, but Gloria said he left real early this morning, around five."

"Probably doing surveillance," I told him. "Did the fire damage all the offices?"

Butch shook his head. "Mostly just the front room. It's not too bad even in there, a little water and smoke damage. The other offices were just ransacked. We need to find out if anything was taken."

"If I can get in Rich's office, I might be able to access his files to see where he's doing surveillance. Did you try his cell phone?"

Butch nodded again. "And I left a page for him." He looked inside. "Let me go talk to Jeremy and see if I can get you in yet. Wait here."

I tried Rich on my cell phone. No answer. Finally, Butch came out and motioned for me to follow him. We moved through the slightly waterlogged front room to the small corridor that lead to the offices. There were files and paperwork strewn everywhere. I sat down at Rich's computer and punched in a couple of commands to see if Rich had entered his smart phone info onto the main computer. He hadn't.

As we were leaving the office building, we heard Rich cursing as he walked up. The two men moved inside to confer with Jeremy. I sighed and found a place to sit nearby on the curb to wait.

Why had someone done this? Rich had assured me last week when he asked me to play secretary that this job would be a snoozer. *Ha! It was anything but a snoozer.* Eddie sticking a gun in my face and now this break-in. I glanced around and greeted a couple of firefighters as they passed.

One of their boots caught my attention, with its yellow sole and yellow stripe running up the front, and a triangular symbol on the side, right below the straps. I flashed back to six months ago. Pinned in my crushed car; a fireman's boot as he stood on the hood while they tried to cut us out. My heart rate increased. I gasped for a breath. *How had I survived? Craig and Robbie hadn't. Why was I allowed to live?* Tears welled up as I remembered picking Robbie up from school, his last words to me, his last day alive.

"Mel… Are you okay?"

I snapped my head up, as I swallowed back the tears. I blinked a couple of times, trying to figure out where I was. It only took a second but it felt longer. "Yeah, I'm fine." I answered automatically, staring up at a blue suit, bright white shirt, blue paisley tie.

Max was standing in front of me with a concerned look on his face. Then he smiled a slightly lopsided grin. "I saw you sitting there looking… lost. Then I heard you sniffle."

"I might be catching a cold." I glanced back toward the office to collect myself. "What are you doing here?"

Max shrugged. "I was passing by... " He stopped and grinned again. "That's a lie. I heard the call and wanted to make sure that you were okay." He looked into the office, then he glanced around the street.

I followed suit. The area was slowly clearing of spectators. There were only two police cars left, and one of the fire trucks was leaving too. "What happened?"

"I haven't a clue. I just arrived a few minutes ago." I looked up at him.

Max nodded, then shifted his weight from one foot to another, sticking both hands into his pockets. He glanced around again, then focused back on me. "Hey, I was wondering Mel... " His cell phone rang, interrupting him. He pulled it off his belt and looked at the number. "Just a minute... Bauer speaking."

I tuned his conversation out but took a better look at him. He looked very comfortable in his tailor-made clothes, even though he had to be hot in the coat. Max Bauer definitely had style. Even the frown that crossed his face didn't dampen the handsome look.

"Okay, I'll grab the kit and meet you there... Sure. Bye." Max closed his phone; his eyes focused somewhere else for a second. "Sorry, I have to go."

I nodded in understanding. Considering my family, my conversations were often interrupted by a phone call as well as my outings with friends. "What did you want?"

"Uh... " Again, Max seemed nervous, but now the phone call had distracted him. "Later. I'll talk to you later. Okay? Take care, Mel." He gave me a slight smile and moved off at a jog.

"Sure." I called to him. I turned my gaze into the office to see Butch leaving. I waved as he headed down the street, also in a hurry. I stood and walked into the office. "Hey."

"I wondered where you got off to." Rich smiled.

The office looked better already. There had been a faint smoke smell earlier, but the big blowers of the fire department had cleared out most of that. The computer in the front room was trashed however. "Where do you want me to start?"

"What?"

"It needs to be cleaned up, right? Where do you want me to start? By the way, this is such a snoozer of a job." My voice dripped with sarcasm.

Rich jerked his head up and looked at me, then he chuckled. "There's never a dull moment with you around. I've always thought that adventure follows you."

"Only in my younger years."

"True. Being married kills that kind of... " I could feel the smile flee my face. Our eyes met. "Oh, I'm sorry, Mel."

I waved it away but my gut twisted in knots and my heart suddenly started hurting again. I shuffled my feet, then looked back at him.

Rich's blue eyes had a sad look too. I could tell he was sorry he had said that. Rich had been walking on eggshells around me, like the rest of my family.

I gave him slight smile. "It's okay, really."

"I didn't mean… what I mean is… it slipped out."

"Stop it, Rich. Craig is dead. You can say his name. I'm not going to crumble on you."

Rich held my eyes for a heart beat then nodded. He glanced at his watch. "I have to get back on surveillance."

"What are you doing and where?"

"I suppose I should be letting someone know, besides John. I'm doing surveillance on a guy who is trying to defraud an insurance company. Fidelity Insurance hired us to take pictures and follow him to determine if he is as badly injured as he claims." Rich rubbed his eyes. "Makes for some really long hours without John taking a shift. Hey, you used to be pretty good with a camera. Want to take a shift for me?"

"Can I? Is that legal?"

"You're an employee. Just don't represent yourself as a detective. Look, I'll be back in the afternoon and give you all the details." Rich looked around the office. "Don't worry too much here. I can hire a cleaning company to come in. I straightened my office and I'll let John do his when he gets back. That way we'll know if anything is missing. If you would though, finish with the files I gave you yesterday. Use my office and computer."

I nodded.

"Thanks, Mel. I really appreciate this."

"Sure."

He caught my gaze. "Are you sure that you're okay?"

I gave him my most reassuring smile. "Get going."

Rich left quickly. I stared at the messy room. Cleaning would certainly keep me from dwelling on my situation. I grabbed some garbage bags out of the bathroom and began cleaning up the place as best I could.

Three hours later, the door dinged and I left Rich's office to see a uniformed cop standing in the middle of the office, looking down and smirking. When he looked up, I saw that it was Mitch.

"Hey." He nodded at me.

"Hey."

"I heard you had some excitement here. Again." Mitch's eyes were twinkling.

I motioned him to follow me into Rich's office. Mitch and I were really close, always had been since childhood. We even hung out together in high school; we're only eleven months apart age-wise. He dated my friends and I dated his.

"I take it Rich isn't here?"

"Nope. Surveillance on a fraud case."

Mitch frowned. "I need to talk to you too."

"Why?" Then I added jokingly, "Official business?"

Mitch's gaze caught mine. There was something ominous in his blue eyes. Bad news. Very bad news. "Eddie Baker is dead."

I gasped.

Mitch nodded. "He was found five hours ago."

I squeezed my fist shut under the desk and held on. I was not going to cry. I swallowed hard and cleared my throat. "How … How did he die?"

Mitch stared at me. "Sorry. You okay, WT?"

I nodded, still squeezing my hand hard, my nails beginning to dig in. "It's just a shock. I mean, Eddie was here yesterday."

"I heard. Rich agreed to help him, right?"

"Yeah." I hesitated. "How did he die?"

"Nine millimeter to the head. You didn't hear that." Mitch gave me a serious look. "Are you sure that you're okay? I can ask you about this later." I shook my head. "He pulled a gun on you?"

"Yeah."

"Lovely." He scribbled in his notebook. Finally, he looked up. "Tell Rich to call me." Mitch stood and headed to the front office.

"Okay," I said as I followed him, still trying hard to ignore the hollow feeling in my stomach.

Mitch's face brightened as he turned at the front door. "Hey, some guys are going skiing on the river on Saturday. Want to join us?"

"I don't know. My right leg still bothers me. And I haven't skied in a long time, Mitch."

"It's just like riding a bike." He smiled and gave me a hug. "Just let me know, 'kay?"

"I'll think about it."

Mitch gave me another hug and a peck on the cheek, and then he disappeared out the door with a tap to my shoulder. It was his way of telling me that he was there for me. I moved back to Rich's office to work on the computer files. But I couldn't work. I sat there thinking about Eddie and the day before. Eventually I gave in, laid my head on Rich's desk, and sobbed.

***

Rich showed up at four and, after talking with Mitch on the phone for several minutes about Eddie, he went over the case he was working on with me.

Charles Lamprey was suing a company for an injury he got on the job. The problem was the insurance company was pretty sure he was faking the injuries. He was on total disability and supposedly could barely walk. Reports from his doctor said that he had chronic back problems. Rich's job was to gather evidence to prove Lamprey's case was invalid. Rich gave me a still camera and a video camera. He handed me Lamprey's file, which contained all the important information on him.

"You did a good job on the front office, Mel. Thanks."

"I was bored. I'd work on the computer for a while then clean for awhile. You'll probably need to get the carpet replaced."

Rich nodded. "Go ahead and leave early if you want to. This'll probably be a bust for you. Lamprey has stuck to his story."

"Is he really badly injured?"

Rich shrugged. "My gut is telling me no, he's faking it, but so far there has been no evidence to support my feelings or those of the insurance investigator. I'll come around and relieve you at around ten. If that's okay?" I nodded. "All he's done is stay at home, so there shouldn't be anything happening. I'll have my cell phone with me if anything comes up."

"Sure, Rich."

I was locking up the office at four-thirty when a nervous woman walked up to me. I looked at her closely. The lady was about my age, maybe twenty-eight or nine. It was hard to tell with her ratty hair and disheveled look. Maybe she was homeless; it sort of looked that way. She was scanning all around, like she didn't want to be out in the open. "Can I help you?"

"Rich. Lookin' for Rich."

"He's not here. Can I do something for you?"

"Uh, yeah, I guess." She seemed to look closer at me. "Aren't you Mel Addison?"

"Yeah." I had been gone for ten years. How did everyone still recognize me? Of course in a town like Quincy, I shouldn't have expected anything less, but I had grown used to the anonymity of Annapolis, Maryland.

"Can you give something to Rich for me?"

"Sure. Sorry, I'm bad with names. How do I know you?" I studied her again. She was thin, almost too thin, and she was wearing badly faded jeans with a ripped T-shirt. Her fingernails were bitten to the quick. That, coupled with her nervousness, made me think she was on drugs.

"They call me Mouse. You probably don't recognize me." She pulled a rumpled envelope from her back pocket with a smile. "Long time ago, I heard about you. You were sort of a legend around places." Her grin grew. "Anyway, this is for Rich."

I took the item, still watching her. "Okay. A legend? Where?" Mouse just shook her head. "You seem troubled. Do you need help or something, Mouse?"

"No. Just need to get goin'."

"How can Rich reach you, if he needs to?" I glanced down at the envelope. There was nothing on the outside, and it was sealed. There was something inside. Round.

"I can't be gotten. I'm leaving, for good. I was told to tell Rich that he'll know what to do with it." Mouse pointed at the envelope in my hand. She moved away, then turned slightly and gave me a little grin. "Thanks. Glad I gotta meet you, Mel."

"Sure," I said and watched her disappear around the corner. I looked down at the envelope again, then put it in my camera bag. *A legend?* I had done a lot of stupid things in my teenage years but nothing that qualified as 'legendary'. I chuckled to myself and continued on my way. *I'll give it to Rich when he relieves me.* I dismissed the incident from my mind.

Nothing happened at Lamprey's house until around eight o'clock. Lamprey came hobbling out on his crutches, in full back and neck braces. I grabbed the camera. Sighting with the telephoto lens, I watched as he slowly made his way down the steps to his car that was parked on the street. *How is Lamprey allowed to drive like this?*

Charles Lamprey, in his mid-twenties, with black hair, seemed to be a sort of body builder, cut and well-developed; even I appreciated a great-looking man like him. This supposed 'accident' must have happened recently because he was still in great shape. I panned with the camera as he hobbled to his car.

He grimaced as he unlocked the door and with what seemed like a great deal of pain, slid into it. He sat there for a few minutes then slowly moved out of his car, looking around. I hoped I was far enough away that he wouldn't be able to tell what I was doing.

He took his time, eyes pausing on each car near him and every house on the block. I slouched down in my seat. When I sat up, he was studying the cars on the other side of the street. I brought the camera back up as he closed the car door.

"Interesting," I said softly.

Lamprey gave one last look around, then with a smile, he walked back toward his house; the crutches were still in the car and his struggling gait was gone. I snapped pictures, following him all the way to the house, then switched over to the video camera.

When he came back out, this time at a run, he had a small box in hand. I waited until he started his car before I started mine. I didn't know how much evidence Rich needed, but I decided to follow him and acquire more, just for the fun of it.

Lamprey pulled away from the curb. I followed, grabbing my cell phone. Rich didn't answer my call. Big surprise. I left a message and paged him too. I tried his home number. No answer either. "I'll have my cell phone with me," I mimicked my brother's voice to myself. "Liar."

Lamprey stopped at a fast-food place, then traveled across town to a small house. When he got out of the car he was struggling to walk once more. I shot more pictures. Lamprey disappeared into the house with a key.

Now my curiosity got the better of me. I wondered who owned the house and what Lamprey was doing. Rich hadn't mentioned anything about this. *Hmmm.* I tapped my fingers on the wheel, then slipped out of the car. Without another thought, I strolled past the house, video camera in hand.

The shades were all drawn, so I couldn't see in any windows on the front of the house. I did a quick scan, noticing the tall fence on both sides, then hurried around the back into a deserted alley. Only a small, waist-high fence was blocking the back view. I crept up to see some people swimming in one of those above-ground pools, but Lamprey wasn't with them. I ducked back behind the neighbor's taller fence.

I peeked out, turned the video camera on, and began filming, just in case. Three people swam in the pool while I watched on the camera's screen. Two women and one man were splashing each other and having a good old time. I was just getting ready to turn the video off when the door opened and Lamprey walked out, looking like he'd just come off a swim suit catalog page. He wore a tight Speedo, and his back brace and limp were gone. I smiled as I continued to videotape them. Lamprey walked over to the pool, grasped the edge, and jumped over it without using the ladder. *Injured, hah!*

There was no way Lambert could talk his way out of this one. I could just imagine Rich's face when he saw the tape. I continued to film, barely able to contain my glee. Then I gasped, almost unable to suppress the chuckle bubbling up. Four swimsuits flung out of the pool. The couples were kissing passionately. Within a couple of minutes, Lamprey and his girl exited the pool to find a place on the grass. The show continued as I filmed it.

My cell phone rang. My heart stopped. I had forgotten to turn it off. I fumbled to switch it off while still trying to keep the video pointed at the yard.

By the time I had turned the phone off, Lamprey was gaping at me in outrage. He stood and started advancing toward me. I continued to film him, even as I backed away.

He shouted, "Hey, you little pervert. You wanna see something-" And started running toward me, looking like he planned to jump the small fence. "Come here! I'll show you… "

I stopped filming and took off running down the alley as fast as my injured leg could carry me. I could hear him still yelling and cursing. I turned and pointed the camera back at him.

He stopped and picked up a brick, throwing it at me. I ducked as it sailed over my head. He stood naked in the alley tossing bricks at me while I filmed it. I waved and smiled. He started to run toward me again, so I hightailed it back to my car.

I drove away still smiling, even as my leg throbbed; apparently I wasn't ready for running yet. I checked my phone, to see who had interrupted our fun. It was Rich.

"You called?" he said.

"Oh yeah, Rich. You owe me big-time for this one."

"Did something happen?"

I started laughing. "How about Lamprey leaping over the side of a pool and getting busy on the ground?"

Rich joined me in laughing. "On video? Please tell me you got it on video."

"Absolutely."

"That's great. Bring it over to my place and I'll take a look."

"Uh, I don't think you really want the kids seeing this." I laughed some more. I could imagine Gloria's face if she saw the tape that I had just made.

"It's okay. Gloria is gone with the kids. This is great. Bring it over."

I closed the cell phone and laughed all the way to Rich's house.

***

It was nearing ten o'clock that night when I pulled into the lot behind the bar and stopped in to say hi to Dad. The bar was mostly empty: a couple of regulars and two cops. Wednesdays are a slow day in the bar. Dad was reading the paper and looked up as I walked in. He smiled. "How's it going?"

"Pretty good." I snickered, remembering Rich's laughter as he had viewed the tape. Between the pictures that I had taken of Lamprey and the video, Rich was sure that the insurance company would also be very happy.

Dad's smile got bigger. "Really?"

I nodded . "I was helping Rich with an insurance fraud case and caught the guy doing things that proved he wasn't injured including 'getting busy' in the grass."

Dad laughed. "I bet Rich loved that."

"Oh yeah."

Dad's smiling face turned serious and he leaned over the bar. "We'd like you to come to dinner tomorrow night at home."

I just stared at the bar top. "I don't know. I think I'll just spend it alone, if you don't mind. I won't be very good company."

"You shouldn't be alone, especially tomorrow. Just think about it, Sweetie." He patted my arm.

I tried to smile for him. "Sure. I'll think about it." I glanced at my watch to change the subject. "Guess I should head up to bed. Did you hear about Rich's office?"

Dad nodded. "Yeah. Jeremy was in." Jeremy, the fire marshal, was Dad's close friend. "He said that they used gas and after wrecking the place tried to burn it to the ground, but that they did a poor job of it." Dad shook his head. "Stupid criminals. Anyway, call us if you need anything or just want to talk."

"I know. Thanks." I walked out the door and headed upstairs. Leaning on the counter in my kitchen, I looked toward the second bedroom door. I sighed. *Can I tackle another box tonight?* I shook my head and decided to hit the sack.

I shucked off my clothes, flopping into bed. Rolling over, I stared at Robbie's drawing in the moonlight coming in from the window. My eyes began to water again. I gently reached out and touched the picture. "I love you Robbie," I said under my breath. "I'm so sorry."

I rolled over, weeping. But I needed all the sleep I could get. Tomorrow would be a tough day.

CHAPTER 4

At four o'clock, I walked into Rich's office, then paused and looked at the floor. "I'm... uh... I'd like to take off early, if you don't mind. All the paperwork is done and on John's desk."

Rich nodded, looking intently at me. "Are you okay, Sis?"

"Yeah. I just, well, I just want to get out of here."

"Sure," Rich said. "Are you coming over to Mom and Dad's tonight?"

I shrugged.

"Try, okay? Everyone is going to be there." Rich's blue eyes showed his concern. "We'd like you to. You should be with people who love you today."

I looked up at Rich, desperately trying not to cry. I could feel the tears crowding the corners of my eyes. I merely shook my head.

"Mel, we're still grieving too. Craig and Robbie were members of the family. Everyone needs to-"

"Maybe, we'll see." I turned and quickly left. I had to get out of there, to be alone. I walked out the office and stopped next to my parent's Taurus. I really needed to get a car of my own. Maybe tomorrow I'd go look. Maybe.

I drove around for a long time, ending up at my old haunt, the mall.

It was a Thursday night, so not many from the younger crowd were hanging out there. I sat in the parking lot away from the main building, mostly numb. I don't know how long I sat there, thinking about my other life. Wondering, asking myself, *Why am I alive?* I felt guilty that they were dead and I wasn't. The tears had long dried, but I had no desire to move.

A green Honda civic pulled up in front of me. I sighed. Mitch was probably the only one in the family who knew where to find me. He was also the only one in the family who understood that I just wanted to be alone today, that I *needed* to be alone.

Mitch paused in front of the car, then walked to the passenger side and got in. My windows were open to the heat and humidity; it felt like we were swimming in warm lemonade.

"Hey," he said softly.

"Hey," I answered back just as softly.

"They were worried about you."

I nodded.

"I told'em you were fine but, you know Mom."

I nodded again.

Mitch rubbed his eyes, then got comfortable in the car. We sat there for a long time. The sunset was just starting by the time I spoke.

"Robbie would have been six today."

Mitch said nothing.

"Last year, at his party-" I sniffled. "The clown Craig hired...Robbie had so much fun with the balloon animal he made. I really miss them." Tears formed in my eyes.

"I know." Mitch rubbed his chin. He was struggling to control his emotions too, I knew from experience. "I remember last year-" Mitch stopped and cleared his throat.

One tear slid down my face. Then another. And another.

"The rat bastard," I whispered, thinking of Craig the night of the accident.

"What?" Mitch asked.

I shook my head as the tears flowed. "What … What about last year?"

"I got him that Lego set. That huge Stars Wars one." Mitch turned and smiled. Now tears were in his eyes too.

It made me let out a sob. Robbie had just been getting into building with Legos. The Lego set Mitch was referring to had been way too advanced for a five-year-old, but Mitch had spent hours on the floor with Robbie, building it with him. Mitch and Robbie were buddies. Robbie had been Mitch's favorite nephew.

Mitch reached out and patted my leg. We sat again for some time in silence. I'm not one who cries much in front of people, even family. It's just the way I am. Lately though, that was starting to change.

Mitch cleared his throat softly. "Are you coming this weekend, WT?"

I gave him a soft smile. "I still haven't decided."

Mitch nodded an okay. "Beside skiing, we might do some tubing too. And if the weather holds, we might have a cookout on Hogback Island." He looked at me as I stared off into the distance watching the road and the cars passing. "We could use another person to help watch with skiing." There was a soft plea to his voice, the kind he used to use on me as a kid.

"Maybe."

Mitch smiled . "Getting closer to a yes."

I chuckled. "Thanks, Mitch."

"Anytime, WT." He patted me on the shoulder then moved to exit the car. "Just let me know before Saturday morning. I'm not sure how early we're hitting the river."

"Okay."

Mitch leaned back into the car. "I'll let the troops know that you're okay. And Mel, call me for anything."

"Okay. Thanks again."

He pulled away in his car, heading to the old homestead to inform everyone that I hadn't disappeared off the face of the earth or gone off the deep end. He was a good brother.

I started the car. Time to head home to an empty apartment. To an empty life.

I headed to the bar first. A beer might help dull the ache a bit before bed. The bar was somewhat subdued; a baseball game was on TV and most of the guys were watching it. I slid onto the bar stool at the end near the door, without looking around, and motioned to Ross, the bartender, for a beer. He slid one to me with a wink. I sighed and nodded back, then began to intently study the bar top.

I ran my fingers over the carving in the wood in front of me and almost smiled. I remembered the day I carved the drawing. The bar used to be owned by a friend of my Dad's and we went here all the time as kids. I had carved the dog into the wood when I was ten. It was just a stick-figure, but the white wood underneath contrasted sharply with the dark, almost black bar top. I got in a lot of trouble with Dad but Buddy, the owner at the time, liked the dog and every time he had the bar top refinished, he always made sure that the dog was left untouched.

By my second beer, I was back to thinking of Maryland. There were some good times, too. Some. I swallowed back the tears at the memories and finished off the beer. As I set the empty down on the bar, a new one appeared near my elbow. I looked up to find that Max had been the one to set it there. "Thanks."

"Sure." He looked closely at me, a concerned look on his face. "Are you okay?"

I nodded as Ross thundered up. Ross was giving Max a hard stare. "Just leave her alone today, okay, fella?"

Max looked confused, then looked back at me.

"It's okay, Ross. Thanks. This is Max Bauer. He's new on the police force."

Ross and Max shook hands. I glanced up and saw Ross still giving Max a look that said, 'Back off.'

"Really, it's okay Ross, thanks for the concern. I was getting ready to head upstairs anyway."

Ross leaned over the bar and gave me a kiss on the cheek. "Want another one for the ride home?"

"In a minute, maybe."

Ross walked away from us, but I could tell that he was still keeping an eye on Max.

"What's that about?" Max asked, sliding onto the stool next to me.

I opened the new beer and took a healthy swig. "Everyone is being overly protective of me today."

"Oh really? Why?"

I looked into his eyes and could see that there was genuine concern. It made me feel warm inside.

"Today is my son's birthday. He would have been six." I took another swig of the beer, going back to studying the bar top.

"Is? Would have been?"

I looked up. "He died in a car accident about six months ago, along with my husband." I was so numb right now that it didn't affect me to say those words the way it usually did. I took another drink of beer. "Give me another, Ross."

He moved to grab one from the cooler under the bar.

Max was watching me. "I'm sorry, Mel."

I nodded in absentminded response, looking away. I was so used to hearing that phrase. "Yeah." I sighed as I looked back at him. "I appreciate the thought and the beer, but I really just want to be alone. Okay?"

Max nodded. "Sure. If I can do anything, let me know."

I tapped the bottom of the beer bottle on the bar top. "You already did." Grabbing the other one from Ross, I nodded in thanks to him, then hurried out of the bar and up the stairs.

My answering machine light was blinking. I listened to the message; it was Craig's parents. With a sigh, called them back. "Hi Phyllis. Thanks for the call. It's been tough today but overall I'm fine. Thanks for the concern. Talk to you later."

I sat in the living room until I don't know when, nursing the two last beers. I knew that alcohol wasn't going to do any good, but that didn't stop me from drinking. I listened to the stereo, staring at Robbie's favorite stuffed animal, Peter Rabbit. I had found it in a box of Robbie's toys.

Petey had been Robbie's favorite cuddle toy as a baby. We couldn't go anywhere without Petey. And we wouldn't have dared to think about putting Robbie to bed without his stuffed rabbit!

Petey sat on the coffee table staring back at me. *Was he accusing me of losing Robbie? Why did Robbie have to die? He had so much to live for.*

I don't remember falling asleep on the couch.

***

I took a deep, nervous breath before getting out of my car at my parent's house the next morning. I already knew what Mom would say, but I felt a duty to show up.

The house I grew up in was great. It consisted of three large lots, a basketball court my Dad and his police buddies had built, two huge trees with swings and ropes strung between them, and lots of grass. The three-car garage that sat on the alley had a tiny attic that we had made into a clubhouse. Next to the garage was a large parking lot, where we all used to hang-out as teens.

Opening the back door leading into the kitchen, I saw Mom doing dishes. "Hi."

"Where were you last night?" She dried off her hands and turned around.

I moaned.

"Everyone was here. Teresa even called from Ohio."

I nodded as I sat down. "Where's Dad?"

"Out getting some supplies for the bar." Mom sighed softly as she walked over and sat down next to me. "How are you doing?"

"Fine." I shrugged, not looking up but studying the pattern on her tablecloth. "I was thinking of looking for a new car soon, so I'll be bringing your car back."

"Use it as long as you need." A very uncomfortable pause followed. "Do you need any money or help with anything?" It was a tone of voice I was familiar with, an 'I know that you can't take care of yourself' tone.

"No, Mom." I looked up at her. "I have enough money." I could see her next thought before she even spoke.

"Then why are you working for Rich?"

"Because I need something to do."

"There's plenty to do at the church."

Now I sighed. I was never very religious to begin with and I hated having it shoved down my throat.

"I'm just saying that you should volunteer at the church, we could use more help." She paused, our eyes locked. "I didn't see you on Sunday."

"Because I wasn't there." I stopped my eyes from rolling because I knew from past experience that it would just escalate the argument.

"You should have been."

I didn't answer or look away. We had had this discussion about three times a year since I left for college. "Everyone else goes; even Teresa takes her new boyfriend to church."

I opened my mouth to say that I knew Mitch didn't go, but didn't say anything. It wasn't my place to get Mitch in trouble. I looked out the window instead so she wouldn't be able to read my thoughts. She was a master at that.

"Think about it. Please, for me. And for you."

"I will, but the answer is still the same, Mom. It hasn't changed."

"Have you heard from Harold and Phyllis?"

I nodded. Harold and Phyllis were Craig's parents. "Phyllis called and left a message on my machine. I called them last night." I regretted it the minute the words left my mouth. I could see the hurt look in her eyes. "Mom, you know I don't like to do the family mourning thing. It's not me. I have always done-"

"It doesn't matter. As long as you know that we're here for you." She stood and went back to doing dishes.

I sighed long and loud. "I didn't reach them. I left a message on their machine. So it's not like I talked with them."

"I'm sure they appreciate the thought, Mel."

I stood. "Tell Dad I stopped by."

"I will. Call if you need anything," Mom threw over her shoulder.

I walked down the sidewalk, mad and guilty. She was so good at that. She always had been. And we probably would never come to terms. But I had done my duty.

When I walked in the office, I smiled sheepishly at Rich. "Sorry, I'm late."

"Not a problem, Sis," Rich said, looking up from Pam's new desk. He leaned back to study me putting my soda in the fridge. "I understand. Are you okay?"

"Yeah, just the normal night thing, enhanced by several beers. This morning I went to see Mom." I rolled my eyes.

"Mitch told us you were okay. Mom was worried. It was sort of a quiet, sad night. It's probably a good thing you weren't there. Mom did her usual thing with looking at pictures and sharing memories." Rich patted my shoulder as he passed me and walked into his office.

I sat down, taking a deep breath to ward off the tears again. I knew that last night I had made the right decision;. It wasn't that I didn't need or want the support of family. I just grieve differently. It seemed that everyone understood that but Mom.

Rich called me into his office. "By the way, Fidelity wants me to congratulate you on the fine job of filming that you did. I think they're going to put you up for an award, or make one up just for you." Rich beamed with pride. I chuckled.

"I found this in the camera bag when I went to get the pictures developed." He held up an envelope.

I looked at it, then slapped my head with my palm. "Doh! That envelope was for you. A lady came as I was locking up," I said. "Her name was Mouse. She asked me to give it to you. She said you'd know what to do with it."

Rich looked at me, then at the envelope, and back at me. "Describe her."

"Uh, blond. Mid to late twenties. Ratty hair. Looked like maybe she hadn't combed it in awhile. Nervous. She said it was a relief to give it to you. And she recognized me, but I didn't recognize her." I paused, thinking. "Oh, she said that she couldn't be reached; she was leaving town."

His stare was intense. He gently laid it down on the desktop and picked up the local paper. He scanned the front page then folded it over, hiding the headline. He held it up and I moved in closer for a look. "Is that her?"

I studied the photo. The picture in the paper looked like a high-school graduation photo. I tilted my head a bit. "Could be." I continued to look at it. "Yeah, it definitely could be. But this girl was... older, rougher."

Rich unfolded the paper and let me read the headline: "Local Girl Found Dead in South Park."

I swallowed, feeling like I had been kicked in the stomach. Tears burned my eyes. "First Eddie's brother, then Eddie, and now this lady? Think it might be related?"

Rich nodded, picking up the envelope by the edge. "Could be. It very well could be." He carefully opened the envelope to reveal a CD-ROM with a sticky note attached. The note said, "Thanks, Rich. Eddie." My brother popped it carefully into the computer, making sure not to touch any part that might hold fingerprints.

I moved to stand behind him where I could see the screen. A spreadsheet with a bunch of letters and several numbers appeared. Rich clicked on the icon for the second file, which had five columns of numbers and a long string of numbers at the bottom. I was lost. It made no sense to me.

Rich looked up at me to see if I had a clue what it might be or mean. I held up my palms and shook my head.

Rich picked up the phone and dialed a number. He mouthed 'Police', and then someone answered. "Pearl? Hi, it's Rich Addison. How are you doing?" Rich snickered at her response. "Hey, is Mitch in? ... He's not. Okay, is Tom Hawkings in? ... Great. Thanks."

Rich covered the mouthpiece and asked me, "Could you grab me a blank CD?"

I nodded and went to the storage room where we kept our supply. I handed one to Rich and he made a copy of the contents of the disk.

He uncovered the phone. "Tom, it's Rich..." Rich smiled. "Going just great. Listen, who is in charge of the investigation on the dead girl from yesterday?...Yeah, Angela Mousina... I don't recognize his name. Is he new? ... Well, I might have some information for him... I don't know... Would you let him know? ... Thanks. I'll be at the office most of the day. Thanks, Tom." Rich hung up the phone and, popping the copy out of the CD-ROM drive, handed it to me. "Would you put that somewhere safe? The lead detective will be in later to talk to us. His name is Max Bauer."

I smiled.

"Do you know him?"

"I met him the other night at the bar." I moved to the door. "I'll run this girl's name through the databases along with Eddie's and his brother's name." Besides, I wanted to be alone. *Was death following me? Was I now cursed?* I shook my head in disbelief.

Rich smiled. "Almost like you read my mind."

"It's the Addison brain. We all think alike." I hurried to Pam's desk.

***

At about one o'clock, I returned from getting sandwiches and heard Max's voice from Rich's office. As I walked by, I called out, "Lunch."

I headed to the conference room and set the bags down, pulling out the napkins from a small cabinet. By this time, the guys had joined me.

I quickly scanned Max as he walked in. He looked very handsome in his beige shirt and darker cream-colored tie. His dress pants were a nice fit. I nodded as Max smiled in greeting. "Are you going to stay for lunch? Rich always makes me buy enough for a whole squad of people."

Max sniffed suspiciously at the bags. "What's in there?"

Rich smiled. "Maid Rites, from Maid Rite."

"Maid Rites?" Max asked as we sat down. Rich was already in the bag. He pulled out the wax-paper-wrapped burgers and looked them over before handing one my way and then putting one in front of Max.

Meanwhile, I handed out the sodas. "Yeah, it's a local joint over on Twelfth Street. Sort of a dive but the food is great. Been at the same location since sometime in the thirties, I think. One of Quincy's best traditions."

I was into the other bag and pulling out the fries and cheddar crisps. I put one of each in front of Rich. The other two I divided between Max and myself.

Max was opening his burger with curiosity. The sloppy joe type burger was packed tightly onto the bun. He watched Rich take a big bite. Max looked at me as I tore into mine. He looked at the burger again.

"They look greasy," he commented, studying the thing in his hand.

"They are, and that's why they're good," Rich said with a knowing grin.

Max shrugged and tasted it. He paused to consider, then took a drink of his soda. He took another bite of the sandwich before saying anything. "Well, it's different." He finished another bite. He studied the sandwich again. "Pretty good, actually."

Rich laughed. "He's hooked."

"Greasy and salty, but something about them makes you want to keep eating." He smiled and ate another bite. He tried a cheddar crisp, a little hunk of cheese, breaded and deep-fried. He smiled at them, then tried a fry. "I've had better french fries but these," he pointed, "these aren't bad at all. What are they called?"

"Cheddar crisps. The french fries will grow on you too. Trust me," Rich said smiling.

The phone rang and I leaned back to pick up the extension. "Security Investigations… Sure. Hold on." I hit hold and hung the phone back up. "Vincent Viking's office," I said to Rich. He nodded, shoving a fry in his mouth, and left the room carrying his sandwich. I went back to eating.

Max was watching me. "Sorry about yesterday, Mel."

I shrugged it off. "You didn't know." I looked up at him. "I don't wear my grief on my sleeve." He nodded, apparently understanding my need to let it drop. Cops were good at reading people. And for that, I was glad.

"Rich says you spoke with Angela Mousina."

I nodded. "Yeah, I spoke with her about at four-thirty on Wednesday."

Max grabbed his notebook out of his pocket. He scribbled in it as we ate. "Are you sure of the time?"

"Yep. I was just closing up. I was doing surveillance for Rich."

He motioned for me to continue as he shoved another bite of the sandwich into his mouth.

I smiled. "Starting to get to you, huh?"

He chuckled.

I described Mouse and how she gave me the disk. He asked me questions about her appearance and demeanor. It wasn't long before the interview was over.

"You have a remarkable memory, Mel."

"It's the Addison training. Dad was a cop. He instilled in us two things: always be aware of your environment, and take note of your surroundings." I shrugged. "Guess some of his lectures stuck."

Rich stuck his head in the room and tossed his trash onto the table. "Hey WT, I have to go serve some subpoenas for Vincent Viking. If Gloria calls, let her know I'll try to be home for supper. Do you need anything else from me, Max?" Rich asked.

"No," Max said finishing up his sandwich. "Thanks again for the heads-up on this."

"Sure. Go ahead and have my other sandwich, Max. The envelope and disk are on my desk."

Max turned to me after Rich left. "That's like the third or fourth time I've heard someone call you 'WT'. What's that about?"

I chuckled. "WT stands for Wild Thing. I used to be pretty fearless when I was younger."

He smiled. "Really?"

"Ask around. The guys will gladly tell you stories, I'm sure. Aside from the old-timer's stories about catching me making trouble, I dated a number of cops before I got married." I smiled at Max. "Trust me, there are plenty of people who can tell you stories. But don't believe all of them. I wasn't as wild as they think." I winked as I took another bite of my sandwich. "Hey, the other day you were going to ask me something?"

Max swallowed quickly as he looked up at me. "Yeah, I, uh, with being called to help with the Edward Baker case, I can't remember what I was going to ask you now."

I held his eyes for a beat. He was lying. "Really?"

He nodded and looked back down at his cheese crisps. "You said this place is on Twelfth?"

"Yeah. Right near Blessing Hospital. North of Broadway." The air was tense but I wasn't really sure why. *Why do I care so much anyway?*

Max cleared his throat. "I'll have to check it out sometime. Care to join me? You can show me the right things to order since I'm a newcomer to these Quincy traditions." He glanced at me with a sly smile.

I gave him a smile back. "Rookie."

Max broke out with a deep laugh.

CHAPTER 5

I showed up at the dock on Saturday dressed in cut-offs and an old T-shirt over my one-piece. The weatherman said it would be another blistering day, so I might want to cool off in the water with a swim.

I saw Mitch and Larry Tolson, another patrolman, already at the dock. Larry had black hair and a mustache that reminded me of a caterpillar. The truck with the boat trailer was backed into the water. Both guys smiled as I walked up to them.

Mitch said, "You remember Larry, right?"

"Yeah," I nodded at him.

"Do you remember Kick?" Mitch asked.

I looked over to the other side of the boat and saw a man bending over. He stood up as Mitch said his name. I gasped in surprise. "Daniel Kickery?"

Kick smiled. He had been in Mitch's high school class but he and Mitch hadn't hung out. Kick was a nerd: big black glasses, plastic pocket protector, and weird patterned clothes included. "Hi, Mel. Glad you could make it."

"Kick, I haven't seen you in ages." I smiled. "You've changed. A lot."

"Thanks," he said, blushing.

"Is this your boat?"

He nodded. "Yeah, pretty, ain't she?"

I laughed again. "'Ain't?' If I remember from high school-"

Kick blushed brighter. "I'm not a nerd any more. I can blend in with you normal people now."

Mitch and Larry both looked at him and laughed.

"Hey! I can. The guys at the shop taught me." He looked at me. "I've inherited my Dad's automotive shop."

"Really? I would have pegged you for computers or something." While we talked, I leaned on the side of the truck, watching the guys work. They were gliding the boat off the trailer and letting it drift further to the side of the dock. Kick held the rope attached to boat to hold it in place.

"I worked on those for a while. I still dabble, but I enjoy working with my hands, believe it or not."

"Really good mechanic," Larry chimed in. He jumped over the trailer that was sticking out of the water and threw a couple of items from the back of the truck into the boat.

"Hey, I'm getting ready to buy a used car. Can I bring any prospective ones in and have you look at them, so I don't get a lemon?" I asked Kick.

"Sure. What kind are you looking for?"

I shrugged. "Something reliable. I couldn't care less what kind it is."

Kick stood up again from the side of the boat and flipped down a white bumper so it wouldn't bump into the metal dock. He looked at me. "I've got a Jeep I've been trying to sell."

I hardened my gaze, evaluating.

"It looks terrible but runs great. I don't want to invest in a paint job though." Kick motioned to my brother. "Go ahead and park her, Mitch."

"But it runs good?"

"Absolutely," Kick said as Mitch hopped in the truck and drove it back up the ramp. The trailer came out of the river, dripping wet. "Come and look at it. I'll give you a good price. I promise. Friend's discount."

"What kind of Jeep?"

"A Wrangler."

"Let me think about it."

We watched as Larry followed the truck up the ramp and headed to his car to pick something up. Kick looked me up and down. "You look good too, Mel."

"Thanks."

Kick cleared his throat. "Are you skiing today?"

"I doubt it. I don't want to risk the leg yet. I'm here to watch the three of you make fools of yourselves."

"That we will. I've only just learned this year. Mitch and Larry are still teaching me."

"Then this will be a blast." We both laughed.

***

Mitch sat next to me after shutting off the engine. He glanced back at Kick and Larry, who were floating and talking on the water. "Max Bauer, the new detective, has been asking about you."

"Oh yeah?" I asked. "He seems to be a pretty good guy, from my conversations with him."

"Yeah, he is." Mitch said, quickly taking a drink.

I watched Mitch fiddle with his soda can. Something was on his mind, I could tell. I sighed. "Out with it, Turd Breath." I grinned.

He grinned back. "Can't keep much from you."

"Never could. What's up?" I glanced back at the two guys but they were still conversing, Larry occasionally pointing at his partially submerged skis.

"Just wondering how you're doing? You know, with everything."

I could tell he was uncomfortable. I squirmed a little too. Then I shrugged at him. "Good. Bad. Most days okay, I guess. Why the sudden concern? And why bring up Bauer?"

"Hey, I can't be concerned? You're my little sister."

I frowned.

"Really."

"Give."

"Lots of people care, me included."

I just stared at him for a few seconds trying to puzzle this one out.

"You'd be surprised how many of the guys ask how you're doing."

I chuckled. "Sure."

"I wouldn't lie to you. Besides, I just wanted to touch base," Mitch said, "and to make sure you aren't going nutso."

I grinned, but it was a forced grin for his sake. He didn't know how close to the truth he was. I doubt anyone in my family knows how close I am to losing control sometimes. He gently patted my leg. "If you need to talk, you know you can talk to me about anything."

I gave him a sly look, changing the subject. "Then let's talk about Tina. Are you two getting serious yet?"

Mitch grimaced. "I meant about you."

I shook my head, setting my soda down to move one of the white bumpers. "Tina. Are we talking wedding bells? Little booties?"

"Give me a break, Mel. We've only just started dating exclusively."

"Give me a break, Mel," I imitated him. "Not likely. I seem to recall when I was dating Marty, remember Marty? I dated him for one week, then you spread a rumor-"

"Not me!" Mitch interrupted, the picture of innocence.

I placed my hands on my hips. "It's about time for payback, I think. Let's see, I think a good rumor to spread would be that Tina is pregnant-"

Mitch stood suddenly, a mischievous grin on his face. He bumped into me, caught my left leg, grabbed my arm, and with a mighty heave, tossed me over the side of the boat.

I coughed as I surfaced. Laughter came from the boat and the two guys in the water. I shook the water from my ears and tried to climb back into the boat.

Mitch shook his head. "What were you saying?"

He extended his hand over the side to help me up. I grabbed on but instead of climbing up, I pulled hard. Since Mitch was already off-balance, he fell, plunging head-first into the water, soda and all. Now I was the one laughing, with an even louder chorus of laughter from the other guys. Mitch surfaced, blowing air to clear water from his face.

"Serves you right, Turd Head."

"Dog Breath." He swam to the back of the boat.

"Stink Hole." I was right next to him.

"Slime Bucket," he called as he left the water. He turned after getting in the boat. "Do you need help back in, Mel?"

I nodded. My right leg had been sore all morning. The guys had tried to get me to ski, but I knew it would collapse on me if I did, especially after I ran on it the other day.

After getting me in, Mitch smiled impishly.

"Do you wanna go back in the water?" I pointed over my shoulder.

Mitch chuckled. "If you could." He moved to the driver's seat and started the engine.

I sat down facing backward to watch the skiers as Larry signaled to me. "They're ready. Hey! I think I'll tell everyone you're in love with Kick."

"They'd believe that about as much as you loving him."

It felt good to be teasing with him again, like old times. I watched as the two skiers finally made it up on their skis. "Wouldn't bother me, but you...The Casanova of Quincy? Bad. Very bad for your reputation and your love life. Women would weep all over the tri-state area." I called back, keeping my eyes on Larry and Kick. "Nobody would care about me."

"Bauer would care."

"What?" I asked, thinking I hadn't heard him right. Mitch just laughed.

***

Once the boat was docked, Mitch disappeared up the hill to get the truck and trailer. It had been a fun day, but I was ready for some quiet time in the shade. I asked if the guys needed any help, but Larry and Kick shook their heads. I slowly made my way up the ramp.

When I reached the top, I noticed a man on a motorcycle parked near my parent's Taurus. When he looked my way, I realized it was Max. He sat with his ankles crossed, leaning against the seat of his bike. He had on jeans and an untucked red button-down top.

I waved and walked over to him.

"Rich told me you were out on the river today with Mitch and Larry."

I nodded and glanced back at the men and the boat.

"What do you do out on the river here? I've seen a lot of boats coming and going while I waited," Max asked, looking down at the bay.

"Ski, tube, swim, bake in the sun, you know." I smiled.

He smiled back, his blue eyes flashing. "But the river is so, well, dirty." He crossed his arms. He was checking me out, even though he was trying to be sly about it.

I put my shoes back on, then looked at him. "That's why it's called the Muddy Mississippi. Was there a reason you tracked me down?"

"Oh," Max said, "Yeah. I wanted to see if you remembered anything else from the day you spoke with Angela Mousina."

I frowned. "No."

The guys had the boat on the trailer and out of the water. They stopped in the parking lot near us to secure the trailer for driving. Once they were ready, they waved and took off, the boat still dripping water.

"Why are you here, really?"

Max looked at me. "Why do you ask it like that?"

"You wouldn't have come all the way here to ask me that stupid of a question." Besides, Mitch's comments from earlier were still ringing in my ears.

"The guys at the station said you were quick. No, it's not the only reason I'm here."

I looked at him and waited.

"Did you look at the computer disk with Rich?"

I nodded.

"Anything?"

"It just looked like a bunch of letters and numbers and stuff to me. Spreadsheets." I shrugged. "Why?"

"None of our people can figure it out either. I just thought that maybe one of you had."

"Sorry. Have you asked Rich?"

"He said to ask you."

I shook my head and checked out his motorcycle. It was a metallic blue BMW R1150RS, a cross between touring bike and suicide bike. Fast yet classy. One of my husband's partners had owned a bike just like it. "Nice bike."

Max looked down at it. "Thanks. Do you ride?"

"Not much anymore. I used to all the time when I was younger."

"Oh really?"

"Another hidden talent that I kept a secret for the most part. Mom would have even more gray hairs if she knew I rode as much as I did."

"Yeah, I've heard some stories about you. I think WT is a very good nickname." He stood up and moved to get on his bike. He pulled the helmet off and held it in his hand. "See you later, Mel. If you ever want to ride, let me know." He gave me a wink as he started his bike.

I watched him all the way down the drive. For some reason my heart rate was elevated and I couldn't take my eyes off of him. He looked back once and smiled. I waved. *It sure would be fun to take him up on that offer.* I felt a slight shiver at the thought.

He was handsome, that was for sure, and he had a cute butt. Seven years ago, before I was married, I would have been all over him. But now-

I hoped in the car and started back home. Something was bothering me about him, but my mind couldn't get past his smile and sparkling blue eyes. Maybe if I let it rest. Now I was just tired and hungry.

***

That night I was working through another of my boxes when I heard a knock on the door. I looked out the peephole to see Beth, my old friend from high school. Five years ago, when I was home visiting, we had reconnected and stayed in touch, and now she was really my only friend in town.

I smiled as I opened the door, motioning her in. "Hi, Beth."

"Hey, Mel. Sorry about just dropping by. I left my kids with Mom to do some shopping and had a few minutes until I need to go pick them up." She wiped her forehead with her hand. "Geez, it's hot again tonight."

I offered her a drink.

"Sure."

"Let's see, I've got milk, beer, tea and Kool-aid."

"Kool-aid?" Beth asked with a smile.

"A holdover from Robbie."

"Tea. I hate Kool-aid. I make it too often for the kids. Just the smell." She gave a fake shudder.

We chuckled as we walked into the living room.

"Hey, I found out some things about that Mousina girl you asked about." Beth was so plugged into the gossip grapevine here in town. I knew she would be able to come up with something on the woman.

"She graduated by the skin of her teeth," Beth said. Her eyes widened in excitement. She knew I was working for Rich and thought that it was great fun to be helping with an investigation. "Apparently she used to run with a pretty bad crowd from Quincy High."

Quincy had two high schools, one public, and one private. Beth and I had both graduated from the private Catholic high school, Notre Dame. It was an expensive school, but most Catholic families could, or struggled to, send their kids there.

"What kind of crowd?" I probably knew a lot of them. I had hung out occasionally with the not-so-good crowd at my school, and we mingled lots with the kids from the public high school, another fact that I had kept hidden from my family, especially Mom. Except Mitch.

"You know, drugs, crime."

"She didn't have a record." I was mystified. I hadn't found anything in the databases I searched.

"Juvie," Beth said, proud that she had information for me.

"Really? How bad?"

"Got caught with a joint in middle school, joy riding, vandalism. You know, kid stuff," Beth said, then lowered her voice. "But the really big news is that she dated that guy who was killed around two weeks ago, uh, Wally Baker."

I leaned closer. "Really!"

Beth nodded. "And, I heard, now mind you this is merely rumor-"

We both smiled at that. Beth's 'rumors' were usually near enough to the truth to at least warrant a serious look.

"-that she was *with* Wally the night he died. And, she was working on something with him that would make it so that she, Wally, and Scott Hiccome, her boyfriend, would never have to work another day in their lives."

"What? What was it?"

Beth seemed to crumble. "I don't know. Apparently, they were pretty closed-mouthed about it. I also heard Scott Hiccome is missing. No one has seen him for a couple of days. Even the cops are looking for him."

That was interesting. "At least we have a little bit to go on." And at least Beth's information did establish a link between the three murders, something that my gut was telling me was right. "I'll pass it along to Rich, and if anything comes of it, to the cops."

With a glance at her watch, Beth stood up. "Gotta go pick up the little beasts."

I stood with her. "Well, thanks for the information and I'll have Robbie's clothes ready for you sometime soon, once I finish with this mess."

"No hurry."

I closed the door and relocked it. *Hmmm, very interesting.* I sat back down on the floor and started working again, flipping the TV on as background noise.

A political commercial caught my attention as I folded clothes. I looked up at the TV. The mayoral race was up for grabs in November and it looked like it was going to be an ugly one. I sighed. The mud-slinging was beginning early this year. It was only August.

Marion Williams was the Republican candidate, running against the incumbent Democrat, Harold Schnabel. Schnabel had fallen out of favor with the public due to his policies regarding rapid city growth and the environmental reform he was trying to force on big business. If the election were held today, Williams would probably win, though I was pretty sure his promises would come to nothing once he got in office.

Politicians. What a bunch of liars! I shook my head and went back to looking through the three boxes of clothes on the floor. I folded most of them back up and put them in a box for Beth's son.

I picked up a small, soft green infant gown, and rubbed its velvety softness on my face. I had brought Robbie home from the hospital in this. Gently I folded it up and placed it in a box of Robbie's things that I was keeping. Next

I picked up a small overall set. It had been Robbie's favorite outfit to wear this past winter. I had given it to him on Christmas and he had worn it for four days straight, not even letting me wash it or taking it off to sleep. I held the shirt in my hands, tears flowing down my face, while I folded and placed it reverently in the box.

After I wiped my cheeks, I sealed up the box of clothes to go to Beth and wrote her name on the outside of it, then I pushed it over to the kitchen. The other box I left unsealed and put with the others in the second bedroom.

I sighed, leaning against the door post. I slid down to the floor to stare at the piles. They were all I had left of my husband and child, other than my memories. Tears flooded my eyes again, but I sniffled them back. I sat staring at the box for a long time before I stood up. I had to get on with life. Feeling sorry for myself wouldn't bring them back.

Supper that night was a can of soup. I washed it down with a glass of Kool-aid. Cherry, Robbie's favorite.

My mind flashed back to the parking lot and Max. I smiled softly, thinking about him. *Stop it.* Here I was, a Saturday night, nothing to do but think about a handsome man riding a motorcycle. I jumped up and headed down to the bar.

CHAPTER 6

Sunday morning I woke up early. Unable to go back to sleep, I got up and ate breakfast. *Why was I awake?* There was no longer a reason for me to be up and about at this time on a Sunday.

Craig used to go to church almost every Sunday. I didn't go with him. He was a Baptist; I'm a Catholic. What a stir we caused in the family when I married him.

A laugh lodged in my throat. Craig was a big, fat hypocrite, going to church as though he were a God-fearing Christian.

Church. Without further thought, I got dressed and found myself standing at the back door to St. John's, where I had attended church regularly until graduating high school.

Mass was just about over. With a deep breath, I quietly opened the doors and scooted in to stand at the back. As I looked around at the familiar surroundings, I thought of Craig.

"I promise to be true to you in good times and in bad, in sickness and in health. I will love and honor you all the days of my life, until death do us part ." Craig's words rang in my ears. *What a hypocrite!*

"Mel, I haven't seen you in a long time." An older man greeted me. "Welcome back."

I shuddered, realizing everyone else was filing out of the church. The man looked familiar, but I couldn't remember him.

"Uh, hi. Yeah, but I'm not back. I'm just-" With a blush, I turned to go.

"Mel?" The voice was extremely familiar. I grimaced before I turned back. *Mom.*

"What are you doing here?" Her baffled expression was replaced by a huge grin. "If I knew you were here, you could've joined us up front." She pointed up the long church aisle to where Dad was still standing and talking to someone.

"Uh, well, I just stopped by. I thought that- I mean you and Dad always-" Anger bubbled inside of me, anger at myself. I had gotten caught by Mom, and now I was stammering like an idiot.

Her face softened and she reached for my arm. "Are you okay?"

"Yeah."

She pulled me off to the side by the stairs that led to the choir loft. "Is something troubling you?" Her eyes locked with mine. "Can I help? Tell me. I can tell that you're upset about something. What?"

I glanced down at the ground. This was not something I wanted to talk about. Not with anyone, especially Mom.

"Let me get Father Joe. You can talk to him." She started to walk away.

"No. I don't want to talk to a priest."

"Then tell me," she returned with an 'I'm waiting' kind of look.

I shook my head. "I'm just going to go- "

"Melissa Ann Addison." She caught my arm, then stopped, lowered her voice and softened her tone. "You came here for a reason. Tell me. I'll do anything I can to help you with what ever problem you're having. I'm your mother."

I caught my breath. The church walls seemed to be moving in. She was smothering me. "No. There's nothing wrong."

"Then why are you here?"

"Maybe to please you."

She shook her head. "That's not it. You know I'm always right. Is this about Craig? His death? Honey, every marriage goes through rough spots."

"This was a mistake." I took a step away from her. "This has nothing to do with Craig or my marriage. It's over. He's dead. Nothing can change that or what he did. Just let it go." I sprinted toward the doors.

Before they closed all the way behind me, Dad was at my side.

"What's going on, Mel?" Dad matched me, stride for stride.

"Nothing."

He stopped with me at my car. "She is just trying to-"

"Yeah, too hard."

"I know." He sighed. "You have to do this your way. Just know that we love you and are here for you."

I blinked the tears back. "I know, Dad."

"First Craig, then Edward Baker and that girl. Death, huh?"

I looked down at my feet, swallowing back tears.

"Sweetie, look at me." He kissed me on the cheek. "Take it slow. Time will heal." He patted my arm and walked away, gathering Mom who was walking toward us. I heard him say, "Just leave her be. She'll be fine."

I got in the car, glanced at the church one more time, shook my head and left.

***

Monday morning I relayed Beth's information to Rich. He went into 'cop mode'; his eyes hardened, his posture tightened, and I could almost see his wheels spinning faster as he sifted through the facts.

"You shouldn't be investigating this, Mel. This is a police matter." Rich leaned back in his chair behind the desk.

I shrugged, trying to be casual. "How could it hurt? I mean, I'm just asking around. Besides, it felt like we had let Eddie down. Maybe if we had acted more quickly-"

"It does matter, Sis," Rich said. "I could lose my license. PIs only investigate murders on TV-. Still." Rich smiled at me. "Don't use the firm's name or anything."

I smiled back as the front door dinged. I immediately stood up and headed to the reception area. A well-dressed man who looked slightly familiar was standing there, tucking a piece of paper into his suit pocket. I almost grimaced when I recognized him. It was Marion Williams, mayoral candidate. I saw his fake, 'I'm your man, vote for me' smile become fixed into place.

"Hi, I'm Marion Williams. I'm running for mayor in November and I'm visiting most of the downtown businesses today. Is Rich or John in?"

"Yes." I turned my head toward the hall. "Rich."

"And you are?" Williams asked, with the same smile in place.

"Melissa Addison."

"Melissa Addison." He repeated as though he was trying to place it. "Related to Rich?"

"He's my oldest brother."

Williams snapped his fingers. His face showed recognition. Rich walked in then. Williams nodded and stuck out his hand.

The men shook, and Rich showed Williams into his office. Less than ten minutes later, Williams headed out of the door to hit up our neighbors, the Print Shop. Rich walked him to the door and then turned to me after he had left. "That is one slick character."

"You feel the political slime trail too, huh?"

Rich chuckled as he made his way back to his office.

"Hey Rich," I called out to him. "When is John due back?"

"Tomorrow, actually late tonight." His voice drifted the length of the hall.

I hadn't been working more than ten minutes when the phone rang. "Security Investigations."

"Mel, it's Beth. The dead girl used to hang out with Tommy Bressler and his group of hoodlums."

"Really."

"Didn't you used to hang out with them?"

"Occasionally. I saw Tommy's picture the other night on the news. Do you know where he's staying in town?"

"Yep, 'cause I knew you'd be asking." Beth gave me his address and phone number. "So you know who he works for, I take it? Can you believe it?"

"It is weird. Thanks for the info Beth." I got a file folder out of the desk drawer and wrote up everything we had so far on the three murders, along with Bressler's contact info. I glanced at the water cooler where I had hidden the disk, taped to the back. *Nah, better to leave it there for now.* I quickly put the file in the cabinet and went back to work.

Tonight, I would track Bressler down and ask him some questions about Angela Mousina.

***

I drove over to Bressler's place, but he wasn't there. As a last resort, I headed to the local Democratic headquarters downtown to see if he was working late; it was after six. As I drove, I called Kick and made arrangements to check out the Jeep Wrangler later that night.

I walked in the Democratic office and looked around. For still being three months away from election, they seemed to be awfully busy. A young man around eighteen-years-old approached me.

"Can I help you, ma'am?"

I gave him a half smiled, half grimace. I still wasn't used to being addressed like my mother. "I'm looking for Tommy Bressler."

"He's in a meeting with the mayor right now, but he should be back in a few minutes. Can I get you something while you wait?"

I glanced back out the door. A deli was right across the street. "Uh, thanks, but I think I'll get a sandwich at the deli there." I pointed at the business. "How long do you think he'll be?"

The young man shrugged.

"Okay. I'll check back in when I get done eating. Thanks." I headed across the street.

I was nearly done with my Italian sub when a smartly dressed man walked in and looked around. His gaze fell on me as I was the only person there this late; the supper crowd had already come and gone. He walked over to me with a frozen, plastic smile in place.

He had changed a lot. The picture on the news didn't do him justice. His haircut was conservative; gone was the long hair. He wore chinos and loafers. He was no longer the rebellious teenager; he looked respectable.

"Hi. You must be looking for me. I'm Tom Bressler. Johnson said that a very lovely brunette was asking for me." Bressler stuck out his hand for a shake. "Please tell me it was you."

I chuckled. "Not desperate are we, Tommy?" He scrunched up his face, seemingly at a loss. I shook his dangling hand and motioned for him to sit in the booth across from me.

"Do I know you?" Bressler asked, studying me as he sat.

"Yeah."

"Gonna give me a hint?" He had always been into games of any sort.

I paused to think. "Okay. A motorcycle. Six kids, a tow rope, and a small surfboard." I smiled at him, wondering how we had survived that particularly stupid night.

Bressler continued to look at me, trying to figure it out until his eyes glazed over. Finally he blinked and looked closer, in disbelief. "Mel? Mel Addison?"

I laughed. "That would be me."

He reached out and punched me in the arm. "Long time no see. How are you?" He chuckled through a broad grin.

"Fine. Politics?" I motioned with my head to the office across the street.

Bressler leaned his head back and laughed. "Yeah, who would've thunk, huh?"

I leaned closer. "Do *they* know about the Washington Park adventures?"

"No one knows about that, Mel," he said, half-joking.

I leaned back, rubbing my chin. "Hmmm."

"Blackmail?" he asked.

"Nah," I smiled.

Bressler looked at me closer. "I don't see a ring. Married, divorced, single?"

"Widowed." My heart missed a beat but I played it cool.

His face darkened. "I'm sorry. Recent?"

"Six months ago." Time to change the subject. I nodded toward his hand. "And you?"

"Free and clear."

"I thought all politicians were supposed to be married. Image, you know."

Bressler laughed and shook his head. "I'm not a politician. I'm a political consultant."

"I heard. And what is that, specifically?"

"A public relations person. I have no political aspirations. Heck, no." Bressler shook his head. "Too dirty. I take care of press conferences, literature, stopping bad press, solving annoying problems, etcetera." He paused. "You?"

"I'm actually between jobs right now. Just moved back to Quincy from the East Coast."

"Okay then, what did you do?"

I grimaced. "You won't believe this either."

"What?"

"Mother and housewife."

"You? No way!"

"Yep."

"How old is your kid?"

I hesitated for just a second, to harden myself. I had said it so often you would think I'd be able to now without this catch in my throat. "Died in the accident with my husband. He would have been six." I nodded at Bressler's sympathetic look.

He leaned his head into his hand and looked at me. "Okay, so why did you come looking for me? Unless you want to-" His eyebrows lifted twice.

"I didn't then and I don't now, Tommy. You're still such a cad. That hasn't changed." He looked disappointed. "I was working for my brother and ran into Angela Mousina the day she died. Rumor has it she used to hang with you."

A dark look crossed his face. "Yeah. Poor Mouse. I heard she was having a rough time of it lately."

"What happened to her after she graduated?"

"You said you are working for your brother. Rich?"

I hesitated for a second then nodded. "Not like you think. I'm answering his phones until his secretary gets back from maternity leave. I met Angela on the street as I closed up that night."

"Mouse got in with some bad characters."

"Worse than you?" I interjected as a joke.

Bressler laughed. "Oh yeah, big-time drugs. As you know, I was never into drugs." He winked and I chuckled with him. "Anyway, Mouse was into cocaine from what I heard. That was after I went to college though." He saw my uplifted eyebrows. "Hey, we all grow up, you know. I hear she was even selling."

"Really? She seemed more like a user to me."

Bressler shrugged.

"Have you talked to her anytime recently?"

He quickly shook his head. Too quickly. "I saw her on the streets a couple of weeks ago as I passed, but I haven't spoken to her in ages."

"Where did you see her?" I saw him hesitate; he took a shallow breath. "I'm trying to find out where she was living, because she dropped something and it looked like it belonged to a female, maybe her roommate." Lies have always come easy for me when I'm being devious.

"Oh. Well, I saw her down near the river. You know that bar down there, uh, Hammerheads."

"Hammerheads?" I shook my head no. That was a new one to me; I used to know all the bars in the area.

"It used to be Biker's Haven."

"Oh!" Now I knew where he meant. I had visited that place a couple of times.

Bressler glanced at his watch. "Look, I have to get going. I have an early meeting with some of the democratic reps in Springfield." He reached into his pocket and pulled out a business card. "Call if you need anything else or if you want to reminisce sometime."

We said good-bye and I watched him walk across the street. Tom Bressler, political consultant, hadn't learned to lie any better then Tommy Bressler, kid rebel. But what I couldn't understand was why?

CHAPTER 7

I sat in front of Hammerheads late that night in my 'new' car. The Jeep was in desperate need of a paint job, but as promised, it ran like a dream. It felt good to be independent again.

The media was pressuring the cops for information, according to Mitch, and they had no clue as to where Scott Hiccome was. He had vanished from town. So, I decided to look for him too.

I tried his home address. I spoke to his parents. I tried everything else that the police had tried and apparently got the same answers. No one knew where he was or why he would disappear. Now I was looking at the bar where Bressler had last seen Mouse. If she hung out here, maybe so did Scott. It was a long shot but hey, it was all I had. I took a deep breath and got out of the Wrangler.

I patted it's side. I was getting to like this car. With it's horrible paint job, no one would think to rip it off. My vehicle fit right in here.

Hammerheads was still a hangout for bikers it seemed; there were ten Harleys parked outside the front door. Being on the riverfront, it attracted the less-than-high-society types.

The outside was still run-down and dumpy. It was a two-story building with a dance floor and bar on the first floor. The second floor was a balcony where people could sit and watch the dancers. In the old days, most of the balcony was reserved for the bikers. They had several tables where no one else dared to sit. It still looked like what it was, a hole-in-the-wall bar.

The music hadn't changed; hard rock leaked out the doors. It wasn't quite midnight yet, so the place was just hitting its stride for a weeknight. I opened the door to find that the inside hadn't been remodeled either.

I sauntered up to the bar and ordered a beer. Then I looked around but I didn't recognize anyone. Not surprising, really. I asked the bartender as he gave me my drink if he knew Scott Hiccome. He shook his head, but directed me to the back of the establishment.

As I watched the group at the table he had indicated, I noticed that the four men and three women were all drinking heavily. It also looked, even from this distance, like they were participating in other recreational habits too. I frowned. I didn't want to get over my head on this one. If Mouse was indeed selling, then it was possible that all of this was drug-related, and I definitely didn't want to get involved.

But Bressler's lie was still rubbing me the wrong way. What was he hiding? I slowly nursed my beer, keeping an eye on the group.

They had a lot of visitors to their table; it seemed that everyone in the place knew them. The more I watched, the more I realized that a lot of their visitors came into the building, stayed just long enough to drink a beer, then, after visiting the table, left the bar. I was quickly becoming convinced they were selling as I watched.

I finished my beer and six propositions later, I saw two ladies get up from the table and head to the bathroom,. So I handed my empty beer to the bartender as he passed, and shook my head to indicate I did not want another. I looked around, then followed the women. I knew from experience that there was no better place to gather information.

I finished up my business before they did and took my time washing my hands. From the amount of time that they were spending in the same stall, I figured they were doing drugs or something else sketchy.

Eventually they walked out. I smiled at them as they washed their hands. They giggled. "I was wondering if I might ask a favor of you two?"

A sniffle greeted me from the redhead. "What's that?" She added more makeup to her already caked-on face.

I dried my hands. "I'm looking for Scotty Hiccome. I'm his cousin. Our uncle died and he inherited some money. I came in town to tell him that, but I can't seem to find him. Do either of you know where he might be?"

The redhead giggled again but it was the blond who answered me. She cleared her throat while adjusting her almost nonexistent, strapless top that she had paired with too-tight jeans. "Well, we ain't seen him in a bunch of days. He's usually here but since Mouse died, nothing."

I frowned. "It's a lot of money. I know he probably needs it. Any idea where he might hang out if he's not here?"

The blond shook her head this time and Red wiped her nose with the back of her hand. Her eyes were lost in drug wonderland. "Swims. He sometimes goes swimming with Mouse in the river."

"Mouse is dead, you idiot." Blond pushed Red's shoulder.

"Oh right, I forgot." Red smiled and looked closely at herself in the mirror, moving her nose one way and then the other. She looked at me. "You think I should get my nose pierced?"

I looked closely at her, as though I cared. She was flying so high she had better watch for airplanes. "Might lose some blow if you do the nose."

"Oh, you're right!" She recoiled in horror. "Maybe then a nipple ring, I guess." She giggled again as they left. "Thanks for the thought."

I shook my head as the door closed. *I knew I was behind the times, but what was the thing with piercing?* I figured I was done here, and left.

Sitting in my Jeep before I drove away, I thought, *So Hiccome sometimes swam. What did that mean? Or was it just a drug-induced comment from a cokehead? What if Scott and Mouse used to swim at the spot where Bressler and company used to hang out and drink? Was it still being used as a hangout by the kids?*

There was only one way to find out. It had been a while since I had traversed the Quincy Bottoms area, and I hoped I could still find it. I started my vehicle and slowly drove away, winding my way along the river. At this time of the night, there weren't many people out on Bottoms Road.

It wasn't long before I crossed the first of two levies that kept the river contained in its bed, except for during the flood of 1993.

It looked like this part of the Bottoms had been reclaimed for fishing camps. I crossed the last levy and worked my way around several rebuilt camps. Over ten years old now, they had taken on an air of neglect. Slowly, I drove past them, counting down the camps.

Finally I came to number eleven, still the last in this row that sat looking out onto a 'shoot', or finger of the river. There was an island about fifty yards away, across the water. The elevated camps were where they always had been; someone had rebuilt them only to abandon them again. Some things never change.

Parking the Jeep, I looked around. After shutting off the engine, I waited until my eyes adjusted to the darkness that always settled in the trees down there. I leaned on the truck remembering the fun times I had. Never a dull minute at Eleven Bottoms, as we had called it. Grabbing my large flashlight out of the back of the Wrangler, I headed toward the camp building itself.

I don't know what I was looking for. Maybe I was just curious since I had spent a few nights down there. I walked up to the building and climbed the steps to the camp.

The door was broken, as could be expected. I turned on the flashlight and wandered though the three room building. Nothing unusual. It didn't appear that anyone was living there, except maybe mice and an occasional raccoon. After leaving the building, I turned off the flashlight and let my eyes readjust before heading down the stairs. I could tell that the kids still hung out there. Their cans and trash were everywhere. The kids nowadays didn't pick up any better than we had all those years ago.

I glanced around, swatting at the ever present mosquitoes. I walked up to the water's edge as an afterthought. *Same as always.*

I squatted down. The tranquil, steady lapping of the gentle waves against the bank murmured softly. It smelled like river water and stagnant pools of river debris. That too hadn't changed. There is a certain smell associated with the Mississippi, one that really can't be described, but is sort of musty and fishy. A smell to me that meant home.

I was heading back to the Jeep when I sniffed at the breeze again. I stiffened. That wasn't normal river-smell. And it wasn't even dead-fish smell. *That smells like, well, it just smells dead.*

I followed the scent. I was heading toward the woods to the right of the camp. There was a block of trees thickly overgrown with shrubs and weeds. I swatted a bunch of mosquitoes that swarmed as I walked.

As the smell got worse, I turned on my flashlight again. My heart was beating much faster now. *It's just a dead animal, a dog or raccoon or something. Yeah, just an animal.* I put my hand to my mouth and nose. Whatever it was, it was most certainly dead. I flashed the light ahead to find the source of the horrible smell.

The first thing I saw was a pale hand.

I stopped and stood still. *A crime scene.* I was standing in the middle of a crime scene. I flashed my light up the arm. The body was bloated. I didn't have any real knowledge about these kinds of things, but I knew that the person had been dead a while. I slowly and reluctantly moved the light beam toward the face.

Scott Hiccome.

CHAPTER 8

I had dug Scott's picture out of the Quincy High yearbook, so I was ninety-eight percent sure it was him. I swore under my breath and backed off the way I came, trying to stay in the same path I'd made. Dad's voice was screaming through my brain. *Retain the crime scene.* I reached the Jeep before I released my hand from my mouth and nose.

I paused to think. I had to call it in. But who should I call? *Mitch? He was just a patrolman. I have to call Bauer. It's connected to his case.*

From what Mitch had told me in confidence, Mouse had been killed with a thirty-eight to the chest. Scott had a gun shot wound to the chest too. I saw a big, dark, bloody stain. I didn't know what caliber or anything, but it was too much of a coincidence that Scott had a hole in his chest too; not to mention Scott had gone missing the same time as Mouse.

I swore one more time as I dug into my purse. *Did I still have Max's card with me?* With a last look back into the woods, I dialed his number. I couldn't smell the odor anymore.

As I waited for Max to answer, I shook myself to get rid of the smell that seemed to linger on me. I knew it wouldn't do any good, but instinctively I tried it anyway.

"'Lo," came the sleepy reply.

I swallowed; I forgot that it was after one in the morning. I smiled to let it seep into my voice. "Hi. Max?"

"Yeah. Who's this?" He sounded semi-awake now.

"Mel. Mel Addison."

"Mel? What time is it?"

"Uh, after one in the morning." I smiled because I could almost hear his puzzlement.

"You aren't calling to take a ride are you?" There was a smile in his voice.

"I wish." I paused. I wasn't quite sure how to report a dead body. I had never done this before. "I, uh, found a dead body and I think you might want to see it."

"You what?" Max asked with what sounded like astonishment. "Where are you? Who is it? Why did you-"

I interrupted him. "Can I answer one question at a time?"

"Yeah." There were noises in the back ground like he was rummaging around, then a loud crash. "Well?"

My eyes scanned the woods. "I'm down in the Bottoms. I was, well, the story is a long one, but the bottom line is I found a body here. And, I'm pretty sure it's Scott Hiccome."

"What were you doing looking for him?" His voice was muffled by something dragged across the phone. "Never mind. Where are the 'Bottoms?'" I heard a zipping noise, then a snap.

"Down by the river. The camp is on one of the Mississippi River shoots."

"Shoots?"

"Offshoots of the river. Kind of like a smaller river. There's an island that separates this area from the main river, a shoot. There are a bunch of fishing camps." I paused, having grown up here it seemed natural, but now that I was explaining it to a stranger it did sound weird. "Let me give you directions. You'd better write them down. They get complicated after you leave the main road."

I spent the next few minutes telling Bauer where to go. The last part was mostly 'turn left at this branch, turn right at the next split' types of directions. He read it back to me and took my cell number before he hung up. He also said that he was coming to see the body before calling it into the station. And he stressed in no uncertain terms that I shouldn't go near the crime scene again.

Like I would want to. Ugh, the smell was horrible. I hung up and got settled into the Wrangler. It had no top, another thing I needed to fix before winter.

Thirty minutes later, I saw a vehicle slowly making its way down the road. I flashed my lights so he would see where I was and the Trooper eased in next to me. Max got out. He looked at me with a hard glare. I could see his eyes in the moonlight shining through a break in the canopy of trees.

"Where's the body?" Max asked, his flashlight panning the area.

I pointed to the woods to our right. "About fifty yards or so in that direction."

Max nodded then panned the light back to me. "Out of curiosity, and since you never answered me on the phone, what are you doing here?"

I paused before answering. "The truth?"

His face tensed. "You'd lie to me?"

"I thought about it," I said through a smile, trying to lighten the mood. "Bad habits die hard."

Max smiled back, seemingly relieved. "Go on. The truth."

"I was out looking for Hiccome. Some friends I ran into yesterday told me he was dating Angela Mousina." I saw Max nodding. "So, I dug deeper into the rumor mill of town and got a lead on him. Only it dead ended. As I was peeing at a bar that he and Mouse hung out in, I asked two cokeheads about him. They hadn't seen him in a while but the redhead, who was really flying high, mentioned that Scott liked to swim. I guess she was so far gone that she forgot that Mouse was dead."

"Mouse? The Mousina girl?"

"Yeah, her nickname. I remembered that we used to swim here all the time, besides other things." I pointed at the elevated camp.

"Other things? Like what?"

"You know, smoking, partying, dumb teen things."

"Ah!" Max looked back at me. "Go on."

"So I came down here." I shrugged again. "I thought that maybe Scott might be staying down here. I checked out the building, then decided to see if the shoot had changed any. As I was leaving, a breeze blew the smell my way. I investigated and found the source."

"Show me." He motioned for me to lead the way.

I got out of the Jeep and turned on my flashlight. Soon we were close enough that he could smell it too.

"Ripe."

"Yeah. With the hot weather-" I didn't need to go on.

"What did you do when you found it?"

"Stopped in my tracks. I knew it was a crime scene,. I smiled at Max. "'Think like a cop,' Dad always said." I stopped. Max had already flashed ahead and saw the body. He muttered under his breath. I once more put my hand to my mouth and nose. I watched as Max crept closer.

"Man, there goes my night," he said softly to himself. "Gunshot to the chest it looks from here."

We backed up and as we headed back to the vehicles, he called the police station to get the other detectives on their way. We waited together. He continued to question me about what I had done and where I had been. He was taking notes the whole time. Finally, he stopped and looked at me. "You shouldn't be looking into this. It's a police matter. Does Rich know about you doing this?"

"Nope. He'd have said the same thing." I leaned on the Jeep, keeping my eyes locked with Max's. I learned the hard way with my Mom, the queen of getting the truth out of people. If you are going to lie, do so looking them right in the eye. I was well practiced at it.

"You'll have to stay here for a while, Mel," Max said with an authoritarian tone.

I nodded. I knew that. I settled down into the seat as the first cop cars arrived. It would be a long night.

In the dark, I watched the police do their work. Finally, seemingly forgotten by Max and the others, I curled up in the front bucket seat as best I could and dozed off.

When I opened my eyes, the sun had risen. Max was leaning against my door, watching me with interest, his smile deep.

"What?" I asked, slightly grumpy.

He shook his head. "Just letting you know that you can go. Sorry, it took so long. We got busy and…"

"You forgot about me, didn't you?" I wasn't really upset. I had slept about as well as I do in bed, except for my leg.

He blushed. "Sorry."

"That's okay." I looked back toward the woods that were crowded with police officers. "Was it Scott?"

Max merely nodded.

"Shot?"

Max hesitated. "I can't tell you that." He was staring into my eyes. "Headed home?"

I glanced at my watch. "Yeah, just to shower. Time for work." I grinned. "By the way, sorry for interrupting your sleep."

He smirked. "Yes, thanks for the lovely time, though not the way I had envisioned spending the evening with you." He winked then walked away.

***

I had to stifle another yawn. I was tired, even with the little nap I'd had in the Jeep. I rubbed my eyes and took another drink of iced tea with caffeine, lots of caffeine. The door opened and an equally tired Max Bauer stepped into the office. I waved. At least I wasn't the only one struggling to stay awake.

"Hi," I said.

Max flopped down in the chair in front of the desk. "Yeah. Hi. And thanks again for the lovely evening spent together."

I smiled at his lopsided grin. "Hey, anytime. No charge."

Max rubbed his eyes. "Is Rich in? And the other partner?"

I nodded. "John Huddleston. Rich, John!" I called out. I looked back to see Rich already in the doorway, and John's chair was making scraping noises.

Rich moved into the room as John came down the hall. Rich introduced the other two: "John, this is Max Bauer, a Detective with the police. Max, John Huddleston."

Max stood. They shook hands. With a weary sigh, he sat back down in the chair. "Do the two of you know what Mel was doing last night?"

"She told us this morning," John said, glancing at me.

Max looked up from the chair. "Good. I know I don't need to tell you this, but we can't have you investigating this case."

Both men nodded and murmured in agreement. Rich gave me a dirty look. "We've already talked to Mel about it. It won't happen again. Will it, Mel?"

"Yeah." I tried to look like I had been chastised. In reality, John and Rich had been impressed. We discussed the situation and Rich had suggested a couple of places where I should go to ask questions. I had to investigate off work time and never mentioned the firm. And I had to keep both of them up to date, just in case.

"Good," Max said then stood up. "I'm heading to bed." He turned to me. "Despite the fact that what you did was wrong Mel, thanks for the help. If you think of anything else that might help us, give me a call."

"Sure."

With that, he left, and John turned to me with a smile. "As I said before, way to show up the cops. Maybe we should advertise this: 'If you can't find that dead body, hire Security Investigations. We can find anything!'" We laughed and went back to work.

I spent the next hour researching information about a fugitive on a skip trace for John. So far the search was going nowhere. I sighed in frustration as the door opened again.

This time a man in a white dress shirt and tie walked in. I looked up at him. Mayor Schnabel. "Good morning. May I help you?" I asked in the sweetest voice I could muster, considering how tired I was.

The politician-smile was in place and working. "Hi, I'm Mayor Harold Schnabel."

"I recognized you."

"Good. I'm walking through downtown today talking with all the local business owners. Is John in?"

"Yes. So is Rich. John, Rich!" I called again. Maybe they should get an intercom. Both men appeared at the door and after shaking hands, the three men retreated into the conference room. As a lowly receptionist, I wasn't privy to the meeting.

The phone rang. "Security Investigations."

"Mel?"

"Yeah?"

"Tom Bressler. You really are working for Rich."

"Yep, but not for much longer. Just until Pam gets back. What can I do for you?"

"The mayor is walking the streets today and I was wondering if he has been there yet? I have an urgent message for him and he left his cell at the office." I could hear the frustration in his voice.

I chuckled. "The mayor is here. He just walked in a few minutes ago. Do you want to speak with him?"

"Could I?"

"Sure, hold on." I hit the hold button and stood up. I knocked on the door frame of the conference room. "Excuse me, but the mayor has a phone call."

"Thanks, Mel," John said. He leaned over, picked up the phone and handed it to Schnabel.

I nodded at them and left the room.

***

At suppertime I was eating my sandwich at the kitchen counter when someone knocked at my door. Before I could get up, the phone rang. Momentarily startled, I grabbed the portable phone off the counter, answering it as I looked through the door's peep hole. Max Bauer was standing on my landing. I opened the door and motioned Bauer in, then returned to my stool.

"Mel, it's Jason Landry. You called the other day. Sorry it's taken so long for me to return your call. What can I do for you?" Jason was one of my husband's two partners in the law firm he had started right out of school. It had grown fast, and now was very successful, with seven associates. They handled all sorts of cases.

I motioned for Bauer to sit on the other stool. "Yeah. Hi, Jason. I called because I was going through some boxes of Craig's and found some files that I think should probably have been at the office when he died." I covered up the phone and whispered to Max. "Want a drink?"

"Sure."

I got out a glass, then pointed at the refrigerator for him to get whatever he wanted. I watched him move, admiring him in his khaki shorts and red T-shirt.

"What kind of files, Mel?" Jason asked me.

"Well, I'm not really sure. I can read you the names off the tabs. I haven't really gone through them. As soon as I saw them, I called your office." I stood up and hurried into the living room to grab them.

"Yeah. Hold on for a minute while I go into my home office, Mel," Jason said putting me on hold.

I returned to the kitchen and set the pile of files near my food. Jason came back on. "Okay, ready."

"How do you want me to read them? By case number or name?"

"Just the names right now," Jason said.

I quickly went through the dozen or so files. I could hear Jason scribbling down the names. "Hmmm. They sound like copies of our files. Let me look into it at the office tomorrow and I'll let you know if you need to send them our way. Otherwise I'll just have you destroy them. Okay, Mel?"

"Sure. That's what I wanted to know."

"So how are things going for you?" Jason asked.

"Fine, most days. By the way, thanks for helping with the house sale. I really appreciate it." I took another drink of my Kool-aid.

"Not a problem. And you should be getting another check from one of Craig's previous cases. It just settled in court. I'll send Craig's share as soon as I can. And just so you know, your lawsuit is still where it was the last time we talked. If anything new comes up, I'll call and let you know."

"Thanks, Jason," I said. I turned to Max. "Sorry about that." I returned the portable phone to its charger on the counter near the door.

"What's with the Kool-aid?" He pointed at the drink sitting in front of me.

I took another drink. "My son got me addicted to it. It's a hard habit to break. Here, let me move these files out of the way."

"They look like law files or something," Max intoned as I set them on the far counter. I had noticed him peeking at them. I guess his cop radar was always on.

"Craig, my husband, was a lawyer in Maryland." I paused. I needed to get my thoughts away from my dead family. I was still tired from the long day, and I knew that it wouldn't take much for me to get depressed again. "What did you need to ask me?"

Max looked sympathetic, but cleared his throat and pulled a pile of pictures out of his T-shirt pocket. "Can you ID any of these people?"

I took the pile, slowly going through them. Several were photos of people I didn't recognize, but then they began to be more familiar. "This is the redhead that told me about Scott and Mouse swimming. And this is the blond that was with her." I indicated the two pictures. "I think this might have been one of the guys seated at the table with them in Hammerheads but I'm not totally certain of that." I continued to page through them. The last one caught my attention. "I know this person." I stared at it for several seconds. Finally, I figured it out. "This is Carly Smythe. We used to call him Weedman." I handed the pictures back to Max.

Max had been taking notes of the ones I had picked out. He looked up at me. "Weedman?"

I nodded. "He sold the best pot."

"Not that you bought off him," Max said with sarcasm. Max thumbed back to the two girls and the guy I had identified. "These three are drug dealers along with Mouse. 'Weedman' sells more than weed now. He's a major distributor of drugs here in Quincy. Mouse and Scott were both dealing for him." He paused to take a drink of cold water. The ice chimed against the glass. "We didn't tell the press, and please don't, but we found several bags of cocaine on Scott's body. Enough to know that he was definitely selling."

"So you think that Mouse and Scott's deaths are drug related?"

"That's the theory right now," Max said rubbing his eyes. "You look fairly rested. Who are you, superwoman?"

I laughed. "John kicked me out at lunch. I took a five-hour power nap."

He laughed with me. "I'll sleep really good tonight, unless you find another body."

"Not if I can help it. That's my quota for a while." I paused looking at him, his blue eyes studying me from his side of the counter. "But how is it connected to Eddie Baker?"

Max shrugged. "If it hadn't been for you talking with the Mousina girl and the note from Eddie, I'd say they were unrelated. As it is, they still might be. It could be a coincidence that she was just delivering that disk to Rich as a favor for Eddie and the two are truly unrelated. Quincy is a fairly small town." He shrugged again. "How did you know about Hiccome, Mousina, and their connection with Hammerheads?"

"I was talking to an old friend and an off comment by her reminded me that if Mouse ran with 'the wrong crowd' she might also have hung out at some of the 'wrong crowd' places. I found out that Hammerheads had changed names but not much else. It was a long shot." I didn't want to tell him about Tom Bressler. Not yet. Something about my old friend and his lie made me suspicious.

"Okay. One thing, though, Mel. Do you generally go to biker bars by yourself, then out into the dark of the night all alone?"

"You sound like my mom. I'm not your typical shrinking violet, Max. I never have been. It's gotten me in some situations that I probably shouldn't have been in, but overall I can take care of myself."

Max shook his head. "Well, you'd better stay away now. This is getting very ugly. Two people were killed due to drugs. I'd hate for you to get hurt because you were 'curious.'"

"I'm always careful."

"You'll stay away."

I mumbled something noncommittally. Max sighed. "How come I get the feeling that you are just humoring me?"

I said nothing to him and my eyes betrayed nothing either.

He stood up to leave. "Just don't, okay. I really don't want to see you get hurt." Max touched my shoulder and then left the apartment, closing the door behind him.

CHAPTER 9

The next morning, when I brought John a file he had requested, he said, "In my opinion, the four bodies are unrelated."

"Why do you say that? There have never been this many murders in Quincy within the same year, let alone weeks." I settled into the chair in front of his desk and crossed my arms.

He leaned back in his chair. "The two sets of bodies were killed with different calibers. The two brothers were killed with nine millimeters, the lovers with thirty-eights. It makes no sense that the killer would change MOs."

I grunted. He had a good point, but I still disagreed.

"The only common thread between them is that they knew each other. But we're talking about Quincy here. In this size of a town, everyone knows everyone." He shrugged. "Do you want my opinion on the deaths?"

"Yeah."

"The two brothers were killed by someone who knew they had something. The other two are drug related. As I said it just happened that they knew each other."

"But what about what Beth found out?"

"In my experience, losers are always working on something that will set them up for life."

I mumbled an 'okay', then headed back to my desk. I still wasn't sure about it. Quincy just couldn't have so many unrelated murders.

***

Sunday night I was waitressing at the Full Moon. The place was busy because of a softball tournament in town in which the police department had a team playing. After winning the tournament, they came to the bar to celebrate. The trophy was being passed around the tables as the men congratulated each other. It was very noisy.

Dad motioned me to join him behind the bar. "Can you run the bar for awhile? I promised some of the guys that I'd treat them to sandwiches."

"Sure Dad," I said with a smile. For the next hour I was constantly moving, getting beers and mixed drinks, and at the same time cleaning glasses and emptying recycling bins of bottles and cans.

"Hey, bartender!" a voice called out to me.

I grimaced and turned. I hated it when men yelled at me like that. It was Bauer and he was smiling at me from the other end of the bar. I smiled back and held up a finger for him to wait as I finished making a whiskey sour. I gave the customer his drink, then headed down the bar to wait on Max, refilling others' glasses as I went. Finally, I was in front of the handsome detective. "What can I get you?"

"What's on tap?"

"Bud, Bud light, Coors, Busch, Michelob," I went down the list by memory.

"Bud," Max said, then glanced around the bar. "Looks like we won."

"Yep. The trophy is floating around here somewhere." I stepped away from him to get his beer, then set it on the bar top. As I handed him back his change, he held onto my hand.

"You aren't working the case anymore, are you?" His blue eyes bore deeply into mine, and his touch grew warm, pleasantly warm.

"I've been too busy," I said, while extracting my hand. "Why? Did you find out anything new?" I glanced down the bar, but everyone seemed okay for the moment.

He looked blank. "I can't talk about it."

"So, you have found out something." I wiped the bar top with a rag and swept the crumbs onto the floor before setting a small bowl of pretzels on the bar. As Max reached for the pretzels, I pulled the bowl away.

He took a drink of his beer. "I can't be bought off with pretzels."

"What with then?"

His blue eyes twinkled and he lifted his brows.

"Not hardly, Max."

"Well, you asked," he said smugly.

I placed the bowl back in front of him. A customer down the bar signaled for me, so I left. When I slowly made my way back, Max's beer was almost gone. "Do you want a refill?"

"Sure." He drained it and set the glass in front of me.

I headed to the tap, glass in hand. As I filled it, I glanced back at him because I could feel him watching me again. "What?" I called out.

I sat the glass in front of him. After I got his change, he looked around the bar area.

"Where's your tip jar?"

"Nothing that fancy. Most people leave it on the bar top."

Max shook his head and motioned me closer.

Feeling suspicious, I leaned closer to him. He reached over the bar top and shoved the money into my shirt's collar. I jerked back and gave him a dirty look.

Jeers and cheers greeted him from the surrounding patrons. Apparently, the other cops had been watching us interact. Many were calling out to him to watch out, that I'd take his head off. The others were just catcalling me. Someone asked if this was the new way that I accepted tips. With a dirty look toward Max, I reached into my top and extracted the money. I snorted, calling out in a loud voice, "And he's cheap too."

Max blushed. The laughter in the bar increased.

He smirked. "Funny, Mel. That was a good tip."

"Yeah, but they didn't know that." I winked at Max and headed back down the bar.

Dad finally rejoined me. I asked him if I could cook up a tenderloin for myself because I was starving. He nodded, so I went and made two, then set one in front of Max and pulled up the stool next to his. He gave me a puzzled look.

I smiled. "It's a peace offering. The cheap tip thing was kind of rude."

Max looked under the bun, curious.

"It's a tenderloin," I explained to him as I pulled out the ketchup, mustard, and relish bottles from my apron and set them in front of him. I liked mine plain, the only way to eat them, in my opinion, and took a bite. "I take it you haven't had a tenderloin yet?"

Max shook his head.

I motioned to try it.

Taking a bite out of the sandwich, he looked closer at it as he ate. "Pretty good. But it needs ketchup." He grabbed the bottle and added it to the sandwich. Then he took another bite. He nodded at me as he chewed. "What's it made of?"

"Pork, sliced thin. Breaded and deep-fried," I said taking another bite of mine. "The Full Moon was voted 'Best Tenderloin in Town' for the third year in a row."

He took another bite and reached for his wallet.

I shook my head. "On the house."

"Thanks." He seemed to really be enjoying the sandwich.

"First Maid Rites, now tenderloins. Stay much longer here in Quincy and we'll have you eating like a native."

***

Monday morning after I got all the usual work done for John and Rich, I pulled the CD-ROM from its hiding place behind the cooler. I booted it up and took another look at it.

The letters and numbers seemed random. I sat back staring at the screen intently. There had to be something there; after all at least two people were killed for it. Not to mention the damage done to the office. I figured it was all because of the disk, although in reality it was just a guess. The more I looked, the less it made sense. Nothing.

"I've been wondering about that too," Rich said from behind me. "Go back to the first page again." He pointed at the screen. "They seem random but there is something there, I just bet." He frowned. "I'm supposed to know about this, huh?" he asked rhetorically.

"Is this the disk?" John asked us as he stood next to Rich.

Rich nodded. "Mel, go to the second page." He looked at John. "The only thing I can think of is that maybe it's an accounting sheet or something."

John crossed his arms while looking at the computer screen, studying it. "Without labeled columns, it could be anything, but it definitely has something to do with money. Go back to the one with all the letters." He shook his head. "That's it?"

Rich and I nodded.

"Got me," John said, and went back toward his office. "Let me know if you figure anything out." Rich shook his head and left too.

I stared at the screen for a few more minutes, then shut it down. After hiding the disk once more, I went back to work.

***

That night I pulled into Daniel Kickery's small automotive shop to see if he was still there, because I needed to ask him about a shake I noticed while driving the Jeep. Kick apparently did all sorts of work on cars; the sign out front mentioned at least half a dozen. The shop had three work bays and all were open.

As I pulled up, Kick saw me from the bay where he and another guy were working on an SUV. He smiled as he wiped his hands and headed outside. "Hi, Mel. What can I do for you?"

"I just wanted to ask you to look at these tires or something. I thought I had a shimmy in the Jeep the other night when I was down near the river." I stood looking at the right front tire. I had no clue what was wrong with it. I only assumed the tires were the problem.

Kick nodded and squatted down to look too. "This one looks okay to me." He moved around all four tires. "Doesn't look like they're separating or anything. What kind of shimmy?"

I shrugged.

"How about we go for a ride and see if it'll do it again?" Kick asked.

"Sure. But you know things never go wrong when the mechanic's in the car." I smiled at Kick as we hopped in the Jeep. But I was wrong. Before long the Jeep did the little shimmy when I made a hard right turn.

Kick nodded as I drove. "I know what that is. Do you have a few minutes when we get back to the shop?"

"Sure. I didn't have anything planned."

"I'll get you fixed up," he said.

I stood in the bay talking to him as he put the Jeep on a lift and worked on it. The shop had closed, but Kick wanted to get my vehicle fixed. He said he felt bad because he should have fixed it before he let me buy it. We had a pleasant conversation for the thirty minutes it took him to change the shock.

As he was lowering the vehicle I looked around, realizing that everyone had gone home. "Kick, I was wondering if I might ask you to help me out with something else?"

He looked perplexed but nodded. He motioned for me to follow him into the office. "Man, is it hot tonight. Have a soda while we talk." After getting comfortable in the chairs, he leaned back and looked closer at me. "What kind of help, Mel?"

I glanced around the shop. "You're still really good with computers, right?"

"I dabble."

"I have a disk that has some letters and numbers on it. Rich, John, and I can't figure it out." I could see that I had piqued his interest. "But the thing is, well see, I'm not supposed to be looking into this. I don't want Rich or John to lose their license."

"Does this have to do with a case of theirs?"

I made a face. "Well, not really, but then again, yeah."

Kick smiled. "So was that a yes or no?"

I smiled back. "Eddie Baker had it delivered to Rich. But we can't figure out what it means. Eddie said that Rich would know what to do with it, but Rich is stumped."

"Eddie was killed."

"Yeah."

"Did you turn it over to the police?"

"Yeah, but we made a copy first. The cops haven't had any luck either. We aren't supposed to be investigating because it's a police matter, but-"

Kick chuckled. "You always were insatiably curious."

"Rich and John are curious too, but they have to be careful so they don't get caught. If I'm doing it, they can claim they didn't know and fire me. So we have to keep this quiet. Not to mention whoever wants it probably killed for it and might have tried to burn down the office."

Kick's smile faded. "This is serious."

I nodded. "I wanted to be up front with you about it. I'll understand if you don't want to help me."

Kick looked off into the distance, then smiled back at me. "Then we'll just have to be careful."

"Good." I stood up. "Where and when do you want to see it?"

"Tomorrow, at my place. All of my computer stuff is there." He stood too, wrote his home address on the back of a business card, and handed it to me.

I thanked him for the fix and left. Maybe Kick could figure it out.

CHAPTER 10

The next day Rich sent me on an errand to 'pick up some supplies'. In reality, he told me to stop at a house on the west side of town to talk to a man named Tootie. According to Rich, if there were drug sales going on in this town, Tootie would know about it and be able to head us in the right direction about Scott and Mouse.

I knocked at the door and waited. The dilapidated red brick, two-story house had seen better days. At one time it had been a nice, one-family home but since the area had fallen on hard times thirty years ago, many homes had been converted to apartments. This particular one was only divided into two separate units.

The door opened to its security chain. A grungy, older lady looked out. "Yeah?"

"Hi. I'm looking for Tootie." I smiled at the lady.

"What for?" she asked, as she put the cigarette she was smoking back into her mouth.

"I just want to ask him some questions. Rich Addison said he would be home and that Tootie was the man to talk to," I said still smiling.

"You ain't no process server, are you?"

"No, ma'am."

"Repo people?"

"No."

"Cop?"

I chuckled. "No. Absolutely not."

"I like you. Tootie's around back puttering in the garden." She pointed around the side of the house and closed the door.

"Thanks," I said and headed around the house. I pushed open the falling-down gate. I walked cautiously into the back yard, not knowing what was there or what I might have to walk, hop, or fall over. Over all it was a neat yard, not a lot of trash anywhere. Most of the grass looked dead, except for one spot of green. That area was obviously well tended. An older man of at least sixty weeded the garden on his knees. "Tootie?"

The older man, just graying at the temples, turned slightly. "Yeah? Who wants to know?"

"Mel Addison. Rich's sister." I walked up closer and squatted down by him, holding out my hand. "Rich said that I could maybe ask you some questions."

"Rich, huh?" Tootie stared at me for a long minute. He wiped his hands on his pants and shook my hand. "Okay. Let me finish here first." He quickly finished weeding the row he was working on, then stood up.

I was already standing.

The old man stretched his back and rubbed it. "So, Rich's sister. He was always fair with me when he was a cop. What's he doing now?"

"A private detective here in town."

"Good for him. What can I do for you, little lady?" He paused. "Let's go sit under the tree back there." He pointed to a set of lawn chairs under an almost dead tree.

"I'm trying to find out who killed four people."

Tootie was nodding already. "Wally and Eddie Baker and Mouse and Hiccy-boy."

I smiled. "Hiccy-boy? I haven't heard that one."

Tootie laughed and pulled out a pack of cigarettes. He offered me one but I shook my head. "Yeah. I don't know anything about Wally and Eddie. I mean, I knew them from the streets but other than that-" He lit his cigarette. "Mouse and Hiccy, now they sold."

"Really? Did they die because of it?"

"Don't know. Could have. Streets are getting real mean lately. Weedman expanding and the regulars don't like it. Glad I'm out of it. Good thing I retired years ago." Tootie shook his head, looking off in the distance. "Nope, ain't no place for an old man like me."

"I heard that Mouse and Hiccy sold for Weedman."

"Yep. Started out with just weed, Carly did, then he decided to sell more than herbage. Wanted more money, so he contacted some people from Chicago. Don't know who exactly. They are always changing up there. Used to be the same ones all the time, but now that my generation is gone, it's just all gone to seed. Can't tell the players anymore. Some gang one week, different gang the next week. Then they're all fighting about territory." Tootie shook his head again. He puffed on the cigarette, then looked at me. "Ain't no good no more, nope."

"Who was Weedman expanding against?"

Tootie stared into my eyes for a few seconds. "Dangerous people."

"I'm not going to do anything by myself. If I get any good leads, I'll turn 'em right in to the cops. You know us Addisons. I'm just curious because I spoke with Eddie before he died." I swallowed back the guilt, again.

Tootie slapped me on the shoulder with a grin. "You sound like your daddy."

"Thanks, I think." I smiled at Tootie.

Laughter greeted me. "Weedman is trying to take away the street sales near the river. Been hanging out at Hammerheads. He bought out Steinman's area. Rumor has it that the Hessors don't like him moving in on that area, they were getting ready to take over for Steinman."

"You mean Madeline Hessor and company?" I asked, astonished. "I thought they got run out of town years ago."

Dad had a big case dealing with Madeline Hessor. He almost lost his life over it. As it was, there had been a big gun battle and three Hessor family members went to jail. Try as hard as they could, no one on the police force could connect them to the St. Louis drug groups. Everyone knew they were connected, but no one could prove it.

"Well. Sort of." Tootie nodded, seeming to be impressed that I knew that part of Quincy history. "They never really left or lost their control. It just passed to other people. Now Bart Hessor is in charge."

Hessor had been one year ahead of me in school. He attended the public high school, but we had dated, unbeknownst to my parents, for about two weeks. I met him at Eleven Bottoms where we partied together. "Bart, huh? So Weedman is butting in on his game."

"So I hear. You want to find the killers, I say look toward Hessor and company. But that's just my opinion," Tootie said taking one last drag on his cigarette. He tossed his butt into the dirt at his feet. "Hammerheads is Weedman's place. Hessor likes to be seen at Su Casa's on Broadway."

I knew the place. "I appreciate the history lesson, Tootie." I stood up with him.

"Tell Rich hi. And anytime you want to stop by, do so. I always like to have an Addison on good terms with me. I remember you too, Mel." Tootie winked. "Wreck any more cars lately?"

I cringed and pointed a finger at him. "Don't tell my Dad that. He still thinks it got taken by some lowlifes. If he ever finds out it was me, even now, I think he'd skin me alive."

Tootie laughed and after shaking hands, he moved back to his garden.

I headed out toward the front yard and tried to shake the feeling of guilt that I had about smashing up my Dad's car. Worse than that, I had lied right to his face about it. One of the few things that I truly felt bad about. I wished that there was some way I could make it up to him. Most of the stuff I did as a kid was harmless, but that was serious. Sometimes the past comes back to haunt us.

***

I found a parking place at Su Casa at the end of a row of brand-new, expensive cars. My rust-spotted Jeep was out of place there.

I had changed from my usual jeans and T-shirt into nicer jeans and a dressy shirt. It was too hot out to wear a jacket. I smoothed the creases out of the shirt, patted both of my back pockets to make sure that my cell phone and wallet were there. Then I took a deep breath and entered the air-conditioned cool of the bar. It was just after happy hour, so the place was not quite packed.

Su Casa was an upscale bar with a Mexican theme. It was the kind of place where the yuppie crowd would hang out, where businessmen might take their clients. It was situated on Broadway, the busiest street in town. Su Casa looked clean and respectable. Not my usual type of hang out, but maybe I could spot Hessor. I just bet the beers were overpriced.

Once inside, I let my eyes adjust to the dim light, then moved up closer to the bar. As I walked, I looked around.

Rich wasn't happy when I told him I was going to Su Casa; he got angry even when I mentioned in passing that I knew Bart Hessor. Rich had agreed to let me go if I only stayed for two hours and called him the minute I was away from the place. If I didn't call in two hours and one minute, he would barge in and physically pull me out. It's nice to have big brothers to worry about me. Of course, when I needed them to worry about me, back in high school, they could have cared less.

I ordered a beer and some nachos. The place was known for its nachos, a big heaping plate of refried beans, all the sauces, chips, and tomatoes. The beers were slightly higher priced then at my Dad's bar, but not as bad as I had expected. I sat on a stool near the end of the bar so that I could see most of the room. I didn't recognize anyone.

I got comfortable and watched the ballgame playing on the TV over the bar. It was the Orioles. Even if Hessor didn't show, I decided to stay and watch the game since it was on ESPN and I didn't have cable at home. I missed watching the local Baltimore team. It reminded me of Maryland. A couple of times I got misty thinking about that, but mostly I just enjoyed the game.

Almost two hours later, a man moved in next to me to get some drinks. I looked closely at him. *Could he be Bart?* He was looking at me the same curious way.

"Do I know you?" I asked. I was pretty sure it was Bart now. He wore his blond hair differently when he was younger, but he still had the same walk and attitude I remembered.

"I certainly hope so," he said with a smirk. "My name is Bart Hessor." He held out his hand.

I let the astonishment play on my face. I was so good at lying. "No kidding!" I shook his hand.

"You apparently do know me," Bart's smile stretched from ear to ear; his eyes raked me up and down. "Good. I always like it when beautiful women know me. The question is, do I know you?"

I laughed in spite of myself. "You haven't changed one bit, Bart."

He looked closer, but it was clear he hadn't a clue who I was.

"Mel Addison."

"No way!" Hessor took a step away and looked me over again. "Wow, you're gorgeous. If I had known how good you would look now, I'd have made it to more then second base with you. Where did you disappear to?"

"College, out of state."

"Home for good or just a visit?"

I waved to the bartender for another beer. "Matt, put it on my tab," Hessor said to the bartender.

"Thanks Bart, but you don't have to do that."

He shrugged. "I own the bar. Gotta have fun sometimes." He took the beer from the bartender and handed it to me. "So, is this a visit or back for good?"

"Back for a while at least."

"Good. Married, single, what?"

I hesitated for an instant. Proclaiming my usual 'widowed' just didn't seem right. So I decided to go with a different slant, and the lie didn't bother me in the least. "Single. Again."

He nodded. Hessor looked back toward the far end of the place and held up a finger for someone to wait. He turned back to me. "Why did you stop here? Doesn't your dad own a bar?"

"Yep, but I wanted a change of pace. Cops are there all the time."

Bart's face changed for a split second, then he went back to smiling. "Still having fun with that?"

"Not really. I'm not a kid anymore, Bart. No, I'm a law-abiding citizen. Still, sometimes they give me the willies." I gave a fake shudder.

"You haven't changed much either." He reached out, placing his hand on my arm. "Tell me, are you still as fun to be with as when we were younger?" His smile had taken on a sly look as he leaned in closer.

"Older and wiser," I said. I knew how to flirt too.

"I bet," Hessor winked. "Do you still like to party?"

"Depends on what you mean by 'party'? Do I like to go to parties? Yes. Do I still drink like I used to? No. And just so you know, I still don't do drugs," I said seriously.

"Come on. Really?" Hessor hesitated then nodded. "Okay. I can handle that."

I lifted my eyebrows. "And that means what?"

He laughed loudly, amused at my expression. "I'm having a barbecue Friday night at my house. Why don't you come? It starts at five for my private guests. But the whole thing really gets going around seven. Show up then. By ten, most of the losers will be gone. Bring a swimsuit; I have a huge pool."

I looked doubtful. "I don't know." I checked my watch. I needed to be heading out soon.

"Got a date?"

"No. Mom and Dad are having a get together at the old homestead and they're expecting me." I sighed in fake boredom.

"Family is important. I'll walk you out." He set his drink on the bar and ordered the bartender to deliver the others to the table from which he had come. With his hand on my back, he walked me out the door. After holding the door open for me, he placed his arm around my waist. "Which car is yours?"

I chuckled. It was easy to fall back into the old friendly ways with Bart. "You wouldn't believe it, if I told you."

His eyes scanned up and down the line of cars. "Let's see-" His eyes stopped on the Jeep. He looked at me, amusement once more in his eyes. "The rusty Wrangler?"

I nodded and we headed that way.

"You definitely haven't changed at all," Bart said walking even closer to me. He stopped me before I could get into the car. "Look, I know that we never got to know each other very well, but-" He switched his hold on me so both hands were on my waist, and we faced one another. "Come to the party. Have a few beers. I promise you a good time, for old times' sake."

I considered. "Well, maybe." I looked into his eyes.

"Good." He leaned down and kissed me on the lips: a sweet, gentle kiss. "For old times' sake." With one hand, he reached into his pocket, and then released the other hand from around my waist. He helped me into the Jeep, then handed me the card. "My address. Seven. Bring a swimsuit, or not. Whatever."

"Maybe," I said and started the Jeep, tucking the card into my pocket. I glanced back to see that he was watching me drive away. I gave him a little wave and accelerated down Broadway, heading west toward home.

After getting several blocks away, I called Rich. It was getting close to the time that he was going to barge in. I got his answering machine on his home phone, so I tried his cell. I got his voice mail on that one too. I shook my head. *Really reliable, my brother.* "I'm out of Su Casa, just so you know. Hopefully, you'll get this before you bust down the door with the intent of dragging me away. Call me tonight or I'll just tell you about it in the morning." I hung up with a sigh.

As I drove, I thought about Bart. He really hadn't changed. He was still a playboy, 'every girl wants me', kind of man. And he now had the money to back up his lifestyle. He was dangerous.

And the kiss?

It had been a long time since I had been on the dating scene. Up until this point, I hadn't even thought about men, not seriously. But the kiss had gotten to me. Now I was confused. I still felt like I should be mourning for my husband, and yet the desire to be held was working its way to the foreground. I frowned as I turned the corner on Twelfth Street, heading for home.

Once inside I tried to wind down, ignoring my inclination to think about men and kissing. Just as I was getting a bite to eat, I heard a loud pounding on my door. *Who would be banging like that?* I glanced at the clock before I looked out the peephole. It was after nine o'clock at night.

Max Bauer was standing on my doorstep and he did not look happy.

I smiled as I opened the door. "Hello."

He just looked at me. His tie was loose around his neck. His shirt was wrinkled and he looked pissed off. I motioned him into the air conditioning. "Can I get you a drink?"

"No. What are you doing?"

I cocked my hip and looked at him. "Doing? I'm having a late supper. What are you doing?" His anger caused my own to rise, although I had no clue as to why he was mad. "I didn't invite you here."

"Tonight. I told you to stay out of it." Bauer was staring down at me, hands on hips, his blue eyes hardened.

"Stay out of what?"

"You were at Su Casa tonight."

"Oh that." I paused, considering how to go about this. "Yeah." I looked him in the eye. "I stopped there looking for someone. So?"

"You found someone." There was genuine anger in his tone.

I looked at him in confusion. Okay, I knew he'd be mad when he found out I was still working the case, but what was this? "True, but not the person I was looking for. I went looking for an old girlfriend of mine. She was supposed to be in town for the week, visiting her parents. She didn't make it." *Liar, liar pants on fire.*

Max gave me a stern look, like he was trying to decide if he should believe me.

"While I was at the bar an old friend, a male that I used to hang with occasionally, saw me. We exchanged pleasantries." I shrugged, trying to appear casual.

"Do you know who the guy was that walked you to your Jeep?"

I nodded with a wry smile. "He kissed me. I had better well know who he was or he'd have gotten flattened to the ground."

Max's eyes lightened just a bit at that. His hands left his hips.

75

I motioned for him to sit at the counter. "It was Bart Hessor. Like I said, I used to hang with him occasionally. I actually dated him for a short time." I paused. "Don't tell my family that."

"Why?"

"His aunt used to be a major drug dealer in town. My Dad busted her and a couple other members of her family. Hessor and I dated shortly before that. Dad would kill me if he knew that, even now." I sat down across from Max. A thought suddenly popped into my head. "Hey, how did you know that I had been to the bar? And why do you care?"

Max's eyes burrowed into mine. Now it seemed he was trying to decide just how much I knew. "We're watching him."

"Why?"

"I can't tell you that."

I frowned and looked thoughtful. Then I tried to look like I had had a revelation. "Did he take over for his aunt?"

Max barely reacted, but the surprise showed just slightly. "I can't tell you that."

"Aha!" I snapped my fingers. "This is related to Mouse and Scott Hiccome, isn't it?"

"I can't tell you that."

I leaned forward just a bit. "Anything else?"

"Why did you let him kiss you?"

"He just did it."

"But you let him. I don't know you all that well, but I know you well enough to know that you knew it was coming and you let him do it."

I shrugged. "Yeah, so. Bart and I have a history, short as it was. I told you that."

Max had a disgusted expression on his face. "The guy is suspected to be one of the major drug dealers in the city!"

"We were teens, it was a long time ago."

"So you have slept with him!" Anger erupted again from Max.

"No." I shook my head. *What is going on here?* "I wouldn't let him. Even back then I had more sense then that."

Max gave me disbelieving look. "Then why did you let him kiss you tonight?"

"Am I under arrest because I kissed a man?"

"Hardly. I'm just trying to figure you out," Max paused, then added a bit too fast, "And I'm trying to keep you safe."

I laughed. "Safe? Keep me safe? I don't want your help or need it, Detective Bauer."

"What did he hand you?"

I gave Max a hard look. "Do you want to pat me down for drugs?"

"Mel, I'm serious here."

"I am too. Are you arresting me?"

"No. I'm asking you," Max said with a softer tone. His blue eyes turned sincere.

"He gave me a business card. Bart wants me to call him sometime. I'm sure he still wants to go out with me." I pulled the card out of my pocket. "See. No drugs. I don't do drugs, Mr. Police Officer."

Max glanced at it, then nodded. "I'm serious, Mel. Stay out of it and away from Hessor."

I sighed. "I just met the guy and spoke with him. We talked about old times."

"He's not a nice guy. I have no idea what he was like back when you were younger, but he's not going to be good for you now," Max said and stood up. He rounded the counter and looked me in the eyes. "For your own sake, stay away from him."

I just stared at his blue eyes, delving into mine. "Is this a new policy of the police force? Watch out for the Addison girl?"

Max smiled at that. He reached out and tugged my hair just a bit. "No, I just don't want you involved or hurt." He walked out the door, closing it behind him.

I sat there slightly stunned. He tugged my hair. *What was that about?*

CHAPTER 11

After discussing the evening events, 'we' decided that it was too dangerous for me to go to Bart's party. Rich was adamant about that. So I placed a call to Hessor and left a message on his machine that something had come up, I wouldn't be there on Friday. Next, I called Bauer's home phone but he was gone. After talking with Mitch at the police station, I found out Max was there, so I walked the short distance from our office to talk to him and to let him know about Bart's party.

I pushed open the door to the police headquarters and greeted the receptionist. Pearl had been keeper of the front desk since I was a teen. She directed me down the hall to the squad room. I entered, remembering all the other times I had entered in search of one of the members of my family. Granted, this wasn't the old station I was used to, but the atmosphere was the same. Several officers greeted me by name and directed me to Mitch. After informing them that I wasn't looking for my brother, I got some strange looks, but when I asked, they directed me toward the detectives' room.

Butch was the only person in there. I smiled at him. He stood up when I entered.

"Mel! What are you doing here? Did you get arrested again?"

"Again?" I smirked. "I've never been arrested."

"You should have been." He chuckled.

"Maybe." I gave him a wry grin. "I'm looking for Max Bauer."

"Bauer is right here," Max said, walking in the door behind me. He gave me a smile that extended all the way from his soul out through his eyes. The embrace of the deep blue warmed my heart. "To what do I owe this pleasure?"

"Business." I gave a quick glance around. Butch was pretending to work, but he was also actively listening to us, I could tell.

Max became guarded, wary. "Okay." He paused at my quick glance around. "Here?" He quickly glanced at his watch. "Or do you want to do it over an early lunch?"

I hesitated. Now that I had figured out he was flirting with me, I didn't want to encourage him, but I didn't want a lot of people to know that I knew Bart Hessor as more than a passing acquaintance. "Hmmm, lunch. A business lunch."

"Okay," Max said and grabbed his light windbreaker off a nearby chair. Today he was dressed in a charcoal-gray polo shirt and khaki chinos, impeccable as always.

I looked him up and down quickly as he swung his jacket on. *Is there any outfit that doesn't suit him perfectly*? I gave myself a little reprimand as I followed him out the door, which he held for me. I smiled a thank you as I passed him, which he returned graciously. I took a shallow breath to compose myself. Thinking such thoughts was wrong. Dead wrong. Just like my dead husband. *Get a grip on yourself.*

We walked to a nearby cafe. Since it was already crowded, Max suggested we buy sandwiches to eat in the small courtyard near his office. There were several benches there and since it was still early, it was deserted. We settled down on one, Max sat right next to me, which didn't help.

I felt weird. I enjoyed being with him. Max made me feel cherished but another part of me was feeling guilty about being with him, like I shouldn't be enjoying his company.

"So," Max said after we sat down. "You had a specific reason for coming to see me, and you didn't want too many people to know about it." He smiled. "Have I guessed right?"

"Yeah, I wanted to let you know-" I paused to take a bite of my sandwich. "-Bart called last night." *I really have to stop lying like this.*

Max stopped chewing. He looked closely at me. "And?"

"He's having a party at his house on Friday. Invited me to go. I begged off. He made it sound like it was semi-business. The party starts at five for 'special' guests. The main party is around seven. He made it sound like it would last most of the night, but 'the losers would be gone by around ten'." I shrugged. "I just thought you'd like to know, since you're watching him."

His blue eyes continued to bore into me as I went back to eating. "You aren't going, right?"

"I said no. I told him I had other things to do." I made a point of making sure I was not looking at Max. To be honest, I still hadn't decided whether or not I would go, even though everyone was saying not to. Talking with Hessor would give me the opportunity to find out about Mouse and Scott Hiccome. "He did say that it would be mostly an outside party. He mentioned swimming."

Out of the corner of my eye, I saw Max grimace. "Look at me, Mel."

I turned.

"You will not go."

"I already said I wasn't." Our eyes were locked in silent combat.

Max broke eye contact, and made a 'huff' noise. He went back to eating. "Anything else?"

My gut twisted. *What was I feeling and why was I feeling this way? Get a grip.* "Yeah, but not about Bart."

Max's eyes rose back to meet mine once more.

"Uh, look, I've, uh, been off the dating scene too long and I just last night, uh, realized that you've been flirting with me. Sorry I didn't pick up on it sooner." I felt myself almost blushing.

Max's eyes turned a deep blue. Amusement was once more in the forefront. "Okay. I understand. Not a problem."

"And I, uh, I'm not ready for dating and, uh, the whole thing. So I'd appreciate it if you'd, well-" I stopped but my eyes were still locked with his.

"Back off?" He smiled one of those lopsided, loveable smiles. Even his eyes were smiling.

This time I knew without a doubt that I was blushing. I could feel the heat in my cheeks. I *never* blush. "Yeah."

"Sure, Tiger." His tone indicated that he was still flirting.

I could feel my anger rising fast. The question was, and I barely wanted to acknowledge it, was I angry at him or myself? I shook my head at myself. *Him.* It had to be him and his refusal to stop flirting with me. "I mean it, Max. I do not want to do this. I'm not ready yet. What I mean is-"

"You got it, Tiger." Max winked.

"You don't get it. Just stop flirting!" I tossed the rest of my lunch in the nearby trashcan and walked away. I knew my anger was getting ready to hit me full blast. Not a good thing, I knew from past experience.

Max caught up with me and clutched me by the arm. "Wait, Mel. I didn't mean anything by it." He looked me in the eyes.

My anger was ready to explode like a volcano. And if he continued to flirt, I would hit him, police officer or not. Tears of frustration welled in my eyes but I willed them away. "Look, I don't need this." I pulled my arm out of his hand. "So just stop."

Now the look on Max's face was one of puzzlement. He hesitated, then gave a sort of nod. "I understand that you're still-I did stop when I learned about you, but when you kept flirting with me, I just thought that-"

"I was not!"

Max merely looked at me.

I looked off to the side of him and thought back to all the times that we'd been together. I *had* been flirting with him. A slight blush crept across my face again. *How could I have been flirting like that? Craig. Robbie. How could I have abandoned their memory so fast?*

"Mel."

My eyes flicked back to Max's even as I felt myself getting ready to cry again. Tears filled my eyes.

Max was watching me with a serious look. "I'll stop. I understand that you're still grieving. I got it. I just thought that you were over him-or maybe that you-" He shifted his weight on his feet, obviously uncomfortable. Then his face softened. "It's okay to cry, Mel. It's part of the grieving process. There's nothing wrong with letting out all the hurt and pain." He held out his hands.

A tear fell slowly, and I quickly wiped it away. I shook my head no.

"Mitch said that you were a closed person, keeping things inside. Just know that I'm here if you want to talk or well, anything. Okay?" He reached out and touched my arm.

I just looked at him, then with a sniff, I glanced at his hand. He quickly dropped it off my arm, getting the implied message.

"So when you are ready to move on with life, you know, dating or even just flirting, let me know. For now, we'll just be friends. Everyone needs friends. I do." Max held out his hand. "Deal?"

I hesitated. "No flirting?" My anger rapidly dissipated and that warm feeling was settling into every nook and cranny of my heart. It felt nice having something other than pain there. *But why the warm feeling?* I quickly wiped my wet eyes again.

"None. Friends." His hand was still out.

I shook, and felt the same rush that I had before. It had to be just his warm hand. It had to be. I was impressed that he didn't let his grip linger in mine. I was grateful for that. He held my gaze.

"But you will not go to the party."

"No, Mr. Policeman, I won't go."

"Good." Max smiled. A friendly smile, even though his eyes spoke volumes. "Be careful walking back to the office, Mel."

"Yeah. Thanks," I said and continued on my way, relieved by the way it had turned out. I felt lighter, like a weight was off my shoulders. I rubbed my hand on my jeans. *Yes, we can be friends but nothing more. He's right. I do need friends.* And in my heart, I knew Max would be a great friend.

I reviewed the conversation again as I neared the office and the warm feeling grew.

***

That night I closed up the office by myself. Rich had surveillance to do, and John was gone on one of his trips. Trying to drum up business, I guess. I locked up, and walked down the block and around the corner. I only had two more weeks of this hideous parking situation. Then when Pam was back, I would give a lot more thought to what I wanted to do with my life. I wasn't paying much attention, so when I looked up, I jumped in surprise. A man was sitting in my Jeep.

Bart Hessor smiled. "Hi, Mel."

I suppressed a grimace. I didn't smile. "What are you doing in my car?"

"Not even a hello?"

"Hello."

Bart smiled even bigger. "I was driving by and saw, well, this." He patted the Jeep. "I stopped and decided to wait for you. I figured you probably got off work around five." He glanced down at the vehicle. "You really ought to get this thing painted. I hope it runs better then it looks."

I glanced behind my car and saw a brand-new, green Jaguar sitting there. "Aren't you slumming it, sitting in my car?"

Hessor belly laughed at that. "I have always loved your wit." I leaned on my Jeep, looking at him. "I got your message." His face fell just a bit. "Are you really busy on Friday night?"

I hesitated, but told him the truth. "No."

Hessor just stared at me.

"I gave it some thought after I left Su Casa. I don't think it would be good for either of us if I went to your party."

"Why? Because of your brothers?" Bart crossed his arms.

"That would be one reason."

"And the other?"

I sighed. "Look, it was stupid of me to date you in high school. My Dad and your family certainly have no love lost between them. I don't want our names to be Capulet and Montague." I saw Bart smile. "And I suspect that your 'job' is diametrically opposed to me and my values."

He frowned.

"Honestly, Bart. Do you do drugs?"

He nodded. "Occasionally, but not often."

"Did you take over for your aunt selling drugs?" His face darkened. "The look on your face is answer enough," I said. "I was stupid to like you when we were teens. I'm not stupid anymore. I can't do that to my family."

"Don't take this wrong Mel, but you never cared what your family thought."

"Back then, probably not," I admitted, even though a huge stab of guilt pierced my heart. "I enjoyed disobeying as a teen. I grew up."

"Still grieving?"

I narrowed my eyes.

"I checked you out. It wasn't hard. The Addisons are a very likable subject in town. I heard about your family. Sorry for your pain, Mel," Bart said. His tone and the look on his face proved that he was being sincere.

"Thanks."

Hessor nodded. "Still, you must move on with life."

"I know." My gut twisted in a familiar way, like at the park with Max, but there was no warm feeling this time.

"Then why not just come to my house to reminisce? Not the party, I understand now. Just come over some night and we'll have a few beers, swim like old times and laugh." Hessor smiled again. "I won't tell anyone about it. That way Daddy dear, Rich, or Mitch will never hear about it."

I shook my head. "I'm not ready for any of that."

"I understand, Mel. I really do. I won't try anything. Really. I've grown up too. Just a beer. Tell me about what happened after you left me high and dry that last night." He grinned arrogantly. No, he had definitely not changed one bit. "You owe me that."

"I owe you nothing, you dirt bag!"

Bart laughed.

"I don't know. Let me think about it."

Bart nodded and got out of the Jeep. "You have my card. Call. I won't intrude on your life. None of your family will know about it, I promise. Besides, you don't think I want anyone to know that I had a date with the sister of a cop." He winked. Bart touched my chin as he moved away. "Call."

I watched as he left and gave a toot of his horn while driving by. I waved and shook my head. I hopped into my vehicle and drove away. Here was a really good lead to the murderer and I was too chicken to follow it up. I really needed to think about it.

My answering machine was blinking when I got home. Dan Kickery. "No luck on the disk. Just wanted to let you know. I'll keep trying. How's the Jeep running? This is Kick by the way. Later."

Good old reliable Kick. He was probably staying up nights trying to decipher it. I erased the message and fanned myself with my T-shirt. The air conditioner was working hard, but I cranked it up another notch. I stood in front of it letting the cold air flow over my body. It was unbearable outside. Maybe I should take the money from Craig's last case and buy a car with an air conditioner. I laid my hands on the window unit and looked down at them.

I stood there for a long time just thinking about Craig and Robbie. This time I cried with no shame. The tears flowed steadily down my face. Five, ten minutes. An hour until they stopped and dried on my cheeks, yet still I stood there. When I finally pulled myself away from the window I didn't feel like eating. I grabbed a glass of Kool-aid out of the fridge before moving into the living room. I switched on the TV and flipped channels. The local news station was running a piece on the mayoral election and the candidates. I sat and watched it for lack of anything better to do. Schnabel was being portrayed as a family man, strong on family values and helping the less fortunate. Williams was being portrayed as a man working to improve the economy, bringing more industry to the area.

The lies were getting bigger and bigger as the election got nearer. *By election time, Schnabel will be the world's savior and Williams will have single handedly brought the nation's economy back to the way it was in the fifties.* I chuckled at my own thoughts. I flipped the channels again, getting bored with the political stuff. Nothing on any of the channels. Maybe I would have to talk Dad into letting me install cable. I switched off the TV and walked toward the stereo.

I stood there contemplating what to play. My eyes landed on the soundtrack to Aladdin. I pulled it out of the stack in the box, gently running my finger over the cover in circles. It was Robbie's favorite CD. In an almost daze, I put it in the stereo. The music washed over me.

My mind flipped back to the day after I bought the movie. Robbie loved the genie. For days afterward, Robbie had tried to imitate him. He would play this CD over and over, singing with the songs and dancing around. Never knowing all the lyrics. Making up some of his own. I smiled remembering his quirky lyrics.

A knock at the door brought me out of my reverie. I opened it and let Bressler in. "Hi." I closed the door, wondering what he was doing at my house.

"Aladdin?" He smiled.

"Thinking of my son." I hurried into the living room and shut it off. Bressler was watching me from the kitchen.

"You didn't have to shut it off because of me."

"I was done thinking of Robbie," I said with a quick swallowing of my pain. I pushed it into the background as I returned to the kitchen. "What can I do for you?"

Bressler shrugged. "I was thinking of you today. So I stopped by the bar looking for any of your family to find out where you were staying. I remembered that I heard your dad bought this bar. Cameron was downstairs; he pointed up."

"You found me. Want a drink?"

"Sure. I'll drink what ever you are," Tom said sitting down on a stool.

Ifter I handed him his glass, I watched as he tasted it.

"Kool-aid!" Bressler smiled. "Let me guess, Robbie?"

I nodded. "Did you want anything specific?"

"Not really. I was thinking about Mouse and the other night."

I kept my face expressionless. "Yes?"

"I felt bad lying to you." He looked down at the glass then took a drink. "This would taste better with gin or vodka in it."

"I don't have any, sorry."

"It's just, well, I can't be seen associating with that kind of person anymore." He looked up at me. "I know that sounds bad, but it's the way it is. I have to think of my career."

"Did you actually talk to Mouse?"

Bressler nodded. "I was at Hammerheads trying to get a hold of one of the mayor's, uh, workers. He wasn't there. I was just leaving the place when Mouse snagged my arm. She's nothing like she was. I didn't even recognize her. She used to be sweet but time and drugs, anyway, she asked me if I had a minute." Bressler paused. "I motioned her outside. She said that she was in a bad way and wanted some advice."

"About?"

He was looking down at his hands as he fiddled with the edge of his shirt. "She said that she had starting using and selling, and that she had been approached by the 'opposition'. Mouse said that she'd make more money with them, but Weedman was like a father to her and she couldn't go behind his back. However, they were really giving her no choice. She said she was scared."

I sat there watching him. He was very nervous about something. I frowned since he wasn't watching me. "Why did she talk to you? What did she want from you?"

Finally he looked up. "I have no idea. She just told me that, then as I stood there, confused to be honest, she kissed me on the cheek and hurried away with a thank you. Maybe she just wanted someone to talk to about it. I don't know."

I ran a hand over my lip. This was too weird. "What did you do?"

"I stood there for a few seconds, not knowing what to do. I just sort of shrugged and walked back to my car. I went home." Bressler looked closely at me. "Sorry I lied to you the other night. You sort of threw me for a loop."

I smiled. "Well, thanks for telling me the truth."

"Sure. Did she say anything to you, the night you spoke with her?"

I thought quickly back to the night I had first seen Tom Bressler and tried to remember what I had told him about Mouse. "Not much. I wouldn't have even said anything about it to you or anything, but she bumped into me on the street as I was closing up. After her picture appeared in the paper, I called Mitch to let him know that I had seen her. Turns out it was the night she died. I picked up an envelope that fell out of her pocket." I shrugged. *Good thing I remembered my lie.*

Bressler waited.

"Did she say who the opposition was?" I took a drink of my Kool-aid.

"No, but I can guess."

"Who?"

"Bart Hessor." Bressler watched my reaction.

"Bart Hessor?" I tried to look shocked. "Didn't you have a thing going with him in high school? Rivals or something?"

Bressler nodded with a grin. "Yeah. He stole one of my girls, so I stole one back. But, do you want to know who the real prize was?"

"Who?"

"You."

"Excuse me?"

Bressler chuckled. "Yeah. The bet was to see who could get the farthest with you. I was so happy when you broke it off with him."

I smirked back. "Why me?"

"You were from Notre Dame. What more is there to say? Who ever could bag you was going to be the man at Eleven Bottoms. The contest was legendary."

Ah ha! That was what Mouse had meant. I was the prize in this contest. "So, what happened? I wouldn't do anything with either of you."

"Yeah, I know," he said. "The bet just sort of got shelved."

I suddenly laughed. "So that was the reason why you wanted me to go with you guys to Washington Park that night."

Bressler nodded shyly. "Yeah, I was hoping to get you alone somewhere. As you well know, it didn't work." He glanced at his watch. "Well, I'd better get going. I've got a brief with the mayor in the morning." He stood up and looked at me as I stood. "Look, if you ever want to go out, just give me a call." He gave me a peck on the cheek. "See ya, Mel."

I locked the door. He was still lying. *Is any of it true?* I did believe him when he said he talked to Mouse. *But is the rest of it a lie? And even worse, why did he all of a sudden come to me to tell me the 'truth'?*

CHAPTER 12

The next day I was still puzzling over Bressler's story. *What should I do? Should I talk to Hessor and just ask him outright? Like he'd tell me if he ordered Mouse and Scott killed. Would he admit to trying to entice Mouse to sell for him, if it were true? Or will he just make a pass at me and make me mad? Again.* And what did I do about *Bressler?* Both men still wanted to date me. *Can I use that to my advantage? I really didn't want to date, but I could fake it to get information.* It was almost too much to think about. If only we knew what was on that disk. I thought about it again. There had to be something on it. Surely two people, maybe four, weren't killed for a random jumble of numbers and letters.

The office door opened and Marion Williams walked in.

"Hi, Mr. Williams. Can I help you?"

"Sure." His fake politician smile brightened the room like a dim bulb. "Is John or Rich in? I know this is sudden, but could I speak with them? If they aren't busy?"

"Sure. John!" I looked back at Williams. "Rich is out on a case."

Williams continued to smile as he waited for John. "Mr. Huddleston, sorry for the imposition. I'd like to hire your firm for a little job." Williams shifted on his feet and glanced at me.

John's face didn't change expression, but he nodded.

I glanced from John to Williams and back again. John was surprised. It didn't show on his face, but I was getting a lot better at reading him.

"Let's talk in my office. Hold my calls Mel," John said, with a quick look at me as he motioned Williams into the hall.

"Sure thing."

I wondered what would prompt a political candidate to want to hire a detective. Hopefully, John would let me know. I admit, I was extremely curious.

Well over forty minutes passed before the mayoral candidate exited the office. Williams exchanged greetings with John and left the office. John stood there looking down at the floor, hands in his pockets. He was either very puzzled by something or shocked.

Finally, John looked at me. "Run his name through the usual databases."

"Okay." Now I was mystified, but excited.

John crossed his arms with another glance out of the window. "And check the mayor's name too. See if you can come up with a list of everyone working on both of their campaigns."

I nodded again, jotting down notes. "Can I ask why?"

John hesitated. "We've been hired to check into his personnel. He thinks there's a leak in his organization somewhere. Williams mentioned several 'secrets' that have gotten over to the other side." John uncrossed his arms. "Sometime today, he'll email us a list of people in his employ that I want you to run through the databases too. I'm not sure how long it will be. It might take a lot of time."

"That's fine, I was almost out of things to do anyway." I smiled. Sarcasm is never lost on John. "I even have a source in the other camp, Tom Bressler. He's some sort of PR person for Schnabel. I could see if I can get a list of people from him."

"Good. Do that." John turned to walk back to the office. "Officially, we are under contract to Williams. Mum's the word to your contact."

"Sure thing," I said as he left me to start the database searches. This would be fun. I was going to get to see all of the dirt on both candidates.

***

It was after three by the time the email came from Williams. John forwarded it to me, so that I could start on the list. I sighed as I pulled it up. There were over two hundred names. I took a hard copy of the files on Williams and Schnabel that I had already found into John. "Here. Prelims on both candidates."

John took them. "I saw the list. If Rich and I both take some tomorrow, we might get finished with all the profiles by Thursday."

"How deep are we supposed to go?"

John leaned back in his chair as I took the seat in front of his desk. "Good question."

"I've got some more information on the two main guys still heading my way. But on the lists..." I drifted off.

"Yeah. Definitely do as thorough a search as possible on the two candidates, down to what they ate the last three years. On the lists, also do a thorough search on at least the top five people. After that, we'll do it on a case-by-case basis." He grimaced. "And we don't have a lot of time. Williams wants to know if there is a leak as fast as possible. So, I want you on this full time. As a matter of fact, maybe tomorrow, could I get you to work some extra hours?"

I shrugged. "Sure, I guess."

"Good," John thumbed through the file quickly. He frowned. "Both men are clean."

"I know. But considering what they want, I would think that any good campaign officer would be able to clean up the files that I searched. I'm digging deeper for dirt."

"Good. The only thing on Schnabel is a parking ticket six years ago." John read from one of the papers. "And Williams in completely clean."

"Yeah. They have never strayed one inch from the law." The sarcasm was literally dripping from my words.

John smiled.

"Could Williams' accusations be true?"

John considered before answering. "Maybe. In my experience, political people are paranoid anyway, but the two things he mentioned might have gotten to the other side by an inside source." John shrugged. "Our job is to find out."

I stood up. "I'll talk to my contact tonight and see if I can get a list from him or something."

"Thanks, Mel."

I headed back to my desk, hesitated, then picked up the phone. It rang three times before it was picked up; there was a lot of yelling in the background. "Beth?"

"Yeah … Stop it, right now!" Beth yelled at one of her kids. "Who is this?"

I chuckled. "It's Mel. Call my cell when you've corralled the kids."

"Okay. Thanks," Beth said, hanging up the phone as she yelled at her kids again.

I dug up Bressler's card next and placed a call to his cell. I got his voice mail and left a message for him to call me. I went back to work. It would take a lot of time to work through this list, and if it was any indication, the workload would be doubled when I got a list from the Democrats.

***

Tom Bressler and I met at his downtown office around six. We walked to a restaurant not far away and after ordering, sat looking at each other.

"So, why the call?"

I shrugged. "I didn't want to eat alone tonight or stay near the bar. They're going to be busy tonight, and I didn't want to get roped into working."

Bressler smiled, his hazel eyes contrasting with his white shirt and light green tie. "Good."

"So, how did you get messed up in politics? Seems a long way from the Tommy of old?"

Bressler laughed. "Yeah, no doubt." He paused to take a drink. "In college, yes, I went to college, I didn't know what to do. Got interested in business, but nothing hit my fancy. Then I met a PR man with a large firm. I got an internship with him in Chicago. During that time, I was running with the crowd outside my usual. And I liked it. I met another guy who worked for the Democrats in Chicago. I guess I impressed him or something. The next summer I ended up working for him in their elections. I found that I liked the atmosphere and everything." He shrugged. "After graduating, I did some more work for him, then through other contacts he introduced me to some down-state Democrats. I ended up here, working with the mayor."

"And after this election?"

"I've got my sights on a really good prospect for the governor's race in two years. A contact of mine has been trying to get something going. But I've got to get the mayor reelected first."

"How's it going? I hear Williams is giving him a run for his money?"

"Absolutely," Bressler said. "It's gonna come right up to election time on this one, unless Williams does something stupid. It's definitely going to be a knuckle biter."

"You sound like you like that."

"I do. It sort of reminds me of all the stunts I used to pull when I was in high school. Doing things just to see how far we could go before we got caught." He grinned. "Remember?"

"Oh yeah." I smiled back. That was probably the biggest reason I misbehaved as a kid. To see how far I could push the envelope, but I knew when to stop. I very rarely crossed the line. "But this kind of thing has to be kept above board."

Bressler nodded. "Yep. Full disclosures to the commission and such. All public knowledge. They need to know where the money comes from, why they sent it, who is on staff, and what it is spent on it. It's sometimes a nightmare, all the paperwork."

"Doesn't that give Williams the information too?"

"Yeah, of course, and any other citizen. But we get full disclosure on how he spends his money too." Bressler winked. "I have someone scouring the Republican web site every day for new information we can turn into 'dirt' on him." *Cool!* He had given me the places to go for information. This had definitely been worth it.

"What about you, Mel? What have you been doing since graduation?"

"A little of this and a little of that." My heart twisted with my gut. I did not want to do this. I didn't want to talk about it, but how was I not to answer questions? I hardened my emotions before continuing.

Bressler gave me a look. "Come on, we have the time."

"Yeah. I don't know. I moved from one thing to another. I went to college in Maryland. While I was there I worked part time as an EMT. I met Craig there and we, well, we got married right before he graduated law school. I was working other odd jobs while I was in college."

"What were you studying?"

"Teaching. I was going to be a teacher, but I dropped out." I shrugged. "Guess it just wasn't for me. Craig's practice took off. I worked for Craig as a legal assistant until the firm got on its feet. He and three other guys started it out of school. Then I got pregnant with Robbie and I just settled into the motherly thing. It was nice." I tensed my right leg hard. Pain laced though it, shattering my concentration. *Don't cry!*

Bressler reached out and gently rubbed my hand. "How did they die?"

"In a car accident. We got sideswiped by a truck that ran a red light. Hit on the driver's side. Robbie was sitting behind Craig in his booster seat. He died instantly. Craig hung on for a while. We were both trapped in the car." *Good, keep it like a report. Just the facts ma'am.*

"That guy must have been going fast!"

I nodded, looking down at the glass in front of me. "We were pinned really good. Craig was taken to the hospital first and died in surgery. It took them over an hour to get us out of the car." I paused. "I remember every minute." *Stop. No more. Stop.*

"Did you know about your son while in-"

"Yeah. I didn't learn about Craig until later, days later." I swallowed hard and blinked back the tears. "It's been tough." I stopped.

We sat there for a few minutes in silence. I was working on not letting the tears out, or allowing the emotions to overwhelm me. I could feel the tide subsiding by the time the food came. I cleared my throat. Bressler did the same. It was obvious he was uncomfortable too.

The conversation turned to other things, brighter and less depressing subjects. By the time dessert arrived, the past was once more tucked safely into the background. We parted after the meal and I drove away. Only then did I fully relax.

I called Dan Kickery's number as I drove but got his machine. "Kick, it's Mel. Just checking in on the disk. Give me a call when you get the chance. Thanks."

***

The next day at work we divided up the names and the three of us worked the computers. All morning the only sounds were of the keyboards clacking away. Our only break came when John called us into his office to listen to his favorite talk show. The DJs were doing a bunch of prank calls over the phone. It was very funny and John laughed so hard he was almost crying.

At about noon, Rich headed out to grab a bite to eat before doing some surveillance on a different client. Moments after he left, however, he hurried back into the office. "Mel, call the cops."

I looked up at him in surprise. As I reached for the phone, I asked, "Why?"

"My car was broken into. A window was smashed and the seats are torn up." He shook his head and headed down the hall to talk to John.

It wasn't long before Mitch showed up. Rich, John, and Mitch left to examine the car. Rich took the camera with him to get pictures of the damage for insurance purposes. I peered out the window at them as they surveyed the vehicle.

As they walked back in a few minutes later, Mitch was asking, "Any ideas at all?" Rich and John shook their heads. Mitch shrugged. "Okay. I'll file the report and ask around."

"Thanks Mitch," Rich said. He motioned for me to follow John and him back into the other office area.

I stood up, smiling at Mitch as he left.

John and Rich were already seated at the table. John spoke with an extremely serious air, "This is one of two things: either someone is still looking for the disk, or we are now a target of one of the candidates. It is possible that Schnabel's people know that Williams hired us."

"But why attack Rich's car?" I asked, trying to be the voice of reason.

"Who knows?" Rich said. "We just want you to know what we are thinking so that you are more alert. Either of these things could be serious."

"Okay. Anything else?"

"Not unless you've got a line on Williams' leak yet."

"I had a thought about that." I leaned toward the table and placed my elbows on it. "Has anyone thought of a bug in his office or headquarters?"

John glanced at Rich. "Yeah, we did this morning. I called a friend of mine who does room sweeps to check them out. But good thinking, Mel. We'll get you trained yet."

I chuckled back. "Well, you've only got another week."

"We've been talking about that, Mel," Rich said. "How about staying on until we get this Williams thing done, even after Pam comes back? We can set up one of these rooms with a computer and you can work out of here."

I looked at both men. "I don't know. Let me think about it."

"Good enough," John said and we all stood up. John and I went back to the grunt work on the computers; Rich headed out to keep an eye on another suspected fraud case.

About two hours later the phone rang. It was Beth. "Sorry about cutting you off the other day. I've been asking around and so far I haven't gotten any dirt on either man, but-" She paused and I could hear the smile in her voice.

"But?"

"But tonight I go to the PTA meeting." Beth chuckled. "There are lots of gossips there. I'll call tomorrow if I get anything juicy."

"Thanks, Beth. Remember no one can find out."

"No way. My mouth is sealed." Beth loved to hear gossip but usually could keep a pretty good secret herself. "Gotta go, the kids are way too quiet."

So far the candidates were still hospital-clean and the top men in Williams' organization were too. Some had a few minor violations, but overall they were well respected citizens.

At three, I shut down my computer and headed to John's office with the small stack of folders in my hands. I handed them to him as he leaned back in his chair.

"Anything of interest?"

"Nope. I'm heading to the courthouse to get the Democrats' list, and I think I'll snoop in the records department." I winked at John.

"Records? Why?"

I shrugged. "I know the lady in charge of the department. Carla is a good friend of Dad's. She was always connected back when Dad was on the force. Dad says she still works there, so I'll gently quiz her. Also, I'll run a check on their properties, marriages, and other papers."

John nodded. I could tell he was impressed. "I never thought of that. Good idea, Mel."

"Want me to make copies of them?"

He hesitated. "Yeah, do so. Just keep a receipt and we'll reimburse you for the expense."

Two hours later, I wandered back to the office. I had a whole file full of copies, thanks to Carla in County Records, and she had given me several other places to look as well. This was actually fun. I had hardly more than glanced at some of the papers she copied for me. Carla had wandered in and out of her rooms having fun finding stuff on both candidates. I think she had been immensely bored and this was a nice change of pace.

I pushed open the door to the office and John poked his head out to see who had entered.

"Hey, Mel. Did you find anything?"

I hefted the file.

"Man."

I chuckled. "Yeah, Carla was really helpful. She got me lots of stuff."

John moved closer. "Anything interesting?"

"Not that I saw in my quick search. Thought I'd take a bit closer look here," I said as John nodded and headed back into his office. I sat at the desk to investigate the various papers in the file. I separated the paperwork into a pile for Williams and a pile for Schnabel.

I had paperwork on their properties. Schnabel had been married in Quincy, so I had his marriage certificate. The list and the pile went on and on. There was more on Schnabel than Williams. Carla had also copied all of the records of his successful election last term.

By the time I looked at all of them and gotten the information in some presentable order, I headed back to John's office. As I walked, I glanced at my watch. It was after seven. I knocked on the door frame. "Hey. I finally got all the paperwork looked through."

John took the files I handed him. "Anything?"

I shook my head. "I didn't see anything unusual. But, I'm not really sure what we're looking for."

"Me either," John said as he rubbed his eyes. He glanced at his watch. "Why don't you head on home? I'm about to call it a night."

"Sure. By the way, I'll be late coming in tomorrow. I'm stopping down at the county clerk's office to check on some political filings that the mayor did during his last bid. I also have to call on the state office in Springfield. They're supposed to send me some paperwork too."

John smiled. "Great. You're pretty good at this."

"Just nosy." I gratefully headed home. I was tired.

I climbed in to bed that night feeling good about myself, until I saw Petey. I grabbed the stuffed rabbit and then cried both of us to sleep.

CHAPTER 13

Saturday afternoon found me sitting behind the bar watching a baseball game on TV. The bar was slow at the time; only three people were there drinking. The kitchen hadn't opened yet.

I sat on a stool with my feet up on a cooler. The door opened and I lazily glanced over to see who it was. Max Bauer stepped into the cool of the bar and let out his breath. He was dressed in baggy jean shorts and a white T-shirt. Even in his grungy clothes he looked good. Yummy good.

"Not used to the weather yet, huh?"

"I'm used to humidity but this?" Max shook his head as he sat on the stool in front of me.

I nodded in agreement; it did take some getting used to. "What can I get you?" My feet came off the cooler.

"Soda. Diet, whatever you have."

I leaned forward, opened the cooler, and grabbed two. After handing him one, I popped one for myself and sat back onto my stool. Max reached for his wallet, but I waved him off. "First one is on the house."

His brow furrowed. "Are these new house rules?"

"Nah. I'm feeling lazy right now. I don't want to walk all the way down to that end of the bar to make change." I smiled, what I hoped was only a friendly smile. Since our little discussion, I definitely didn't want to encourage him.

Max laughed, took a drink of his soda, and looked around the bar. "It's slow today."

"For a while. It'll pick up tonight." I hesitated. "Is this a friendly visit or official?"

"I just stopped by to say hi," he said. His eyes were a liquid blue.

"Hmm," I said noncommittally.

"Mitch said that Cam had off today, but that you'd probably be manning the bar this afternoon," Max said as he took another drink.

"Yeah." I glanced down at my drink, then after taking a sip noticed that Max was staring at me.

"Something wrong, Mel?"

I shook my head.

"Can't fool me."

I sighed. It was strange, but I really did feel like I could talk to Max about anything, even things that were very painful, that I wouldn't admit to my family. I guess he was a good friend. I sighed again. "My niece is having a birthday party. The family is all together at Rich's house."

"What? They don't like you?"

I gave him a quick grin to show that I knew he was trying to lighten my mood.

"What else? Why aren't you there?" His blue eyes were delving into mine, and I couldn't look away.

It felt comforting. Suddenly, I wanted, no I needed, to talk about it. "I didn't want to go. Lizzie's birthday is too close to Robbie's. I don't know if I could handle it. They are, they were, the same age." My throat constricted, and I took a swallow of my soda to cover it up. I could feel the tears forming in my eyes.

Max nodded in understanding.

We talked for almost an hour as we watched the game. Just small talk, nothing important, but the sad, painful feeling was replaced by that warm feeling again. It felt right, somehow.

By now the bar was empty except for Max and me. But it didn't feel empty, like it usually did when there were not many customers.

Eventually Butch walked in and said, "Hey Mel, did you have something delivered upstairs?" His expression was wary.

"Delivered?"

He frowned. "I saw two guys leaving your apartment. I just assumed-"

I sat there stunned for about half a second. "Watch the bar." I hurried out of the building and around the corner to the back where my stairs were located.

Everything looked okay, but my door was slightly ajar. I scrambled up the stairs. When I reached the small landing at the top of the stairs, I saw the damage to the door frame. Anger welled up inside of me.

I pushed on the door and stepped into my apartment, gasping in shock. I barely noticed Max coming up behind me on the landing. My living room was trashed. Every box had been dumped, and stuff was spread all over the floor.

Then my shock was replaced by anger, which hit me like a truck. I opened my mouth and released a string of expletives exploded. Someone had deliberately violated me.

The second bedroom was equally chaotic. My anger grew to a monumental proportion. Every box had been dumped. Back in the living room, I saw Max looking around.

"Get out of here! Just get out!" My anger was a rolling boil and he just happened to be in the way. Max stared at me, startled. He retreated to the kitchen, already pulling out his cell phone.

I stomped into the main bedroom and sat down on the bed. Robbie's stuffed rabbit lay at my feet. I picked it up and caressed it, tears in my eyes. Whoever had done this had ripped Petey nearly in half. I cradled him, feeling the anger slowly flowing away. But replacing the anger was a desire for revenge. I would find out who did this and make them pay.

"Mel?" A soft voice broke into my reverie.

I wiped at my eyes and looked up to see Max standing at the doorway watching me. His blue eyes were full of concern.

"I didn't hear anything for a while. Are you okay?"

I nodded.

"I called your parents; someone from your family will come right away." Max leaned on the post, pausing he said, "Can you tell if anything was taken?"

I looked around, still silent, then shrugged. "Probably not. The only real things of value that I have are the TV, DVD player, and stereo. They're still here. Rich's car was broken into the other day. Now this."

Max frowned. "Do you think this is connected to the Eddie Baker murder?"

"I don't know. Maybe. Or a new case that the guys just got this week." I walked toward the kitchen, feeling tired. I wanted to get away, briefly, from the mess. Max moved in front of me and we sat at the counter. Suddenly I stood up. "The bar."

"Taken care of. Butch's watching it until someone gets here," Max said, gently patting my arm. We heard hurried, pounding footsteps on the stairs outside.

The door flew open and Rich came bounding in with Dad and Mitch behind him. They all looked at me with concern and worry.

"Are you okay?" Rich asked nervously.

"Yeah. I was doing bar duty when this happened. I didn't hear or see a thing."

Dad and my brothers walked through my apartment while Max and I stayed seated. When they walked back into the kitchen, Dad was cursing to himself. Rich looked worried, and Mitch was pissed.

"Any idea who did this?" Dad asked, probably just beating Rich and Mitch to the same question. His tone was tense, yet still gentle.

I glanced at Rich, then looked back at Dad. "Not a clue."

Dad turned to Rich. "Is this connected to your vehicle burg, Son?"

"Maybe," Rich said with a glance at Mitch. I couldn't tell what the male communication meant.

Bauer didn't speak, but I could tell he was watching the family interactions.

"Anything taken, Mel?" Rich asked.

Mitch turned to Max. "Call it in?"

Max merely nodded.

"Good. Well, Mel?" Mitch turned to me.

"I doubt it," I said and looked down at the stuffed animal cradled in my hand. My eyes burned. "Doesn't even look like they did much damage, except to Petey." I set him reverently on the counter top.

Dad pulled me into a hug. His arms wrapped around me tight. His head rested on top of mine. "It'll be okay Sweetie. Petey can be sewn back up."

I sniffled once to fight back the tears.

"I can take it and have Dot fix him for you," Dad said. His hug tightened on me. I felt Mitch's hand rub my back.

I shook my head. "I'll fix him myself." I ran a finger along the soft, plush animal. The hug tightened briefly then with a sigh, Dad released me. I looked up into his eyes, as I wiped my own again. "Thanks, Dad."

"I'll have a locksmith here within the hour to fix the door and put better locks on." He glanced at the others, then back at me. "I'll be downstairs if you need anything."

"Thanks again, Dad."

Rich shifted on his feet as Dad left. "Want us to help clean up, Mel?"

I shook my head. "No. I have to wait for the cops anyway. Go ahead and head home. I'll be fine."

Rich leaned over and gave me a kiss on the cheek.

Mitch gave me a hug. "Are you okay?" he asked as his eyes asked even more.

"Yeah. Thanks."

"Call if you want help." I noticed he glanced at Max, who nodded back. Everyone left Max and me alone. Max hadn't moved an inch, or said a word, or even breathed it seemed. I looked up into his blue eyes; his warmth replaced the violated feeling to a degree.

Max smiled. "That was quite a string of curse words earlier."

I gave him an embarrassed smile. "I like to be inventive when I'm mad. Sorry I yelled at you. I have a very short fuse."

"I noticed."

A knock at the door caused Max to move for the first time. He let a uniformed cop in and the paperwork began. As it turned out, the mess was relatively easy to clean up. It seemed the guys, whoever they were, picked up a box, dumped it, and moved to the next one. After the first couple of boxes, the area cleaned up fast.

At one point Max paused, turning to me. I was squatted down repacking a box of books. "Mel, uh, I think something else got damaged."

I turned to look at what he was holding. Slowly I rose and stepped closer to him. "What is it?" It was small enough to fit in the palm of his hand.

"A medal of some sort." He moved his hand, letting the medal dangle by the chain from his finger. "It looks like it got stepped on or smashed."

It took me a second before I realized what dangled from his finger. It was Robbie's St. Christopher medal that he'd gotten from my mom on his fifth birthday. He always wore it. My heart skipped several beats. I froze, my breath catching.

"Mel?"

I barely heard him, as though he were at a great distance. My stomach constricted with a familiar wrenching pain. Our eyes met.

Max looked uneasy; his eyes darted between the medal and me. I stepped back, but my hand reached for it of its own accord. Then I heard a sob.

I brought my other hand to my mouth in an effort to contain a moan. Still my eyes remained fixed on the mangled piece of metal.

He twisted it for a closer look, then his voice broke through my fog. "It looks like there's some dried blood."

I snatched my hand away, pounding it on my chest as I struggled to regain some composure. I could feel the tears flowing down my face. I hate crying. I wiped furiously at the tears with both hands. My eyes locked onto Max's, and it felt like he could see the depths of my pain.

"Mel, are you okay? You're white. What's wrong?" He took a step toward me. Now we were only inches apart. "Mel? Talk to me."

"I... It's Robbie's... It was his... St. Christopher medal... He... I thought it was lost... or... no one told me... the coroner must have... He never took it off... I thought they buried it with..." I could barely speak through my sobs.

"Oh," Max whispered and took me into his arms.

I cried quietly on his chest for a long moment before realizing what I was doing. I pushed him off. I needed composure. I needed space.

Max raised my hand and peeled open my clenched fist, tenderly placing the mangled medal into my palm. Gently, he curled my fingers around it. For a few seconds he held my hand. A tear fell from my chin and he caught it with his finger. "It's okay to grieve, Mel. Don't hold it in. I understand." I felt the familiar deep, piercing pain in my heart. "I understand that you don't like to cry in front of people, but you need to let this out." He traced my jaw with the same finger. His eyes said something I couldn't quite identify. We were so close that I could still feel his warmth.

We both hesitated for a second as though about to hug again, then he turned and squatted down to finish with the box he'd been working on.

I could feel myself shaking and wrapped my arms around my body. I opened my hand and reached with my other index finger, reverently touching Robbie's medal, vividly remembering that last day, remembering Robbie as I put him into his car seat, all sleepy-eyed and adorable. The medal in my hand was so broken and twisted, just like my little boy had been in the accident. Tears flowed again as I closed my fist tight. I kissed my hand, then held it to my chest as I sunk to the floor.

My mind wandered back to the day he'd gotten it; he was so proud that he could wear it, that he would be protected as we traveled back and forth from Maryland to Illinois. I opened my hand to stare at it. The medal didn't protect him as promised though. Or maybe it had. The doctors finally told me that he had died instantly. No pain. That was a good thing. Craig and I had been in horrible pain as they extricated us from the car. But Robbie had been spared that.

Mitch told me several weeks after the accident about Robbie's and Craig's funeral. I was still fighting for my life when they buried my family. I assumed that they had buried his medal with him, or that it had been lost in the accident.

This was the last possession of Robbie's that I had.

I looked up to see that Max had left the room and the boxes were all picked up. *How long had I been sitting there?* Getting up to my feet, I wiped the last tears from my face, and I gently put the medal into my pocket.

Max was seated at the kitchen bar with two glasses. I sat across from him before looking up. "Thanks." He pushed one of the ice waters to me. I looked at him. "Uh, I uh-"

Max shook his head. "I understand." He smiled softly as he patted my hand. "Hungry?" He glanced at his watch. "It's after six. Pizza?"

I nodded and reached for the phone. "What kind?"

"Order your favorite." After I ordered we moved to the living room. Max clicked on the TV. A political commercial for Schnabel blared at us, extolling his virtues. Max shook his head, pointing at my TV. "Man, the mayor's race sure is gearing up fast."

"Yep."

"Is Quincy always this political?"

"Nope, not that I remember." I took a drink. "Of course, we do have a very colorful history."

"Really?"

I could hear the skepticism in his voice. "At one time we were the biggest city in the state, being on the Mississippi River."

"It must have been a long time ago. Bigger than Chicago?"

"Yep. In the famous Chicago fire, we actually sent two fire teams up there on a barge. No kidding. And we had one of the Lincoln-Douglas debates here. There's a statue in Washington Park commemorating it."

"Hmm."

"Not to mention our own share of mobsters, dirty mayors, and general bad guys." I noticed the skeptical look he was giving me. I nodded again. "Yep. This city has always been a contentious area with the various mob groups, being between Chicago and St. Louis. Oh, and some of the houses here were on the Underground Railroad during slavery times."

"No kidding?"

"No kidding." I stood up at the knock on my door. It was the pizza. We ate in silence.

Max turned to me. "Mel?"

"Yeah?"

"What do you think they were looking for?" Max's blue eyes were delving deeply into mine.

"If I had to guess, I'd say the disk."

"Surely they'd have to know that you'd turn it over to us?" Max said, shaking his head.

"Unless they think we assumed it wasn't connected to anything."

Max shook his head again. "Even still, any criminal on the street knows about Rich and his former profession."

"What if they think Eddie hid it without us knowing? That would explain the fire at the office and breaking into Rich's car," I said, starting to eat another piece of pizza.

"True, but that doesn't explain here."

"Maybe I brought it home with me. Mouse did give it to me as I shut down the office."

Max thought about that seriously. "So, you think the two sets of bodies are related."

"Let's just say I'm real suspicious."

"They aren't, Mel. A source has clued us in to the fact that Hiccome was already working for Hessor. They think he was playing both sides of the fence. The only reason Mouse's body was found first was because of those kids playing in the park. Their wounds are identical. Thirty-eight to the chest."

"But if Hiccome was already working for Bart, why did he kill Hiccome?"

"Bart?" I could tell he didn't like me using such a familiar tone. "We don't know that yet." Max sat back. "And you didn't hear any of that. Okay?"

"Got it."

Max looked at his watch. "I've got surveillance in an hour. I'd better run home first." He looked me in the eyes. "You're not going to look into this, right?"

"Right."

"Yeah, right. Anyway, thanks for the pizza."

"Thanks for the help and, well, everything."

Max paused, then reached out for my hand that was resting on the couch cushion. "Are you going to be okay here by yourself?" He looked deep into my eyes.

"Yeah. Thanks for being here."

Max nodded. "That's what friends are for. Being there in times of need. Mel, seriously, if you need anything-" He gave my hand a pat, then laid it back down on the couch. "Anything at all, even just a sympathetic ear, about anything, call me. Okay?"

I touched his hand. "I appreciate all you've done. But really, I'll be okay."

"I know that. You're one of the strongest women I've ever met." He hesitated, then gave me a smile. "Or maybe just the most stubborn."

I laughed as I walked him to the door. "Thanks for making me laugh." He gave me a wink and a smile and headed out.

CHAPTER 14

Monday I worked hard to find the leak in Williams' organization. Max had said that Scott Hiccome was already working for Bart. Was that true? It occurred to me that there was a quick way to find out, if I wasn't chicken. *Should I?* I glanced down the hall toward Rich's office. *Hmmm.*

I dug into my fanny pack and got out Bart's card. With just a moment's hesitation, I dialed his home number. I didn't expect him to answer.

"Hello."

"Bart?"

"Yeah. Who is this?"

"Mel Addison."

"Mel!" I could hear the change in his voice, from a stiff business tone to a more casual one. "What's up?"

"I was just thinking that I might take you up on your offer for reminiscing over a drink."

Bart chuckled. "Good. How about tonight?"

"Maybe. Where?"

"My house. I think the cops are watching the bar." Hessor was smiling, I could tell by his voice. "How about seven? I could grill some steaks."

"Okay, but I can't stay long. I've got work to do at home."

"Stay as long as you want, Mel. I'll buzz you in. Just drive up and park next to the garage. I'll be in the back yard."

"Okay, see you then." I hung up the phone. If I was careful, I might find out about Scott and Mouse. I would have to fend off Bart's advances, but it wouldn't be the first time.

***

We sat on the deck in the shade. The two-story house was located in one of the more affluent areas of Quincy. It was huge, at least six thousand square feet, with a deck that wrapped around the entire length. It couldn't have been more than two or three years old.

The landscaping was perfect, the swimming pool huge. Bart had not lied about that. One end had a diving board and the other end had a hot tub attached. I wondered briefly if he used it in the winter.

The pool was tempting in the ninety-five degree heat. But even with the hot weather, I didn't want to be inside his house with him, and I didn't want to go swimming either.

"So." Bart sat back after dropping his napkin onto his plate. "You never did explain why you left me high and dry on the island like that when we were younger on our last night together."

I chuckled. "Come on. You really don't know?"

Bart smiled that mischievous smile. "Because I made those advances on you?"

"Advances? They were more than that. It was practically rape."

"It wasn't." Bart made a face. "You went over to the island willingly. What did you think we were going over there to do? Snipe hunt?"

I shrugged. "Not get raped. Besides, I left you your clothes."

"True. And after I could move from the kick in the crotch, I got dressed. I had to swim across the shoot, you know."

"Poor baby," I said with no sympathy in my voice.

Bart laughed. "Still, it was fun."

His machismo made me laugh. "I've heard since then that I was the prize."

Bart laughed very loudly at that. "True. I thought for sure I'd win the bet." He winked. "Bressler tried hard too, or so I understand."

"He tried," I agreed. I watched as Bart took a drink of his beer. I was drinking soda. I wanted all of my faculties working. We sat eyeing each other. A slight tension began to fill the air. *How will I broach the subject?* Bart surprised me by speaking first.

"Can I ask you a question?" Bart asked with a serious look on his face.

"Sure."

"You spoke to Mouse the night she died. That's what the papers said."

I shook my head. "The papers didn't say I did, they said someone talked to her, not me specifically."

Bart smiled his 'Okay, I'm caught' look. "But you did, right?"

"Yeah."

"What did she say?"

"Why?"

Bart eyed me closely. I could tell he was evaluating me. "Seriously, Mel. I want to know."

"Answer my question and I might tell you."

"Okay." Bart set his imported-beer bottle down. "Scott Hiccome was working for me. Selling. Mouse was supposed to be an informant in Weedman's operation for me, and she was checking into another matter for me too, closer to home. She was supposed to have dropped off something to me that night. I was wondering if she gave you anything? Said anything to you about where she was going?"

I hesitated before answering. He had confirmed the information. *Is he talking about the disk? Is it somehow related to Hessor? But why did the note say it was from Eddie?* "She did talk to me. I literally bumped into her coming out of the office. She recognized me. Now I know it was from Eleven Bottoms. We exchanged pleasantries, then she moved on." *Here I go again, lying.*

Bart frowned. "She wasn't carrying anything?"

I shook my head. "Not that I saw. At least, nothing in her hands."

"Hmmm." Bart picked up his drink and sat back in thought. "How was she acting?"

"I don't know. Nervous maybe. She said she was on her way out of town. Mouse looked like she hadn't slept in a while. Her hair was all messed up."

"It's the style now."

"Really? I'm so behind the times. I can't see why." I shook my head in disbelief.

Bart laughed.

I glanced at my watch.

"Wanna go for a swim, Mel?" Bart motioned to the cool, inviting pool.

"Tempting. Very tempting, but I have to go. The guys want me in early tomorrow and I have boxes to pick up at my house." I was watching Bart for a reaction, to see if he had maybe sent someone to my house. He gave me no indication that he knew what I was talking about.

"Okay. Well, let me walk you out then." He stood and motioned to the stairs.

I stopped by the front of the jeep. "Thanks for the steak, Bart. You're a good cook."

He put his hand on the Jeep between me and the driver's door, stopping my movement. "Sure I can't talk you into a swim?"

"Even if I wanted to Bart, I don't have a swimsuit with me."

"You don't need one in my pool."

"Pass." I went to move his hand.

Bart leaned over and placed a kiss on my lips. His hands moved to my waist, holding me tight. He leaned on me, pushing me into the Jeep.

I broke the kiss after a minute. I was caught up in the moment, remembering the times we had spent together as kids. "Are we going to have a replay of the night on the island?"

Bart smiled, licking his lips. "You're still a great kisser, Mel. We could have a replay. Bet I would win this time."

"Pass, again." I extracted myself from his embrace and hopped into the vehicle. "It's been fun, but I don't want anything more. Thanks again for the meal and the reminiscing. See ya," I threw over my shoulder as I drove off.

In my rear view mirror, I saw him watching me. Dangerous. Definitely dangerous, but it had been an informative evening.

***

"You did what?" Rich yelled the next morning.

I shrugged. "I needed to find out if what Max said was true. I called Bart Hessor. I went to his house. We ate steak and talked of old times."

"'Old times'?" Rich leaned forward in his chair.

I glanced up to see John now standing in the doorway shaking his head. He had come in response to Rich's raised voice.

"What do you mean by 'old times'? You used to hang out with that drug dealing scum?"

"Every now and then. In the Bottoms. Sometimes."

Rich exhaled. "After what his family almost did to Dad? How could you?"

I shrugged again. "It's history. Where do we go from here?"

"Dig deeper into Mouse and Scott," John said from the doorway. "See what connection there is between them and Hessor. See if we can connect them in anyway on the night of the murder."

"How?"

"Friends. Family." John smiled. "See if that cop will spill more about their investigation. And talk to Mitch."

"Hmmm." That wasn't what I wanted to hear. That would mean that I'd have to get even friendlier with Max than I was. I had mixed feelings about that. I enjoyed his company to be sure, but there was this feeling deep down that I shouldn't, even though I wanted to.

"I'll talk to Mitch," Rich volunteered. "I need to talk to him anyway." He turned a look at me. "Mel, you stay away from Hessor. He's nothing but bad news."

I stared at my brother. His blue eyes were hard and unyielding. Rich was in full cop mode now, he was being extremely serious. "Sure."

"Don't 'sure' me, Mel," Rich said in a low, almost threatening tone. "I know you. You like to play with fire. You aren't a stupid kid anymore. You'll get burned on this one, trust me. He's done a lot of bad things, even though he hasn't gotten caught. Yet."

"I figured as much," I said looking him in the eye, refusing to give in.

Rich's finger came up to point at me. "You will not see him again."

I made a face. "What are you going to do? Fire me?" I could feel myself getting angry.

"He's dangerous."

"I know that. I don't intend on seeing him again, but, and I repeat but, I will not be told like a child what to do." I stood up and looked down at Rich, my anger once more getting the best of me. "So just stop with the brotherly attitude and leave me alone." I stormed out of his office.

John moved quickly out of my way.

I sat down at my desk, letting out a large breath to dispel my anger. *Brothers!*

John walked out quietly and sat in the chair in front of Pam's desk.

"What?" I snapped.

"Rich is right."

I sighed. My anger melted into frustration. "I know."

John smiled, stood up, and walked back into his office. I could hear him whistling as he walked.

"Shut up!" I called to him. A chuckled floated down the hall.

I sat thinking about things for a few minutes. Resigned, I stood up, walked back down the hall, and knocked softly on the door frame of Rich's office. "Hey."

Rich looked up, still mad. "Yeah?"

I slid into the chair in front of his desk. "I just came to apologize."

"Good."

"Can't you take an apology better than that?"

"Not when I'm one hundred percent right."

I took a deep breath to let him see that I was visibly calming myself. "So, what if you were? I did learn a lot from him." I paused. "You said that Eddie used to use. Could he be involved with Mouse and Scott dealing for Hessor?"

Rich leaned back and thought about it. "Could be, but I doubt it. Eddie said he had no idea what was going on. And I believe him. He was a good informant and usually didn't lie well." Rich's eyes refocused on me. "He used drugs in the past, but I doubt he was actually smart enough to sell. Now, Wally… Maybe. I wouldn't have put it passed him to start selling. He couldn't hold a regular job for longer than ten minutes. He tried so many: bouncer, chauffeur for a local limo company, car salesman." Rich shook his head. "He was smart but he never wanted to do any real work." He paused, still looking at me. "You're thinking that they are related because of the note mentioning Eddie."

"Yep. And Bart did ask if she was carrying anything. Could be the disk."

"Maybe, but the note said it was for me from Eddie, not for Hessor. She said that Eddie said I would know what to do with it, right?"

"Yeah."

Rich shook his head. "This doesn't make sense."

"None of it does."

"Try tracking some of Mouse's friends. Leave Scott alone for now. Of the two, he was probably the more dangerous. Let's see if we can place Mouse and Wally together with more than just Beth's rumors. If so, we can connect the four bodies."

"Okay." I stood up to leave.

"Mel? Don't see Hessor again."

I nodded.

CHAPTER 15

By Saturday night, I didn't want to ever hear the name Mouse or Scott again. I was bored when Dad called me downstairs for a favor. It turned out three men in the bar needed a fourth for a euchre card game. They wanted Dad to play, but he knew the bar would get crowded later on, so he suggested me.

Harold, Gus, and Melvin were my Dad's age, and at first they didn't want to let me play. I was a 'girl' and a 'young one' at that. But Dad assured them, not only could I play, but that I was fairly good. He told them two old and well-respected euchre players had taught me to play. He didn't tell them I was a card shark though. Still, the old guys fought over who 'had' to be my partner.

We were just finishing up the last game and the bar was crowded, when I found Max at my shoulder looking down at the game. "Euchre?"

I nodded.

"Want a beer?" Max asked, seeing that my glass was empty. His baby blue shirt made his eyes glow as he smiled.

"Wait on buying a beer. I'm about to win a round for the house." I smiled up at Max. I held up my last card and as I played it, groans and curses came from Harold and Melvin. I smiled at Gus, my partner, who grinned back, then glanced at the others. "Sorry."

"The infamous Addison luck," Melvin commented.

I shook my head. "Not luck. Skill and a good partner." I shook Gus's hand, while he continued to laugh at the other two.

"I'll get 'stuck' with you any day, Mel." Gus winked at me in a flirting manner.

The losers motioned to my Dad who announced that the next round was on Melvin and Harold. A cheer went up in the bar for Gus and me.

I accepted the congratulations of the group as Max walked me up to the bar. "I've seen you drink just about every beer in the house. What's your favorite?"

"Whatever is free," I said with a smile.

"No, really."

"I acquired a taste for microbrews when I lived in Maryland, but any domestic will do. I generally don't like imports and I absolutely hate Mexican beers." I put my empty glass in the tub at the end of the bar.

"Hey Dad, do you need help tonight or can I boogie? I haven't eaten yet and I'm starved."

"Are you going upstairs?"

I nodded.

"If we get swamped, can I get you to come back down to help out?"

"Sure."

"See you. And thanks for taking my place at the game." Dad smiled, motioning to the crowded bar. A large group of cops and firemen had been hanging around watching us play when they learned the outcome would be free beers.

"Anything to help promote the bar." I winked at Dad as he moved on. "I'm going to grab a six pack. Okay?"

Dad was already waiting on his next customer, but he waved an okay.

Max leaned closer. "How does he determine how much to pay you? Your hours are so erratic."

"I get paid in kind." I winked at Max and pointed at the beer taps. "Cheats the government out of taxes."

Max laughed. "So you haven't eaten. Can I buy you something?"

I couldn't tell if he was being flirtatious or not. Either way, it was a good opportunity to pump him for information. "Sure. I'll have it delivered." I stood up and motioned for Max to follow. As I headed out of the bar, I grabbed a six-pack from a stack in the cold storage room.

Max carried the beer and after we went into the apartment, he put it in the fridge. I immediately headed over to the air conditioner to crank it up. He entered the living room and looked around. "I see you got everything back to normal."

"Yep." I pointed at the stuffed rabbit sitting on the stereo. "Even Petey is back from the hospital. It was a close call, but I think the lady bunnies will get a kick out of his scars." Max chuckled. "Make yourself at home. I need to get out of these hot clothes." I had been wearing a pair of jeans and a polo shirt, so I changed into a relaxed pair of shorts and my usual T-shirt.

"What do you want to eat?" Max asked through the door.

"I don't care. Chinese, burgers, pizza, subs, Italian. Whatever." I came back to find Max in the kitchen looking at my phone book. "Have you decided?"

"I was thinking Chinese."

I picked up the phone. "What do you want?"

"You know the phone number by heart?"

"Yep. I lived most of my life nine blocks from here. What delivered to the old homestead, will deliver here. What do you want?" I spoke into the phone. "Yeah, I want to place an order for delivery... Is this Cassidy? Hi, it's Mel." I smiled at Max's astonished look. "No. I'll take my usual." I pointed at Max for his order.

"Whatever."

"Make it two of the specials. Thanks." I hung up the phone and sat down at the bar. "So? How is Quincy treating you?"

Max shrugged.

"You said Steve Wettle asked you to come to Quincy." I took a beer and motioned for Max to follow me into the living room with his drink.

Max nodded as he sat. After taking a drink he spoke, "Yeah. I met Steve in college in California. He knew I wanted a change of area."

"Why?"

Max's eyes met mine. His normal look was more guarded.

"I mean, why Quincy?"

Max relaxed just a bit. "Just a change." He smiled, shifting his weight on the couch. He was hedging around something.

"No, really. I know Quincy is soooo exciting you just had to leave the coast."

"Quincy isn't that bad."

"You didn't grow up here."

"True."

"Where did you grow up?"

"Lots of places."

I swallowed a sip of beer. "Come on, Mr. Mysterious."

Max grinned. "Seriously, all over." He seemed to draw inward for a few seconds. "I guess the longest stretch of time that I lived anywhere was when I lived in Maryland with my Grandmother, mostly. Mom and Dad traveled a lot."

"Where in Maryland?"

"Annapolis."

"I lived there. Loved the Chesapeake Bay. Hated crossing the Bay Bridge."

Max nodded in agreement. "In college, Steve and I shared a room. We kept in touch since both of us went into law enforcement."

"How long were you a cop in California?"

Max paused thinking. "Ten years, give or take." He took another drink. "What did you do in Annapolis?"

"Don't change the subject, mister." I gave him a stern look, pointing my finger at him.

A slight grin fluttered across his face.

"Why leave a career out there for Quincy?"

"Just a change." The tone in his voice had changed. And his eyes. His facial muscles tensed.

"What happened?"

Max broke eye contact to stare at the ground. After a couple of seconds he raised his eyes to meet mine again. "My partner got shot."

I could see the pain in his eyes and something else, maybe guilt. He didn't seem to want to talk about it. "Died?"

Max bobbed his head slightly.

"Sorry."

Another bob.

This time I broke eye contact. I knew what it felt like to be in pain. And since he always let my painful subject drop when I needed it to, I didn't press. "But Quincy? What do you miss the most?"

"From California?" He took another drink.

"Yeah," I said quickly gulping my beer, nodding for emphasis.

"The ocean. We used to surf and barbeque on the beach. The nights were terrific. The surf, the sand, the girls." He grinned. "Seriously, just the ocean." He paused mid-drink; his eyes were vacant, as though lost in thought. "Ox was great on a board."

"Ox? Your deceased partner?"

"Yeah."

"Let me guess-" I took another drink, then smiled to get him to relax again. There was no way I was opening his can of worms. I had a cupboard full of my own cans. "Blond, muscular surfer dude?"

A nervous chuckle. "Actually, no. Black hair, conservative in everything. Italian. No 'dude' there, more the business executive type. He was a great friend and partner," he near-whispered.

I didn't know him well enough to tell if I should push or not. "Max."

He lifted his head to look at me. His eyes were still guarded, but there seemed to be sadness there too. I couldn't tell what he was thinking.

"Want to talk about it?"

He swallowed as his eyes narrowed just a touch. "No."

"Okay. Just so you know, this friendship thing is reciprocal." I tilted my beer bottle toward him.

His expression softened. An adorable smile crept across his face. "Good to know." He tilted his bottle toward me, then took a drink.

I smiled back, my eyes locked with his as we drank. *Why did he make me feel so good? So special?* And all with just one little smile.

We were eating when the subject of Mouse came up. Max actually brought it up. "So, I hear you've been asking around about the Mousina girl. Again."

I looked up at him from my plate. I laid my fork down. "Yeah." I noticed he was eating with chopsticks. "How do you eat with those things?"

"Stop trying to avoid the subject."

"No, really. I've tried it lots of times. All I ever do is throw food all over the place. I've always wanted to be able to do that. How do you?"

"Let's make a deal."

"What kind of deal?"

"You tell me what you found out, and I'll teach you to eat with chopsticks."

I considered. "Deal. So-" I picked up the second set of disposable chopsticks. I briefly studied his hand trying to imitate him. I was in the process of getting it right when I heard him 'tsk' at me.

Laying his sticks down, he said, "You tell me first. That was the deal."

"Okay," I sighed. I leaned my elbows on the counter. "Mouse was still working for Weedman, but it was a cover. She really worked for Hessor."

Surprised, he said, "How did you find that out?"

"Sources. She was like a spy, I guess. Why, I don't know. Anyway, word is Eddie was with her the night he died."

Max nodded; he apparently already knew that.

"Also, Wally was around Mouse the week before he died. No one will tell me if they were an item, but no one has denied it either. The night Eddie died, Mouse made a phone call on a pay phone to someone. She mentioned that she had information for 'him'. My source assumed it was Hessor. Also, Mouse and Scott were both pretty happy about something that was going to happen 'within a couple of days'."

Max sat back and thought. "This source of yours, is he reliable?"

"She, and maybe. Let's just say she wasn't especially happy to talk with me, being an Addison, but she hates cops even more. I think she just wanted to insult someone and I was the first available person. Still, she gave me a lot of information." I smiled.

"Anything else?"

"Neither Wally or Eddie were selling for anyone, that I could find out for sure. Wally was back to using cocaine, but Eddie was clean. He had been for several months. One of his friends mentioned that he was trying to win back his ex-wife."

"Okay."

I took another bite of food. "One last thing, then you teach me to eat with chopsticks."

Max nodded at me to go on, picking up the chopsticks. He started eating again.

"Mouse was supposed to deliver something to Hessor the night she died. I got the impression that it never got delivered."

He froze, food halfway to his mouth. "Really? Same source?"

"Nope. A much more reliable source on that one."

"Who?"

"I can't tell you that."

"That's obstruction of justice!"

I shrugged. "Hard to prove. I'll deny I said it. No witnesses."

"Mel." There was a threat to his tone.

I just smiled. "The chopsticks." I picked mine up again.

"Did your source say what it was? Did he or she mention if it was the disk?"

I shook my head. "Didn't say, but I got the impression that the package was small, possibly able to fit in a pocket."

Max muttered something under his breath.

I leaned farther across the counter. "Chopsticks. The deal, remember Bauer?"

Max was lost in thought. "Yeah," he said absentmindedly. "I've got to go." He dropped his utensils and stood up. "Thanks for having me over, Mel." He hurried out the door.

"Hey!" I called out to him, but he was gone. Max owed me. Next time, I'd get all the information I needed.

***

"So, here is where we are right now," John said in a short briefing to the group on Monday morning. Pam was back to man the front door and phones. "The big case of course is the paying client, Williams. Everyone is working on it. Concurrently, I'm working on a skip trace for A1 Bonds. Rich is working surveillance on another fraud investigation. Mel is *not* working on the murder cases." John winked and smiled at Pam.

"Jeez, I go away for a short time to pop out a kid and you guys go and get serious on me," Pam said as a joke. "Okay, I see the new desk, computer, etcetera. Same system or did we upgrade?"

Rich chuckled. "We have not hit the big time, Pam. Same system, faster computer."

Pam nodded. "And in which closet have they stuck you, Mel?"

"The conference room across from Rich's office. And welcome back. Those phones never stop ringing."

"Then there are days it never rings," Pam said with a smile back.

Rich gave Pam a serious look. "You're definitely back on coffee duty. Mel's coffee could be used as paint stripper. Please make us a decent pot. Please, Pam!"

The group parted.

I was currently searching Williams' subcontractors. He always used the same caterers, flower delivery people, limo service, carpet cleaners, and office cleaners. I was checking to see if any of the services were also used by Schnabel. If there was a connection, I was to bring it immediately to the guys' attention. Personally, I thought it was the biggest long shot in the world, but I was getting paid, and it did give me something to do. If I worked at Dad's bar all the time, I'd drink too much.

Around noon, I had finished up with the caterers and florist and was getting ready to turn to the limo company when Pam announced that I had a visitor. I stood up, surprised, and walked to see who it was. Max was standing there quietly talking with Pam, inquiring about her baby.

I waved him back down the hallway.

"Nice office, Mel," Max said looking around. "I particularly like the expensive desk and filing system you have."

I smirked. My 'desk' was the conference room table, which also served as my file system. As he got seated in a chair, I reached into my purse and pulled out the chopsticks. I tossed them onto the table in front of him. "Remember?"

Max blushed slightly. "Yeah. That's one of the reasons I'm here. We need to make a date to eat Chinese again so that I can teach you."

"Okay. And the second?"

"Who was your source on the package that Mouse carried?"

I shook my head. "I can't say. I might need that source again and if I tell you, he won't talk to me anymore."

Max frowned. "This is serious, Mel."

"Yeah, I know."

"Do Rich and John know that you are still looking into this?"

"Nope. They yelled at me once already. I do it after I leave here at night, so don't even threaten me with telling them. I don't care. I'll just quit working here." I leaned back and crossed my arms.

Our eyes became locked in a battle of wills. I wasn't about to lose. I had been taught to fight this kind of battle by the best, my mom.

"Has anyone ever told you that you're infuriating?" he grunted.

"Just about everyone. That would be followed closely by pigheaded, stubborn, deceitful, and I think most people would add bad tempered." I winked, knowing what I was doing could be construed as flirting by some people, but it felt more like playful kidding to me, and it seemed that Max knew it too. "Do you agree?"

"Absolutely." He smiled right back, his blue eyes sparkling with amusement.

"Good, then it's a consensus." I paused to change subjects. "So, are there any major similarities between the two sets of bodies?"

Max gave out a big sigh. "I stepped right in to that one, didn't I?"

I just smiled.

The cop studied me for a minute. He leaned back and shut the conference room door. "You didn't hear this and don't spread it around."

"Got it."

"I mean it, Mel."

"There is one thing you have to learn about me, my word is sacred. I once did a two-month stint in detention for a friend because I gave my word I wouldn't tell anyone something." In reality it wasn't a friend, it was Mitch, but no one knew that.

Max sighed again. "Wally and Eddie were both shot with nine millimeters to the head. Point blank range. There was evidence that their hands were tied behind their backs prior to the shooting. Neither died where they were found."

I nodded. I had already found all this out from Mitch. "Okay. Go on."

"Mouse and Scott were shot with a thirty eight. Mouse was shot from the front, point blank range. Scott was shot from the back, plus a chest shot." Max paused. "Both were found with cocaine in their systems and on their persons. Mouse actually looked like she struggled some, several abrasions and such. She was not killed in the park. Scott was killed at the river where you found him. We think, mind you, that Mouse was also killed in the Bottoms and transported to the park."

"Why?"

"We don't know why the body was moved, but we found another blood covered area that matches Mousina's blood. We found the bullet that killed Scott. Mousina's passed through, and we still have two officers combing the woods and ground for the other bullet." Max paused, then looked at me. "One more thing, and no one but the Medical Examiner, myself, and the Chief knows this … Angela had sex with someone the night she died, but DNA tests show it wasn't either of the Bakers or Hiccome."

"Rape?"

"The ME says no; there is no bruising or rough-play evidence."

"Suspects?"

"Yes."

"Can you give me a hint?"

"Not on your life," Max said.

"The disk?"

"That's the million dollar question in the Baker murders. No one has been able to crack it. How about you?"

"Nope. I have a friend working on it, but so far a big, fat goose egg." I tapped my finger on the table. *Very interesting news.* Mouse had sex with someone she knew before she was killed, but later had struggled against her killer.

"Now what's running through that devious mind of yours?"

"I was just thinking that I know of this really expensive Chinese restaurant that I've been meaning to go to." I gave Max a grin. "How does Friday night sound? I'll make the reservations."

Max stood up. "Friday it is. I want to know that source, Mel. I will find out."

"Sounds like a challenge."

Max moved to leave the room, then stepped back into my office. "I always win, Mel. Just a warning."

"Then you've never gone up against an Addison before," I called after him.

Back to the Williams case. I started a routine search on the limo company, Top Hat Limo. The company was locally owned. It was one of three limo companies in town and was used by many of the funeral homes, high schools for proms, and dignitaries in the area. Something about the limo company was nagging at me. On a whim, I gave the company a call.

"Hi, I'm with a local firm here and we might need to rent a limo or two. I'd like some more information, please."

"Certainly. How long would you need our services?" The man on the phone sounded young.

"A couple of days. How much would it cost me?"

"It depends on which car you would need to rent. We have five. Two are stretch limos and the other three are regular size."

"Just the regular ones."

"The cost depends on how long you need the service, but it includes the driver. Tip is extra. The prices are a bit more flexible the longer you rent it. Week long rentals are negotiable depending on circumstances and the dates. If you can give me specifics about the rental, I can give you a more firm estimate."

"Well, we're still in the planning stages. Can you give me some references, you know, former and current clients that I can contact to ask about your service? We want the best. Money is secondary."

"Let's see, we have as regular clients, City Hall, uh, the University is a regular user of us for visiting professors and, of course, all of the funeral homes use us."

"City Hall? As in the mayor's office?"

"Yes, Mayor Schnabel. We have a contract with the mayor's office. We've been his limo service for over two years." The guy was quite proud of that fact.

"Okay, well when we formalize plans, I'll be calling you back. And your name was?"

"Eric."

"Do you get a commission on this, Eric?"

"No Ma'am, although, I'm usually the one to answer the phones. Or you can speak to one of the owners, Frank or Martha Grimes."

"Thanks, Eric."

"Thank you ma'am for calling Top Hat Limousine Service."

I spent the rest of the day was trying to find the connection between the two factions using the same limo. So far it seemed to be the only thing in common. And so far, we were coming up with zero. I was sitting in a chair in John's office, thinking, when he looked up at me.

"What's up, Mel?" I shrugged. "Really Mel, let it out, even if it sounds weird. You're incredibly talented at this, almost a natural."

"It's just, I remember something and it's bugging me, but I can't put my finger on it."

"Something having to do with the limo service and Williams?" Rich asked.

"Yeah, I think. It's on the tip of my tongue but I can't remember."

"Let it sit. It'll come back," John said. "Don't push it."

Rich nodded in agreement and checked his watch for the fourth time in as many minutes. "I've got to go. My fraud guy heads off to work in twenty minutes. I need to follow him." He stood up. "I'll have my cell with me if you think of anything or need me."

"Sure," I called after him.

"Did we ever hear from Springfield about the search on Williams and Schnabel?" asked John.

"No," I said, wondering why it had slipped my mind. "I'll call them up." I looked at John. "What happens if we can't find anything for Mr. Williams?"

"Well, I have to give him a report tonight. We're meeting at his house. It'll be his decision to continue to investigate. If he feels that there is still someone spying on him, he'll probably tell us to continue, otherwise we stop when we get done tonight." John shrugged. "This had been relatively easy work, as cases go. I just don't know if there actually is someone. I tend to doubt it."

I stood up and headed back to my office. By the time I finished with the rest of the information on the vendors for Williams, I was ready to call it a day. John agreed with me. He said to come in tomorrow to see if we were to continue looking into the matter. Gratefully, I headed home.

It hit me as I was doing dinner dishes. Something about Wally. I picked up the phone and dialed Rich's cell. No answer. I tried his home number and Gloria informed me that he wasn't due back until late. I tried John on his cell and he told me the location of Rich's surveillance, so I headed out to talk to my brother. And to tell him to turn on his phone.

Rich was doing surveillance on an auto body shop in an industrial complex just outside of town. They were supposedly repairing cars with substandard parts. Rich's job was to catch them in the act. He was parked on a slight rise overlooking the complex. The road curved at the hill, and it gave him an excellent vantage point to watch from. They did a lot of work into the evening.

I climbed out of the Jeep and took a seat next to Rich on the ground near his car. "Your cell isn't turned on."

"Really, I thought I did." He immediately checked.

"Someday that will get you in big trouble," I said. I handed him a soda that I had brought with me. "Here, have a cold one."

"Thanks. I was getting thirsty."

"You'd think, being an ex-cop, that you'd know better than to stay out of communications with people," I chided him again.

"Okay. I get the point, Mel." Rich took a big drink then looked at me seriously. "So, what are you doing here?"

"I have a question about Wally."

Rich picked up the binoculars again to watch the shop. "Okay."

"You mentioned that he worked for a limo company for a really short time. I checked the information on him and it doesn't mention that. Do you remember which one it was?"

"Hmmm. It's been a long time since I talked with Wally. I think he mentioned Top Hat Limo but..." He lowered the binoculars from his face and turned to me, his expression priceless.

I smiled. "How long ago was that?"

"I don't know, four or five years maybe." Rich set the glasses down on his lap. "That's too big of a coincidence to be wrong. But how does it connect up with..." Rich stopped at the sound of a car pulling up behind my Jeep.

We both stood, but before I was fully upright, someone slammed me to the ground, face down. I tried to struggle, but it was someone very muscular and powerful. My face was being ground into the dirt. I could hear Rich making a commotion too. It sounded like he was putting up a good fight.

"Stop or he'll kill your sister."

I felt a gun barrel touch the back of my head. I immediately stopped struggling.

"Who are you? What do you want?" Rich asked. His voice had an unfamiliar quality. Worry maybe.

I heard more movement, but I couldn't see anything. Finally, I managed to turn my face partway to the side. Four masked men were standing by Rich, two holding him in a choke hold. A third, wearing a hockey mask, pointed a gun at him. The fourth man, wearing a skeleton mask, stood with his arms crossed.

Hockey Mask spoke, "Answer our questions or he'll blow your sister's brains all over the ground."

Rich's eyes flashed to me as he continued to stand motionless. The two men holding him both looked at Skeleton Mask. So did Hockey Mask. Skeleton Mask turned to look at me, finally noticing that I was watching all the action. He motioned to the man on top of me, and the guy forced my face back toward the ground.

There was some general movement over by Rich, but I couldn't tell what it was. I heard Rich yell a 'no', and the light went dark as the pain exploded in my head.

CHAPTER 16

The first thing I became aware of was light. Bright, white light that I could see even though my eyes were closed. I groaned and tried to open them. I needed to find out what had happened to Rich. Because of the pain in my head, I knew I wasn't dead. I sniffed as I groaned. Disinfectant. *I must be in a hospital.* Sure enough I started hearing people moving around, voices in the distance, then intercom noises.

I struggled but finally got my eyes open. I tried to move, but was strapped to a backboard. A face appeared above me, startling me.

"Good, you're awake," the nurse said to me. "I'll get the doctor." With a faint smile, she disappeared from my line of sight.

I tried to figure out what was going on. I remember Rich yelling 'No', and then pain and blackness. *I must have gotten hit in the head.* Taking stock of my body, I found I didn't hurt anywhere else. Okay, my back and side hurt some too. And then my head began throbbing even worse.

A man's face appeared over me. "Good evening, Mrs. Blakemore."

"Addison," I struggled to get out. "I changed my name back to my maiden name. I haven't changed the license yet."

The doctor nodded. "Okay. My name is Dr. Hilton. Do you know where you are?"

"I assume Blessing Hospital Emergency Room."

Hilton smiled. "Good. We're still waiting on your head and back x-rays before I can unstrap you from the board. It'll be a few minutes. First, I'd like to ask you some questions and do a few tests. Okay?"

"Sure. But how is Rich?"

"Richard Addison, Jr.? Is he related to you?"

"My older brother. He was probably brought in with me." I watched him for a reaction, praying Rich wasn't dead.

"He was brought in at the same time, different ambulance. He's in the other room. He was beaten pretty badly. The cops on the scene have made calls to find your family, I've been told."

"How long ago?"

"You only arrived a few minutes ago." The doctor crossed his arms and looked amused. "Now, can I ask you some questions?"

I tried a smile for him.

"Let's start with moving your extremities. Can you move your fingers?"

For the next several minutes, he did neurological tests to see if I had any brain damage. I guess I passed. He seemed pleased and didn't make any worried faces.

Then the doctor turned away. I heard a nurse speaking in quiet tones but with all the other noises, I couldn't hear what she said. He turned back to me. "There's a police officer that would like to talk to you. Do you feel up to it?"

"Sure. When can I get off this hard board? It really hurts lying here."

"As soon as the x-rays are back," Hilton said again. He made a motion to someone at the door, then walked away from the bed. "She's still strapped to the board, and I don't want her moving." He was obviously addressing the police officer.

I strained to see if it was Mitch but I couldn't. Finally, a face appeared over me. A pair of concerned blue eyes, smiling down. Max.

"Hey there, Tiger."

"Hi."

"I heard the call on the radio as I was being relieved from surveillance duty. I came right over. Two patrolman are outside, they'll come in to take your statement in a minute." He paused. "They told me someone has contacted your family. Uh, Mel, this wouldn't have anything to do with-" He trailed off.

"I don't know. I was talking to Rich. How is he?"

"Beaten. He's conscious but not very responsive, according to the nurses. What were the two of you doing?"

"Rich was doing surveillance on a fraud case. John can give you specifics. I don't actually know that much about it. I went to talk to him about another case I'm helping the guys with."

"So, this has nothing to do with Baker or anything associated with him?"

"Not that I know of." I tried to move my head, but the straps were holding me tight. "I hurt. I want to move. My back's killing me."

"The cavalry is here." He gently touched my shoulder, a light caress. "I'll talk to you later."

Dad and Mom came into my field of vision. Both had concerned looks on their faces as they hurried to my side. Dad and Max exchange greetings.

Mom spoke first. "Are you okay?" She gently rubbed my forehead and stroked my strapped down arm. "What were you doing?" There was anger in her voice, which immediately changed to concern. "You look okay. What hurts? They say Rich is badly hurt." She finally took a breath, as she composed herself.

"I'm fine, Mom." I glanced at Dad.

Dad pulled a stool up to the bed. His soft smile betrayed his concern. "What happened?" he asked in a gentle tone, grasping my right hand. His warm, calloused palm felt good on my cold skin.

I gave him a quick, pain-filled smile. Somehow the hurt was more bearable. He had always been easy to talk to. That was what had made him a great police officer. Victims responded to him, I had been told lots of times in my youth. I took a shallow breath, then without looking at Mom, I began. "I was speaking to Rich and some guys showed up." I told them what happened.

Mom sucked in a breath. I glanced between her and Dad. His eyes darted to the doorway. "Dot, Mitch just walked in with Gloria." He nodded with his head to the hallway. "Why don't you go with them to be with Rich? Gloria looks really upset. She could use someone to console her." Mom patted my arm as she turned to look.

"Go ahead Mom."

"Sure?" She glanced worriedly toward the empty hall.

"Yeah."

Mom leaned over and placed a tender kiss on my head and hurried from the room.

"Thanks." I smiled at Dad in relief. I could see that mom was gearing up for more smothering.

Dad kissed my cheek, and squeezed my hand again. "She's upset. She thought the only one she had to worry about now was Mitch. I guess she was under the impression that Rich's business was free of this sort of stuff." Dad sighed. "Now you work with Rich."

I nodded in understanding. A muscle spasm in my back caused me to grimace.

"Tell me what hurts, Sweetie." His fingers gently massaged my bruised hand.

Before I could start, a uniformed police officer entered. He was a regular at the bar.

"Brent," Dad greeted him.

Brent nodded at Dad with a serious look. He turned to me. "Mel, I need your statement. If you feel up to it."

Dad moved the stool closer to the head of the bed, but didn't relinquish my hand.

I swallowed, then took a nervous breath. Unfortunately, I couldn't tell him much. I hadn't seen much. And I couldn't even really identify the voices, except that they were all male. I described them to the best of my ability, including the Halloween masks.

It seemed like an eternity before I was unstrapped from the board and allowed to lie on the ER bed. I was starting to stiffen up too, so the doctor ordered a painkiller for me.

Mitch showed up in the doorway about this time. He smiled as he walked in, then patted Dad's back and said, "Mom wants to talk to you in Rich's room. I'll stay here with Mel."

Dad gave my hand a last pat, kissed me on the cheek, and hurried from the room.

Mitch sat down in Dad's place.

"How's Rich?"

His smile faded. "He's in pretty bad shape. Those guys did a number on him. Broken arm, possible broken ribs, and maybe internal injuries. The docs are waiting on some test results. He's getting admitted."

"Is he conscious?"

Mitch shook his head. "In and out."

I closed my eyes.

"Don't fret. It's Rich." Mitch patted my shoulder. "He'll be fine. Remember when he crashed his bike down the hill at Berrian Park?" Mitch chuckled.

"This is a bit more serious."

"True, but he looked worse back then." Mitch grinned.

I smiled back, realizing that he was trying to lighten the mood. He was good at it, and forever the optimist.

"How are you, WT?" His eyes scanned my face and the bandage on my head.

"Doc says I'm getting released. I got a huge cut to on the back of my head and bruises all up and down my arms." I turned my arms to show him. "My back is bruised pretty good."

"Road rash too." He pointed at the scrapes on my face. "Reminds me of when we were young."

I chuckled in spite of the pain, which was considerably less as the pain killers began to take effect. "Ah, if Mom only had painkillers like these back then."

Mitch chuckled with me.

The doctor entered, stitched my scalp, and told the nurse to release me. His orders were to rest, heal, and see my doctor in five days to get the stitches removed.

Mitch left and returned with Dad as the nurse finished cleaning my other cuts. Dad and Mitch were talking about which car to take me home in as they walked in the room. With a smile at me, Mitch turned and headed out.

"We'll move you into the spare room at home," Dad said as he sat down on the stool. "Mitch is getting his car, then we'll head home."

"No. I want to go home. To *my* bed." I swung my legs over the side of the bed and waited for the throbbing in my head to stop. Even with painkillers I still hurt.

"But-" Dad started, his eyes hardening as they always did when we disagreed on something.

I interrupted him. "Dad, please. If I stay at your house, Mom will smother me. Like after the accident in Maryland. I love Mom to death but..." I paused to look deep into his eyes. "She drives me crazy." My eye twitched several times in a row, as though the beating had caused a nervous tic.

That amused Dad. "Yeah, I know." He winked ; I returned his smile. "But," He paused. "If you go to your apartment, Mitch is staying with you tonight."

I opened my mouth to argue.

He held up a hand. "No arguments. It's Mitch at your house to help you or my spare room. Your choice."

I sighed. I knew I had lost this argument, but Mitch was far better than being smothered by Mom. "Agreed. Home with Mitch."

***

John showed up the next morning, early. "Feel better or worse than last night?" He was smiling, expecting me to feel a lot worse today.

I gave him a 'you know' smile while I sat at the counter sipping my juice. I had just finished breakfast with Mitch, who had hurried off to work. My back was stiff, and my head felt like I had my own construction company building in there. It was pounding, reverberating, and throbbing. "Worse. How's Rich? Have you heard this morning?"

"Bad shape. He suffered a concussion, still possible internal injuries, broken arm, and the list goes on."

"Is he talking yet?"

"Sort of. The doctors have him heavily sedated." John looked at me. "Tell me what you told the cops and everything else."

When John had been at the hospital last night, there was always someone around. He had whispered in my ear that he'd see me in the morning to discuss 'it'. I relayed the incident to him. "That's what I told the cops. And there is nothing else to add."

"You didn't recognize any of them?"

"As I said, they had masks on. Why?"

"The one thing Rich was able to make us understand was that they had knocked you out for no reason," John said, then continued, "He made a comment to your Dad that you had settled down. He was not even struggling any more. Then you were knocked out."

"Why?"

John just shrugged.

"Which case do you think this is connected to?"

"If I had to guess, I'd say the murders, but who knows. As soon as Rich can give a better statement about what happened we'll know. But until then, I want you to be very careful." John stood up and looked me in the eye. "None of these cases are worth getting killed over."

"But-"

"Dead people aren't worth getting killed over, Mel," John said seriously. "It won't bring them back. And the other cases aren't even worth mentioning."

"Someone thinks it's worth almost killing over."

John nodded in agreement. "This is getting serious."

I saw that look on his face. It reminded me of Rich's expression when he was yelling at me about Hessor. John took on that overly protective, brotherly look. "Oh, don't you start too. I can take care of myself."

John motioned to the bandage on my head. His eyes softened. "Mel, I'm not saying stop looking into it. Just back off and rest for a day or two. And I want you to be extra careful. I'm heading out to talk to some contacts. Stay home. Heal."

"Okay," I said, "but you will tell me if you find out anything. Right?"

"Absolutely," John said with a smile. He leaned over and gave me a peck on the cheek. "I'm glad that both of you are okay. I'd hate to have to train two new employees."

I laughed at John as he headed out the door. Slowly, I washed up the dishes. By that time, I was ready for a break. I was tired. It was only ten o'clock, so I headed back to the bed for a nap and another painkiller.

Heal. Relax. Whatever.

The next thing I knew, I heard my apartment door banging open and footsteps thumping through my living room. By the time I was upright in bed, Max had barreled into my room, Mitch on his heels.

"What the...?" I yelled.

Mitch and Max stood rigid, looking at me, fear furrowing both their brows. Mitch leaned against the doorpost and put a hand to his chest. Max let out a deep sigh. They glanced at each other, then both smiled at me.

"What are you doing in my apartment? How did you get in here?" I was still sitting in bed with the covers tucked up to my chest.

Mitch walked over and gave me a kiss on the cheek. "Are you okay, WT?"

"Yeah. I was sleeping! What are you doing here?"

A chuckle escaped from Mitch's throat. He gave me another kiss on the cheek and headed out. "I'll let Max explain. And I'll tell Dad downstairs that you're okay." He gave a loose wave over his shoulder.

Max stood in the doorway, his hands on his hips, breathing deeply. "I came by to say hi. I knocked several times, but no one answered. I called

Mitch. He said you were home. I tried knocking again. Yelling, actually. I called Mitch back. He was already on his way and by the time I got downstairs, he met me. We got the key from your Dad and well, here we are."

I just sat staring at him in amazement. I shook my head. "That painkiller must have really knocked me out." I stared at Max as he stared at me. "That doesn't explain what you are doing here?"

"Hey, I was worried," he whined as he glanced at his watch. "It's almost lunch time. I thought you might want some company?"

"Sure. I guess. It's almost lunch time?"

"Man, I was really out of it."

"How's the head?"

"Throbbing." I waited. "Do you mind? I need to get out of bed."

"Okay." He didn't moved one inch, and his smile increased. I knew he was flirting, but it felt okay. I kind of liked it.

"Get out of my room and close the door," I said pointing to the living room.

Max bowed his head, closing the door behind him.

I swung my legs off the bed. My back hurt far worse than last night. I groaned in pain, knowing I needed another painkiller. I tried to stand up. Too much pain. I tried another way up. No go.

I glanced around my bed looking for my clothes. My shorts were on the box across the room. I looked around, then down. I had gone back to sleep in my nightshirt and underwear. I grimaced, thinking what I needed to do. I gathered my blanket around me and called out for Max.

The door opened and Max stuck his head in. "Yes?"

"I need help getting up. My back is really stiff." I pointed at the shorts.

Max walked in and looked at me with a smile. "This could get interesting."

"Shut up. And don't get any ideas, Mister."

"Who me?" He picked my shorts up off the box and held them in the air. "Do you want these?" He looked pointedly at me holding the blanket around myself.

I held out my hand.

"Can you put them on?" Max moved them closer to me, but still out of my reach.

I huffed and put my hand back in my lap. "Fine. I'll stay here."

Max tossed them to me. "Need help putting them on?"

I scrunched my face.

"Do you want me to leave again or help with getting you dressed?"

"Over my dead body."

"It can be arranged." Max reached out and tapped my nose once, then headed out the door. As he closed it behind him, he whispered, "Just ask."

I struggled to get the shorts over most of my butt without standing. My back was aching and the added work had made my head spin.

"Mel? Are you all right? I was just kidding," Max said through the door.

"I'm fine," I grunted out. "Come help me stand up."

Max walked in. He looked at me sitting there in my shorts and white nightshirt. I could see his eyes linger on me. "Bet it hurt to put those shorts on, huh?"

"Shut up and help me up."

Max walked over and gently grabbed me in a limp hug. I held on to him as he lifted me to a standing position. He let go.

I stood for just a second, then I swayed. My head was throbbing in pain. My right leg was twitching and ready to drop me, again. I grabbing at him to stop my fall.

Max took hold of me, then swept my legs out from under me and carried me into the living room. He sat me gently on the couch, then squatted down by me. His blue eyes were full of concern. "Mel? Do you want to go see someone?"

I shook my head leaning back on the couch. "Just give me a minute. My head is throbbing."

Max stayed beside me waiting, watching.

I finally smiled. "I'm fine."

"Fine?" He grunted. "Anyway, I brought lunch. Feel up to it?"

I sniffed and realized that I recognized the smell. Maid Rites. I laughed. "Got you hooked, did we?"

He grabbed the bags and some drinks from my refrigerator before joining me back in the living room. He handed me one sandwich and a half basket of cheese balls and fries. "I'm even getting to like these fries."

We ate for a while in silence, then Max turned to me. "Can I ask you a personal question?"

My mouth was full of the last bite of Maid Rite so I couldn't speak.

"If I'm treading on painful ground just say, okay?"

I swallowed down the food as my gut twisted. "Okay."

Max took a drink, still eying me. "At the hospital, when I first showed up, I asked about you. They didn't have you registered as Addison but as Blakemore. I assume that's your married name."

I nodded. It felt like a scab had just been picked open on my heart.

"Uh, you don't strike me as one of those women that won't take a married name. And you introduced yourself as Addison. So, I guess I'm confused."

I looked over toward the stereo and Robbie's Petey.

Max touched my arm. "I'm sorry. I shouldn't have asked-"

"No. It's okay. When I got out of the hospital in Maryland, I had Jason Landry, Craig's partner, petition to get my maiden name back. I just haven't gotten my license here in Illinois yet."

Max seemed puzzled, but he didn't pursue the topic.

"I know you're curious," I said, and he looked embarrassed. "For your information, I wanted my maiden name back because-" I stopped. This was a very sore subject with me. I could feel the anger rising fast, but I pushed it back down and took a shallow breath to calm myself. Finally I glanced at Max, who was watching me closely. "I didn't want the rat bastard's name any more. That's all."

"Rat bastard? Your husband?"

"Yeah. It's a long story and I'd rather not go into details."

Max nodded, accepting my explanation.

I turned on the TV to diffuse the tense air. The shows were the usual; I shut it off. "I hate being sick."

Max laughed. "You need cable or a computer."

"Something." I looked around the place. *What am I going to do all day?* "This is so boring." I sighed deeply. I looked at Max. "By the way, thanks for lunch. Since you never answered me before, what are you doing here?"

Max shrugged. "It's my day off. Thought I'd check on my favorite snooping sneak."

"Snooping sneak?"

"I read your report last night." Max looked closely at me. "Did you 'forget' to tell them anything?"

I shook my head in all sincerity. "That was everything."

"Who was the source on the package?"

I laughed. "Good try, Sherlock. I may be stiff and slightly woozy, but I'm not brain dead."

Max sobered. "I'm glad." His tone made me pay closer attention. "Look Mel, I'm going to be honest with you. Since the first time I met you, I can't get you off my mind. I know that you're still grieving and I understand. I want to see you and maybe get to know you better. I'm not talking sex, although that would be great. But I can wait." He finally looked at me, a blush tinting his face. "I don't know why I just said all that. Anyway, I know you're not ready to date-"

My gut twisted tight and continued to wring itself dry as he spoke. I had opened my mouth to say that very thing. I smiled at his smile to me. He apparently guessed what I was going to say.

"But can I see you more often? As friends?"

"Yeah. I'd like that, as friends." I gave him a soft smile, my body suddenly not hurting quite as badly.

"Good. I'll break down your defenses. Now, the source?"

"Fat chance, Bauer."

CHAPTER 17

It was nice having Max around. I talked him into taking me to the hospital to see Rich. We stayed there for a few hours, then ended back at my place for supper. Max cooked some spaghetti and even cleaned up afterward. I was tired and ready for bed. We were sitting quietly until there was a knock at the door. He looked out the peephole. "It's a lady with a kid."

I motioned for him to open the door. Beth stood there with her youngest on her arm. She hurried in without an invitation from Max, giving him a funny look, but her face quickly took on a look of concern for me. "Your mom called. She asked if I could stop by and make sure you were okay. I just heard about you and your brother. Steve and I were visiting friends out of town. Are you okay?"

I finger waved at the baby on her arm. Julian was only seven months old. He was currently sucking on a pacifier. "Hi Jules. I'm fine, Beth. Thanks."

Beth walked around me, looking intently at my hair. I had taken the bandage off, but the stitches were visible. She quietly said, "Ouch." With one hand, she gently moved my hair aside. "Call me tomorrow, and I'll come over and help wash your hair."

I watched as Max slowly sat back down. The look on his face asked, 'Who is this?' as he watched her take command.

"Well, at least this scar won't be noticeable," Beth said authoritatively. "Better than your other two."

"Don't I know it."

"Scars? From what?" Max asked.

Beth trained her eyes on him as though noticing him for the first time. She looked back at me with an uplifted brow.

"Oh, stop. This is Max Bauer. He's a Detective on the police force. Max, this is Beth Majorham, a longtime friend. And the little guy on her arm is Julian, her youngest."

"Hi," Max said, giving the kid a suspicious eye. The kid was looking almost the same way at him.

"I can't stay long. I abandoned the kids so I could come here. This little rat has an ear infection and won't let me put him down. Right?" she asked the baby who cooed at her. She gave him a kiss.

"Abandoned?" Max asked horrified.

I laughed. "At her Mom's. For heaven's sake, Max, get a clue."

"Oh, I forgot." She looked at Max and then back at me. She placed Julian in Max's arms. "Here, hold him. I'll be back in a minute." She disappeared out the door.

I watched as Max held Julian at arm's length like he was a bomb. Julian looked terrified. They both looked suspicious, Max probably assuming that Julian would do something yucky on him, and Julian suspecting that Max might drop him. It was priceless. Doubly funny when they both scrunched up their faces; Julian to cry, Max to beg for help.

"Here, hand him over." I cuddled the little one tight to my chest, making mommy noises. Julian settled right down. He poked his head out from under my chin to look at Max with still wet cheeks. I kissed him and wiped his tears away. "See Jules, he won't hurt you."

Julian looked at me, then back at the strange man, and once more at me. The little boy spoke baby talk to me around his pacifier.

"He says you're funny looking."

"Ha, ha."

"You looked like you were going to cry too."

"Would I get hugged like that?"

I ignored him. "Jules and I are in tight with each other, aren't we buddy?"

The baby laid his head on my chest, content. I smiled at Max.

His eyes softened. "You're good with kids."

"It's a mommy thing." I looked down at the baby in my arms. I missed Robbie. I sniffled once and blinked several times to keep the tears back. "You, uh, you haven't been around too many kids, I take it?"

Max didn't answer right away, but he was watching me as I slowly began to rock. "No. I was an only child. The closest I ever came to kids was a cat that ate my pet goldfish." Max's eyes were locked on Julian. "He's going to sleep. Just like that."

I nodded as I kissed the top of Julian's head. "I could tell he was tired."

"How?"

I shrugged.

"What's with the rocking?"

"Another mommy thing. Beth said he had an ear infection. He's probably having trouble sleeping. Most kids find the motion soothing."

"Looks like it." He sat there silent, watching me put Julian to sleep.

When Beth reappeared at the door, her eyes immediately went to her child. She smiled at me, then winked at Max. "Mom genes never go away." Beth laid the two bags in her hands on the floor.

"No. Max scared him."

Beth put her hands on her hips and turned a disgusted look on him.

"I...all I did was look at him. I swear!" Max held up his right hand.

"Here." She pointed at the bags. "Your mom made me stop by on my way and grab her heating pad, cold pad, and a bunch of other stuff."

"Thanks."

"Sure. Hey look, I'd better get going. I need to get the little monsters home and to bed." Beth moved toward me.

"Can I get your help for a minute, Beth? I had a hard time getting into my bra this afternoon and I would appreciate it if you'd help me get out of it." I glanced at Max whose eyes had brightened. I made a face at him. "I was going to sleep in it, but since you're here..."

Beth nodded and took Julian from me and transferred him to Max. "Just sit there. If he stirs, rock like you saw Mel and shush him." With no more words, she got the baby situated on Max's shoulder. "Think soft and mommy-like."

"But-"

"Shhhh," Beth said.

Max obediently closed his mouth.

"It works on the big boys too," Beth said to me.

I got up slowly, chuckling at the bewildered look on Max's face. We headed into the bedroom. I grabbed my nightshirt and tossed it on the bed next to us. With a grunt, I started to take off the T-shirt that I had worked so hard to get into that afternoon.

Beth immediately started helping, pulling the shirt off. "Got news for you," she whispered to me from behind.

"Yeah?"

"Schnabel is having trouble with his wife."

"Trouble?"

Beth nodded as the shirt came off. "As in marital trouble." She fluffed the nightshirt and over my head it went. "Rumor has it there is trouble brewing at the old homestead."

"Why?"

"He's in his late forties, why do you think?"

"Midlife crisis? Another woman?"

"That's the rumor."

"Interesting. What about Williams?"

"The only thing I could find out about him is that he is worried about something, big time."

I turned around. "About what? Do you know what he's worried about?"

Beth shrugged. "I'll keep digging though. His wife is on a PTA committee with me. She made mention that he wasn't sleeping well. He's been getting lots of phone calls from strange men at odd times. Also, he's been brooding."

"Brooding?"

"That's what Virginia said, 'brooding'. She actually caught him talking to himself the other day. She's really worried about him."

"Okay. I'll pass that along."

"That's a really big bruise on your back, Mel. Are you sure that you're okay?"

I nodded. "Stiff but okay."

Beth inclined her head to the other room. "What's going on with him?"

"It's not what you think. He wants to date, but I'm not ready yet."

"Oh," Beth said. Her tone changed. "He's really good-looking."

"Yeah, he is." I gave her a dirty look. "Just stop."

Beth smiled her knowing smile. "Good-looking and has a respectable job. Not to mention that he is really into you. I can tell. Max has the hots for you. Don't wait too long, Mel. I have lots of divorced friends that would give their eyeteeth for a catch like him."

"I'm not ready. It's not right."

"I know." Beth patted my arm. "Still, he seems to be a really nice guy."

"Yeah." Sighing, I walked out of the door. We both stopped at the sight of Max walking back and forth in the kitchen. When he saw us, his look quickly changed, relief mixed with a pleading to hurry up. Beth grinned at me. I chuckled.

"He woke up and almost started crying. When I stood up to get you, he settled back down, so I just walked back and forth. He hasn't cried, but I don't think he likes me." Max looked down at the baby in his arms who looked up at him, and gave Julian a smile. "Mommy's here. You'll be okay, little guy."

Beth hurried to take the almost sleeping child from Max. Julian immediately snuggled onto her shoulder, sighed deeply, and was out like a light. "Thanks, Max."

"Sure," Max said. He opened the door for her. When he closed it, I was sitting back down at the counter in my nightshirt. Max turned to look back at the door, then sat down. "Babies have a smell."

"It's usually poop, drool, or in Julian's case, medicine," I said, trying to contain my amusement.

Max frowned. "Those aren't the smells I meant. Uh, well, a baby smell."

"Talcum powder in the diapers."

"Really?"

I started laughing. The surprised look on Max's face was incredible. I laughed until I had to hold my sides in pain, and wipe tears from my eyes. "Thanks, Max. I haven't laughed that hard in ages."

Max gave me one of his lopsided, full-faced, adorable smiles. "Beth said you had scars?"

I nodded, my humor subsiding, but my heart didn't constrict like it usually did. "From the car accident. I was pinned in the car for well over an hour."

"Hit and run?"

"No, the guy was still there."

"Drunk?"

I shook my head. "He was on medication. Anyway, I'll carry these scars for life, besides the emotional ones. "*Why isn't this as painful as it usually is?* It still hurt to talk about it, but there was a sense of calm too. *It must be the painkillers taking effect again.*

"Where?" Max hesitated. "If I can ask? Beth said that they were visible."

"You can see one. The other is not available for public viewing." I motioned to look at my leg. I lifted the hem of my long nightshirt over my shorts that I slept in. The six-inch scar was still a bright shade of pink on the thigh of my right leg.

Max leaned over the counter and looked. "Ouch. And the other? The one not for public viewing?"

"My chest."

Max hesitated as he sat back down. "When did you come back to Quincy?"

"Less than a week before we met." I fiddled with the ice pack on the counter.

"Looks like a serious injury. How long were you in the hospital?"

"Over a month and a half. Complications from my surgeries. Then physical therapy. Mom stayed with me for about a month after that." I smiled. "She drove me nuts."

Max grinned back. "Mothers are good at that." His gaze held mine.

"I, uh, tried to stay in Maryland, but the house was too quiet." I lowered my eyes back to the counter as Max gently patted my hand. "One call back home and Mom organized my move. My brothers showed up. Bam! My house was packed. When we got here, lots of the regulars from the bar helped move me in." I shrugged. "I needed distractions."

Max nodded in understanding.

I glanced at the clock, ready to change the subject. "Not that I'm kicking you out but-"

"You're kicking me out," Max finished with a grin.

"Yeah."

"You'll be okay here?"

"As long as you don't come barging in again." I gave him a soft smile. "Thanks for keeping me company all day."

His blue eyes twinkled. "I had a good time, too." He reached out and picked up my hand, leaned over, and kissed it. "Have a good night, Mel. Call if you need anything, or want to tell me the name of your source."

I locked the door behind him. *Max is a good friend.* Before I could turn around, the phone rang. "Hello?"

"Mel, just checking in," John said. "I heard that you were at the hospital visiting Rich."

"Yeah. He looks bad."

"That he does. Is he able to speak better?"

"Not really. The docs said maybe tomorrow. Did you find out anything?"

"The streets are quiet. No one is bragging about beating up on Rich. I figured if it were a hired hit or something, there'd be word about it. Nada. I did find my skip though."

"What did Williams say when you met with him tonight? Are we still working for him?"

"Yes. He wants to know who the leak is at whatever cost. He doesn't think that it has anything to do with the limo service though. He dismissed it rather quickly."

I frowned. "But so far that's the only link."

"Yes, I know. His attitude puzzled me too. I want you to rest one more day. Then I want you to go back to working on that angle. I'll continue working the other avenues of investigation."

***

I was back at work the next day despite John's orders. My back hurt and I still had another four days before getting the stitches taken out, but since I was only doing computer work, I figured I could handle it. John wasn't happy, but I told him I was bored at home. So there I sat, scouring the databases for information.

"Mel, line two," Pam called out to me.

"Thanks." I picked it up. "Hello."

"Mel, Rich wants to talk to you," Dad said.

"Is he able too?"

"Yeah. This morning he's awake and talking. He asked me to get you here before calling the cops in for a statement." There was a long pause on the line. "When I didn't find you at home..." His tone indicated just how upset he was at me.

I cringed even though he couldn't see me. "I was bored. All I'm doing is computer work anyway, nothing strenuous. I promise, Dad. I'll get John to bring me to the hospital."

"Good idea. I'll tell Rich."

I hung up and headed to John's office. I tapped on the door frame to get his attention. "Rich is awake and wants to talk to us."

John nodded in acknowledgment. He started shutting down his computer. "I'm driving, Mel." His stern expression told me he wouldn't take no for an answer.

"Yeah, yeah," I said walking toward the front of the office. "Everyone ordering me around." I mumbled with a passing glance at Pam.

Blessing Hospital isn't far from the downtown area. When we got there, Rich had just fallen back asleep, so we talked with Dad for a few minutes. Mom had left earlier to do some volunteer work at the church.

Rich groaned awake.

I moved over to his bed and looked down at him with a smile. "Hey, big brother."

Rich tried a smile for me. "I'm glad you're okay."

I nodded back, patting his good arm. "What did you want to talk to me about? John's here too." I pointed to the other side of the bed.

Rich looked over at John. John winked back.

Dad excused himself from the room. "I'll call Mitch and let him know you're awake."

Rich waited until the door closed. "Did you recognize anyone, Mel?"

I shook my head. "Not with the masks on. I only heard that one man speak. The one in the hockey mask."

"The skeleton mask guy was the leader. He didn't speak until after they had knocked you out. And he kept having them check to make sure that you were still out. I got the impression that he knew you and that maybe you could ID his voice." Rich closed his eyes, exhausted after our short exchange.

I thought about the guy in the skeleton mask. "From his body shape, it could be any number of guys."

"Who?" John asked.

I shrugged. "He has a similar body shape to Mitch's, height-and-weight-wise, so I guess pretty average. You know, not fat but not thin, and not as cut as you, John. Just a tad shorter than Rich." I thought harder. "All were Caucasian and now that I'm thinking about it, all of them were nicely dressed. No raggy jeans or really dirty clothes. Skeleton mask wore dress pants, maybe chinos. Expensive shoes too."

Rich looked at John, then at me. "Hessor?"

I thought about it. Reluctantly, I nodded. "Could be. Or it could be Tom Bressler. It could have been Max Bauer, Daniel Kickery, or even Mitch."

John shook his head. "Anything else, Rich? What did they want?"

"The video. They wanted to know where we had hid the video."

"Video?" John and I asked in unison.

Rich nodded.

"Not the disk?" I asked in confusion.

Rich shook his head. "The video. Skeleton man was quite mad that I had no idea what he was talking about."

I thought hard. Videotape? "Could it have been, uh, what's his name? The guy that I videotaped on that fraud case, uh, Lamprey."

"No. He's too cut. Skeleton guy had a gut. Not big but it wasn't wash board like Lamprey's."

"Hmmm," John said. "I'll look into Lamprey anyway. Just in case."

"When it became obvious that I had no clue what they wanted, they just beat on me. They told me to stop looking into 'it'."

"It?" John asked.

"I've got no clue. 'It'. Skeleton guy said that twice. 'Stop looking into it. If you don't, Mel is next.' That's what he said."

"He called her Mel?" John asked.

Rich nodded.

John looked at me. "It's definitely someone you know."

"I know a lot of people, John." I looked down at Rich. I could tell he was tired. "Go back to sleep, Rich. Dad will wake you when Mitch or whoever arrives."

Rich nodded and closed his eyes. "I'm glad you're okay. John, take care of her." He mumbled as he fell asleep.

"I'm glad you're okay too," I said softly back and headed out the door with John, who had merely patted Rich on his good arm.

The trip back to the office was short but silent. Before getting out of the car, John turned to me. "If it's someone you know Mel, you could be in a dangerous position. You need to be really careful of what you do, where you go and who you talk to."

"I will, John." I hesitated. "A video. What is that about?"

John shrugged.

"What if the video was the thing Mouse was to deliver Hessor?"

John nodded like he had already thought of that.

"There's one way to find out. Call Hessor. He wants to date me. Badly. Maybe I can use that to our advantage."

John studied me. "You've had more than just a passing relationship with Hessor, haven't you?"

My eyes stayed locked with his for just a second, then I lowered them. "Yeah, but don't tell Rich."

"How intimate were you with him?"

"We were teenagers. I dated him along with Bressler for a short time. Nothing ever came of it. Bart tried to push the issue one night and I, uh well, I left him in a very painful position." I gave John a wry smile.

"Did he try to rape you?" John's eyes hardened.

"No, well, I guess it might be called attempted date rape." I shrugged. "He got the message. Loud and clear." I paused. "When I was at his house the other day, he made it known that he would still like to get to know me better. I could use that to get information from him."

John immediately shook his head. "No way. You're not talking with Hessor again. Rich was right, he's very dangerous. And if skeleton mask man was Hessor and you ask him about the video, he's going to know that you know it was him. Very dangerous. Whoever they were, they have already killed at least twice. They will not hesitate to kill again."

"But-"

"No, Mel," John said. "It's too dangerous."

He was right, but it was the fastest way to find out.

John was watching me closely. "Look Mel, give it a couple of days. Maybe Hessor will call you. If he inquires about your health, see if you can get a feel from him. If he knows too much about the attack, then we'll go from there."

I sighed but nodded. I was in no shape to be doing anything physical anyway. "Okay. You're right, John."

"Why don't you go home and rest?"

"I told you, I'm bored to death at home." I stopped at his stern look. I knew he was going to tell me that I needed to rest. "I'll go home after lunch. Happy?" John chuckled and shooed me out of his office.

As I wandered back to my desk, Pam flagged me down. "Phone's for you. Line one."

I picked it up. "Mel."

"Hi Mel," Dan Kickery said. "I just heard from Mitch about you and your brother. Are both of you okay?"

"Yeah. Rich is still in the hospital. I've got a cut on my head and bruises," I said softly rubbing my eyes. I was getting tired. *Maybe I should head home and rest, like John suggested.* "Did you get my message?" I had called the day before to tell him to be careful, thinking that whoever had done this might be after the disk.

"Yeah, I did. But I was busy and couldn't get back to you yesterday. Were you trying to warn me?"

"I was, but now I don't think it had anything to do with the disk."

"Really?"

"Yeah. They wanted the location of a video."

"Hmmm," Kick said. "Well, I did need to talk to you about the disk. Can you come over here tonight, or I could come to your place if you want?"

"I don't have a computer," I said, my voice fading with exhaustion.

"Really?" Kick asked as though he was surprised that not everyone had a computer at home.

I chuckled. "Yeah. Tonight at your house?"

"Great. Say after nine, okay?"

"Fine. See you then, Kick." I had no sooner hung up when I had another phone call.

"I just heard. Are you okay?"

I hesitated, not quite recognizing the voice. "Tom?"

"Sorry, yeah." His voice sounded like he was smiling. Bressler continued, "I just spoke with a cop here at City Hall. We were talking and he mentioned the incident with the two of you. So, is Rich okay?"

"He's in the hospital."

"Is he talking? Do you know who did it?"

"Not yet. He was just able to let us know about the attack today." I closed my eyes and rested my head on my hand. I was really tired now. My eyes felt like lead weights. I guess that last painkiller was starting to take effect.

"The officer said that all of the guys had masks on. Did Rich or you recognize any voices?"

"No."

"What about you? Are you okay? How's the head and back? Did the two guys hurt you holding you down like that? Any lasting effects?"

"I'm fine. I've got a couple of stitches in my head and my back is bruised pretty good, but over all I'm fine," I said. "Thanks for the call."

"Sure. Let me know if I can do anything. What's going on in this town anyway?" Bressler paused. "I'll let you get back to work. Don't hesitate to call, Mel."

"Thanks again, Tommy." I hung up the phone and rested my head on my arm. I guess I fell asleep, the next thing I knew, John was waking me up.

"Time to go home, Mel." He was bent over, looking at me eye-to-eye.

I lifted up my head and yawned. As I stretched, I grimaced in pain. Apparently sleeping sitting up wasn't the best thing for my back. "What time is it?"

"Noon. I saw you sleeping here about forty minutes ago, but I let you sleep. I'm heading out to get lunch and to talk with an informant. I'll take you home." John was handing me my purse and had a hold of my elbow, raising me from my seat.

"But my Jeep-"

"After work, I'll come and get you or something. We'll get it home." He gave me a brotherly smile.

CHAPTER 18

Dan Kickery lived in a three-bedroom, ranch-style house in an older subdivision off of 36th Street.

After welcoming me at the door and getting me a drink, he showed me into his computer room. He had more electronics in that one room then I had seen anywhere else, except for maybe at a computer store. I looked around in awe. I wouldn't have been surprised if the room wasn't worth more than the entire house! He already had the disk's contents on-screen.

He glanced at me, then away, at the computer. "You look good, Mel."

"Thanks." Kick sat behind the desk and I positioned my chair to sit next to him. Gesturing to all of the equipment, I asked, "What do you run out of here, the Pentagon?" I noticed him looking at all the hardware, as though seeing it for the first time. "You only dabble!" I chided. "So, what have you got, oh computer guru?"

Kick smiled. "Well, I thought I was onto something, but I think I was wrong."

"Tell me anyway."

Kick nodded and pointed at the screen. "This pattern is too random. I was watching a James Bond movie the other night and had a thought that maybe this is in code."

"Code?" The skepticism was strong in my voice. "Why would Eddie put something in code? He wanted Rich to see it. And the note said Rich would know what to do with it." I shook my head. "Rich is not into secret codes, Kick."

Kick sighed. "I know. But look at this." He punched in some commands and the screen reset itself. One word became visible with lots of other letters around it. The word was 'firecrackers'.

"What is that?"

Kick shrugged. "I was running some encryption programs that some friends of mine have. This came up. So did this." He did some other keystrokes and the word that now appeared was 'cease fire'.

I looked at him, then back at the screen. "But why? What about the other page?"

"I asked some of my computer friends about it. The only thing we can come up with is that it's some sort of accounting sheet."

I nodded in agreement.

"And if it is, then someone is taking money from this account." He pointed at one of the long string of numbers at the bottom of the page. "The columns don't add up like they should. One of my accountant friends pointed that out. If this is some sort of tracking sheet, he said that maybe someone is siphoning money. Taking from one account and putting it into another. Or, more likely, we're completely wrong."

"Hmmm." I sat back and looked at the screen. "So, this could be some sort of debit sheet or something."

Kick shrugged. "Something like that."

"Interesting." I took a drink. "These encryption programs. Just how many different words do you get off the first page?"

"I've only run three programs. Only those two words came up," Kick said. "I've got a bunch more I could run, but in order for the system to work, the sender and receiver have to both have the same codes. It makes no sense that Eddie would have used one, knowing that Rich had no idea about it. Like you pointed out, Rich would have to be in on it. So, now that I'm thinking about it, I was wrong."

I just sat staring and thinking.

"Sorry for wasting your time, Mel."

"No. You've gotten further on this then anyone else." I smiled. "Keep working on it. Maybe, think like Eddie. I don't think he was very computer savvy."

"No, Eddie was actually pretty good with computers. One of my friends knew him. They talked computers all the time. Let me talk to Buzz and see if between the two of us we can't figure this out."

"Thanks, Kick. I appreciate it."

I headed home. It was getting dark, and I wanted to be in before then. I guess I was still spooked from the beating.

I was sitting in the bar drinking a glass of water when Max walked in. He immediately moved to my side and ordered a soda. "Got a minute?" he asked with a serious look on his face.

"All night."

"Good. I want to ask you some more questions."

"Here?"

Max looked around.

I picked up on the fact that he wanted it to be in private. I motioned my brother over. "I'm going upstairs. If Dad calls just relay the message for me, okay Cam?"

"Sure, Sis." Cam smiled at me before glancing at Max.

After we were in the living room of my apartment, Max turned to me. "I spoke with the officer investigating your beating. He let me read Rich's statement. Do you have any idea about the video thing?"

I shook my head. "John and I were stumped too."

Max sighed in obvious frustration. "This guy with the skeleton mask? Who do you think it might be?"

"From his average build, it could have been you." I paused, and then smiled. "So, what were you doing that night?"

Max laughed, his mood not so serious now. "Why would I beat you and Rich up?"

"So that you could play the knight in shining armor," I said with a smile still on my face. "Being at the hospital so quick, breaking into my apartment when I didn't answer your knock-"

"I had a key, and Mitch." Max smirked. "Okay, I see where you would get that thought. Possible, I guess. You, I could see beating up on." He smiled, jokingly. "You're a very frustrating woman. But why would I beat up on Rich?"

"Because you could. I'm only kidding."

"But the man had my body shape?"

"Yeah, sort of." I paused, taking a closer look at his body. His jeans fit just right and the polo shirt looked adorable on him. He had a nice, strong-looking body. I swallowed, stopping my own reaction to him. "Well, okay maybe the guy was a bit taller, maybe an inch or so, but not much."

Max rubbed his chin. Suddenly he asked, "Hessor?"

I nodded slowly. "Could be. Or one of a hundred other people I know with a similar body type. It was average."

"Okay. I'll look into Hessor anyway. It'll give me a reason to go and talk to him. I'll get a feel for him about the attack." Max paused. "Did Rich ever investigate him?"

"You'd have to ask Rich or someone at the station. Try Tom Hawkings, they were partners for a long time. From Rich's attitude about Hessor, I'd have to say yes." I tapped my finger on the table in thought.

"Could the video that Skeleton Mask asked about be what Mouse was supposed to deliver to Hessor the night she was killed?"

"Could be, I guess. My source didn't say how big it was."

"Did your source say when it was to be delivered?"

"The night she died, I've already told you-"

"Who?" It came out of him before I had finished my sentence. Obviously he was trying to trip me up.

I smirked. "Nice try." He shrugged in defeat. "Will you let me know about your interview with Bart?"

"Maybe."

"Are we still on for Friday night at the Chinese restaurant?"

"Yes Grasshopper, I will still teach you to eat with the revered chopsticks," Max said in a Kungfu voice. He stood up to leave and laid a hand on my shoulder. "Be careful, Mel. Call if you need me. Someone out there doesn't like you and Rich looking into something."

"Yeah, I know," I said touching my head gently. "Trust me, that message was received loud and clear."

***

I lay awake that night thinking about everything. *Was the beating related to the murders or to Williams' case or what? Could this video thing be something completely different?* I had a gut feeling that everything was related. Somehow, the break-ins and the beating had to be related-not to mention the four bodies. If they weren't, it made absolutely no sense.

Then it hit me. I had forgotten to tell John about the possible connection between Wally's job with Top Hat Limo and the politicians. *Was that the connection? Or was it just a coincidence? This was a small town.* I sighed. It was too much to think about. My head was starting to throb again. I'd tell him the next morning.

CHAPTER 19

I called the office early, but Pam said that John was out. I debated waiting on researching Wally's employment at Top Hat until talking to John, but something told me to try right away. After once more calling into the office to let Pam know where I was going, I headed to the limo address.

Top Hat was located in a mixed residential/commercial area of town on the east side. The place had obviously been a residence at one time. The one story house had only three parking places in front of it, in what used to be the lawn area. I guess this cut down on lawn care too. Behind the house, in front of large garage, several black limos were parked, including one stretch limo. I stepped out of the Jeep and looked around. It was a quiet area with hardly any foot traffic.

The door opened into a small office; the only sign on the place was lettered on the door. It was nothing fancy, but it had the look of a respectable business. It seemed deserted.

"Hello?" I called out.

A man quickly hurried out of a back office. He was older, maybe in his fifties, and he smiled when he saw me. "Sorry, I didn't hear you come in. What can I do for you?"

"I'm trying to find a friend of mine." I smiled, deciding right then to go with a lie, an impulsive, gut reaction. This man looked like I could hook him with a story. "He mentioned that he worked here. Of course, it was a while ago. I can't really remember when it was, maybe a couple of months ago." I paused again and tried to look embarrassed. "I know it's a long shot, but I'm only in town a few days, and I'm trying to find this guy." I shifted my weight on my feet and looked around the room trying to appear embarrassed. "No, never mind." I started to back off.

The man rounded the counter and stepped in front of me with a huge grin on his face. "I like long shots. Tell me and I'll see if I can help you."

"Okay, but don't laugh at me. Like I said, it was a while ago."

The older man nodded.

"His name was Wally. That's all I know. He said he worked here. Top Hat Limo in Quincy, Illinois."

"Hmmm." The man thought. "I don't recall anyone working here by that name." He looked off into the distance, thinking. "Nope. Do you have a last name?"

"Sorry."

"Hmmm." The man turned and called toward the back office, "Martha, can you come here a minute?"

A lady, about the same age, walked out with her glasses perched on her nose. She looked at the man, then at me. "Yes? Is there a problem?"

The man waved his hand dismissively. "Just a funny question. This lady is looking for someone who might have worked for us a while ago by the name of Wally. I can't seem to recall anyone, can you? You do payroll."

Martha took her glasses off her nose and thought. "No." She shook her head in thought. "No, wait a minute. About two months ago we had a guy here, all of our drivers were sick, remember Frank. Everyone had the flu. Tim, one of our regular drivers, had a friend who could drive for us for just a day or two."

I glanced at Frank, but he still seemed clueless.

Martha looked at me. "We just needed a driver for a night job. Tim said his friend could do it, that he'd worked for Mr. Walker, who used to own the place before we bought it four years ago." Martha stopped and looked closer at me. "Are you a police officer?"

I shook my head. "No, Ma'am. Just a friend looking for Wally. You said he drove one time for you? See, he told me he worked here all the time. I just need to talk to him. I really liked the weekend we spent together in the Caribbean." I once more tried to look embarrassed.

Martha made a sweet, 'This must be love' look. "Okay, but we paid him under the table since it was just for one night. Actually, he drove two days for the same client. I don't know if it's your friend, but he called himself Wally."

"Uh, five-eleven, sandy blond hair, hazel eyes, a small scar on his left cheek."

Martha recognized him right away. "Wally Baker. He drove two days in a row for us. I asked him to continue working for us, but he said he was otherwise employed and this was a favor to his friend." Martha shrugged. "I don't know where he lived or anything. Like I said, we paid him cash for his work."

I ran a hand over my cheek, looking down at my feet. I looked up to see Frank still lost about the whole incident and Martha merely watching me. "Do you think he might have spoken to this client about where he lived or he might know the client? Would it be possible to find out who he drove that night?" Here was the longest long shot of them all. I waited with baited breath.

Martha hesitated.

"Forget it. It was a long shot." I swallowed and fluttered my eyelashes. "I thought that I'd like to see if what I was feeling about Wally was more than just a weekend fling." I had pegged Frank as a romantic from the first smile. Hopefully Martha was one too.

Martha's eyes softened. She glanced at Frank. "I know what it's like to be in love. Come with me and I'll see if I can find the old records. But you must promise not to tell anyone where you got the information, especially the client. We try to be very discrete."

I smiled in genuine relief. "Absolutely."

***

"Is John back yet?" I asked Pam as I walked in the door of the office.

Pam shook her head.

"Do you know when he's due back?"

"John never tells anyone much of what he's doing. Or when he'll be back." Pam's eyes widened. "You found something out, didn't you? You have that look."

"Maybe. I might have a connection, but I don't know." I smiled. "I don't really know what I'm doing here. John and Rich are the pros. I'm just being a gossip."

"Women make the best detectives, I think. We're naturally nosy and most people will tell us things that they wouldn't tell men. Five years ago, I worked as a telemarketer for a loan company. I could get people to give me all kinds of information over the phone with no real proof that I was who I said I was. It was so easy."

"Why did you quit?"

"The company went out of business. I'll tell you though, it was the easiest money I ever made. Sitting on the phone gossiping with others about their mortgages and stuff. Some people are so talkative, especially the men. Give them that flirty, 'I'm an airhead' laugh and they'd start to spout information." Pam shook her head, smiling.

"I know what you mean. I just did something similar." I stood up and headed back to my 'office'. I picked up the phone and dialed the hospital to check on Rich. Gloria told me he was having some more tests run and that he'd be back in about thirty minutes. I thanked her and hung up the phone. After thinking about it for a few moments, I called John's cell. His service picked up and I left a message, then I paged him.

A minute later, he peeked in. "You paged me?"

"Oh yeah! Sit. Listen to what I just found out."

John sat, his head cocked in curiosity.

"The night we got beat up, I remembered what was bothering me. Rich had mentioned a while ago that Wally worked for a limo service. He remembered, right as the car pulled up, that it was for Top Hat. I went down there this morning and pretended to be a lovesick girlfriend looking for Wally. He worked at Top Hat two months ago. It was only for two days."

"That would have been fun to see, you acting love sick."

I chuckled. "Yeah anyway, they paid him cash since it was only short-term. I talked the lady into telling me who the client was. It was Schnabel."

John sat back, thoughtful.

"The mayor was being driven to Springfield for some sort of weekend conference thing over there. Wally drove him, then picked him up the next day and drove him back to Quincy."

"How does this connect him with Williams?" John asked.

I shrugged. "I don't know, but the coincidence is too big to be random."

John nodded agreement. "Did she say where the mayor stayed?"

"No."

Silence settled in the room for a few seconds. John looked up. "You said it was for a conference?"

"That's what Martha told me. She read it off a work-detail sheet that she scrounged up."

"Then if it was business related, the mayor's office should have a record of the transaction. And if the mayor stayed somewhere, that's public knowledge too," John said.

Why didn't I think of that? "Yeah!"

John stood up. "Follow it up, Mel. I doubt it leads to anything, but it's worth a look at." His face broke out into a grin. "Good job! I told Rich you were going to be good at this." He winked and left the room.

It was so satisfying to get a genuine compliment like that. I picked up the phone to call my contact, Carla, in county records.

Not long after, I headed to the basement of the courthouse again. At one time the police department and City Hall shared this building along with the courts, the Adams County Jail, and Adams County Police Headquarters. But as all parties started out growing their space, it had become apparent that the QPD needed to find new housing. So the police department and City Hall moved. But the city records and the courts were still located in the old city hall building.

The door opened to reveal Carla waiting for me. I truly think that she must have had a thing for my Dad long ago. She was way too nice about helping me.

"I got it right here." Carla held up the two pieces of paper. "Wasn't even that hard to find." Her gray hair reminded me of a spinster old aunt or a very kindly librarian, but she was neither.

"Thanks, Carla." I pulled out my wallet to pay her for the copies. Within minutes, I was back at my desk reading the file, waiting for John to finish with a client.

It seemed to be a standard trip for the mayor. It matched other trips to Springfield that I had obtained from Carla already. He was meeting with several other mayors at the State office, and there had been an additional meeting with the governor. Nothing unusual. I glanced at the second document to find it was the hotel records. The mayor had stayed at the Clairmont Regency in downtown Springfield, Illinois. The city even had an account with them. *Maybe it's nothing important.*

I heard John walk his client out of the office, so I stood up and waited for him in my doorway.

"Anything on the mayor's trip?" John asked.

I shrugged, following him into his office. "It looks like a normal trip." I handed him the papers as I sat down in front of his desk. "Looks like you were right; it has nothing to do with anything."

John quickly read the papers. "Sometimes things pan out and sometimes they don't, Mel. Don't take it personally. That's the way it is in the detective game." He smiled as he leaned forward to hand them back.

"So, where do we go from here?"

John sat back in his chair. "I don't know. On the political case, we'll keep digging into people's pasts. I know you thought this was connected to the murders, but it seems to have come to a dead end. Have the cops found out anything new?"

"Max Bauer wouldn't tell me even if he knew. I'll call Mitch and see what he's heard on the grapevine." I sat looking at the papers in my hand. "I really thought that I had found the connection between the two political campaigns though. I mean, how convenient is it that Wally worked for the company that is used by both parties?"

"Many times the easy way is wrong. Then again, sometimes it doesn't take much to connect pieces together. Have you talked to Rich today?"

I shook my head.

"Has your friend come up with the name of Schnabel's mistress yet? Or the 'thing' that is bothering Williams?"

Again I shook my head no.

"Okay." John sat up. "Let's try this from a new angle. Dig into Williams' past. See where he graduated high school and check his acquaintances. See if any of them connect up with Schnabel's people. Do the same for his college friends and business partners."

"That will take hours! Do you want me to file workers comp for eye fatigue?"

John laughed as I left his office still looking at the papers in my hands. I felt like I was getting close. As I sat at my table, I pulled the file of the four murders and shoved the papers into it. I needed to acquire a lot more names from Williams' past before I could do any matching.

***

Williams had graduated from a private high school outside of Chicago. After spending a couple of years working as a manager in his father's fast food restaurant, he attended college and got his MBA. It appeared, according to his press releases, that it was at this time he really became interested in politics. Also, he moved to Quincy at that time.

But no names matched up, no matter how hard I tried. Just as a further study in masochism, I decided to do the same with Schnabel.

He graduated from the local public high school, went to college in Indiana right out of his military service, and moved back to Quincy afterward. He married and was elected to an alderman post shortly after his move home, and he had been in the political arena the entire time.

Frustration is not my strong suit. I just wanted to forget the entire week. But the 'date' with Max was set for six o'clock at the Golden Wall Chinese Restaurant. I had heard it served great General Tso's chicken and I really felt like something spicy to top off the hard day. I told him I would meet him there.

I walked in to find him casually dressed up. He was wearing a sports coat and chinos. With his blue shirt underneath, he was more than handsome. Max stood when I approached and my eyes involuntarily took him in, entirely. I also noticed that his eyes widened in appreciation when he spied me.

I was wearing my black 'dress' jeans and a white oxford top. It was as about dressed up as I get, unless I'm dragged, kicking and screaming, into a dress. His blue eyes panned quickly, taking me in, and he moved to pull out the chair for me.

Smiling, I sat down. "Such a gentlemen, Max."

He gave me a slight blush in return. "A date is a date, even if it is as friends." He got comfortable at the table. "You look nice tonight." Max chuckled. "But I lost the bet."

"Oh, really?"

"Yeah, I had a bet with Mitch that you'd come in a dress. He had you pegged: jeans and dress shirt."

I laughed. "I hate dresses."

Max nodded. "That's what he said." He held my gaze. "I haven't had the chance to see you all week. You seem to be doing really well. How's the back and head? How's Rich?"

"The bruises on my back are still a little sore. But the stitches are gone, and my head only hurts when I touch it. Rich came home from the hospital today. He's really sore and all, but he'll be okay. Thanks for asking."

I took the menu from the waitress and looked it over, but I already knew what I wanted. After she left, I looked closely at Max. "So, did you talk to Hessor at any point this week?"

Max made a face. "I knew you were going to talk shop."

"Well, you did say that you'd tell me," I said coyly.

"I said maybe."

I sipped my water as I waited.

With a sigh, Max leaned closer. "But no more talk of the case after this, okay?"

"Deal."

"Hessor has a very strong alibi for that night. I've checked it out. Of course in his profession, I'm sure he has lots of convincing people to back him up. Anyway, he didn't appear to know about you getting beat up. He had heard about Rich, but since we kept your name out of the papers, he didn't react like he knew about you. Again, he could be a really good actor, but I'm not sure. I'm pretty good at reading people and unfortunately, I'd have to say he was telling the truth."

Was this good news or bad? "So, it wasn't Bart?"

"I guess not. He was very convincing."

"Did you specifically tell him about me getting beat up?"

"No, I implied that someone was with Rich. He seemed unfazed."

"What excuse did you use to go talk to him?"

"I said an informant told us Weedman was moving in on his territory. Hessor, of course, denied knowing what I was talking about. That time I could tell he was lying. He kept looking down and to the left. The rest of the time he stared me right in the eye. Anyway, nothing else came from the interview." Max paused as the waitress brought our food to us. "Thanks, that was fast."

"Anything for you," the waitress said, winking. She was standing so close to Max she was practically in his lap.

I stared at her as Max nodded absentmindedly, picking up his chopsticks.

She leaned in just a bit and fluttered her lashes. "Anything else I can get you?"

"No. Thanks." Max reached for his drink.

She cocked her head at me, raised her nose just a smidge, and walked off. I desperately tried not to laugh. Max turned his head in her direction. "What?"

"Nothing." I picked up the chopsticks lying near my place mat. "Now, chopstick sensei-"

Max laughed as he picked up his set. "Not at all. It's really easy. The thicker part of one chopstick rests at the base of your thumb. The thinner part rests on your middle finger's tip. See?" He took one in his hand. "Bring your thumb forward to trap the stick. And you need two or three inches past your fingertip." He watched me do it. "Good."

"Feels funny."

Max grinned. "Now put the other chopstick against the side of your index finger by the end of your thumb. Kind of like holding a pencil. That's right," he said as I picked up the sticks awkwardly. "Now put the ends on the plate and push the tips so that they are even." He smiled. "Not hard at all."

I struggled with them. "How did you learn to do this?"

"When I was growing up, I had a Chinese nanny. Mrs. Lin had me eating with chopsticks before Mom taught me to eat with a spoon, according to my grandmother." Max's smile was soft, like he was enjoying a happy memory. "Anyway, Mrs. Lin watched me off and on for a number of years. Whenever she fed me, we always ate with chopsticks." Max looked at me struggling to work them. He smiled and reached across the table to grab my fumbling hand. "Relax." I looked at him. "Loosen up. Don't hold on so tight." Max's eyes never left mine. "That's better. See how much easier they are to use when you're relaxed?"

I looked at his hand, still touching mine. The warm flush was starting to spread through the rest of me. "It'd be easier if you'd let go of my hand."

Max blushed and dropped his hand from mine. "I didn't mean it that way."

"Sure, Max." I smiled. "But it's okay. Relax when I hold them. Got it." I moved the chopsticks a little in my hand. It did feel more comfortable. "Okay. I guess I can do this." I pulled my plate closer to me.

"Etiquette says that you never stick your chopsticks in the bowl like this." Max demonstrated, sticking his chopsticks straight up in an imaginary bowl. "And never wave them around while you talk."

"I bet Italians have a hard time eating with chopsticks." I gave eating a try, but the food dropped back onto the plate.

Max laughed. "Watch." Slowly he picked a piece of meat up off his plate and placed it in his mouth. While he chewed, he demonstrated the pincher technique again. Max swallowed. "Italians have trouble eating with forks and spoons, if Ox was any indication."

I tried the noodles. This time I met the food halfway to the table with my mouth. I looked over to see Max trying to hide a big grin. "Shut up. I'm trying."

Max nodded, letting the grin out. "You are and I give you credit for that. Noodles are hard. Try the meat. That's usually easier."

I took his advice. It was awkward but easier.

"See," Max said. He proceeded to eat away with the wooden instruments of torture. "If you set them down, put them in the chopstick rests here." Max pointed to a small piece of wood that had been set near both of us on the table. "And, if you need to get more food from the community bowl, such as rice or something, use the square end of the sticks. Like this." Max pretended to pick up a bowl. Using the back end of the sticks, he mimicked pushing some out onto his plate. "Anything else is rude."

I tried eating with them for all of another three minutes before giving up. I wanted to eat, not starve to death with my food in front of me.

Max merely shook his head. "You'll only learn by practicing."

"Fine. I'll practice at home. But I want to enjoy my food tonight, since you're paying." I smirked.

***

That night I lay in bed thinking over the last week. My mind replayed all of the information we had gathered on the four murders. It was infuriating. *How do cops do this all the time?* The digging was sort of fun, but not knowing if what you found out was worth anything, that was the hard part. I sat up and glanced at the alarm clock. Close to one o'clock. I stood up and walked out to the kitchen to get a drink.

It suddenly dawned on me that I had never really investigated Eddie and his whereabouts the night of his death. Or for that matter, I had never done a very good search on Wally either. Mouse and Scott I had looked into pretty thoroughly. *Could the answer lie with one of the Bakers? Could Wally be the missing piece? Could the four truly be connected? Or, was I just chasing my tail? Did any of this matter? What was the price of tea in China?* I sighed and headed back to bed, now determined to find out more about the Baker boys.

CHAPTER 20

"Well my boys were different, that's for sure," Mrs. Baker said while we were sitting in her living room. She was in her seventies, and she had a head full of gray hair to prove it. The air conditioning was on, but in my opinion it was set to 'roast'. It seemed only five degrees cooler than the afternoon air outside, and it was in the mid-nineties today. Mrs. Baker looked off in the distance and sniffled. "Now with my husband gone, all I have is Roy."

"How old is Roy?"

"He's twenty-four. Goes to college at Valparaiso. He was my late-in-life baby. Wallace and Edward were my problem kids, especially Wally. He was forever in trouble at school. He was smart though, just didn't like schooling and other matters like that. We tried, my husband and me, to steer Wally into the military. I think it would have done him good, but he didn't think so. Wally was a night owl, usually," Mrs. Baker said, leaning toward me and lowering her voice as though it were a state secret.

I smiled.

"He was forever needing money, until recently."

"How long ago?"

Mrs. Baker sat back and thought about it. "I don't know, a year ago, I guess." Her smile suddenly brightened her face. "Wallace used to always bring me flowers. When he lived here, during high school, he grew them on his balcony in a planter." She pointed upstairs. "He said he liked to see me smile and that I didn't smile enough. Wally was always the thoughtful one. Daffodils, roses, tulips, whatever he grew or picked up."

"What about Eddie? Can you tell me something about him?"

"Eddie was my quiet one. He was thoughtful, although not as thoughtful as Roy. Roy's my baby. Still is, although he hates to be called that. Eddie liked to fiddle with things. I always thought he'd go to college, but right out of high school he got Valerie pregnant and well-" Mrs. Baker sighed. "Eddie tried real hard though. Val left him when he was laid off one time, got caught with some drugs. Just shameful. Eddie cleaned up his act, but Val was right to leave him. Still, my boy tried. He got a really good job at the factory and worked hard at staying clean." Mrs. Baker brought her Kleenex up to her nose. "I'm sorry." The tears started to come. "I still can't believe that they're both gone. I miss my boys."

I swallowed hard. I could feel myself getting misty too. "I understand, Mrs. Baker. I really do." I patted her hand. "Do you have any idea why they might have been killed? What I mean is, did they have any enemies that you knew of?"

Her head shook almost imperceptibly. I once more patted her hand.

"Do you know if the police know who did it yet?" Mrs. Baker asked, sniffling and wiping her tears.

"No. I'm sorry, I don't know. I just feel that maybe I can help, since Eddie came to my brother and me the day he died. I don't know if I'm doing any good, but I keep trying. If I find out any thing I'll tell the police, and I'll also keep you up to date if I can." I gave her a gentle smile.

"Thank you."

***

"Wally was a loser, plain and simple." Kerry Henderson snapped. We sat on the bleachers at Waverly-Moorman Park, watching his son's baseball game. I sipped my coke, keeping an eye on him, and I tried hard not to compare the six-year-old kids out on the baseball field with Robbie.

"Why do you say that?"

Kerry just stared at me, then turned his attention back to the game. He frowned and yelled some encouragement to his son, who played center field. He glanced back at me. "Look lady, I don't mean to speak ill of the dead and all, but Wally was only interested in himself. He couldn't keep a girlfriend, let alone a job."

"I heard he went through quite a few of both of them," I said wryly.

Kick had given me the names of some guys who knew Eddie, and they in turn had given me names of some people who knew Wally. It was nearing supper and I had been at this all day. The list still had three people on it, but I doubted I would get to them by the end of the day. My patience level was dipping low. "Can you remember any of his jobs?"

Henderson sighed. "Let's see, he worked as an auto mechanic for a while. He actually wasn't a bad mechanic, when he wanted to be. He drove a school bus for about a week. Got fired from that job when he showed up drunk. Stupid jerk. It was a good job. Wally worked for about three months with Eddie at the factory. Didn't like the hours. Did landscaping work for a couple of seasons, with Green Lawns, I think."

"Green Lawns? How long ago?" I tried to keep the excitement out of my voice. This was interesting. Marion Williams used Green Lawns to do his home lawn.

Henderson shrugged. "A year or two ago. He drove for a limo service a long time ago. He really seemed to like that job. I think he worked there for over a year. Old Man Walker sold out and Wally quit." Henderson yelled at his son to pay attention, then said, "I think Old Man Walker was the only one who put up with Wally's absences."

"Where did Wally get his money? I mean, he had to live and all."

"Wally was never one to talk much about his sources of income."

"But you were his friend. One of his closest friends from what I've been told."

Henderson just looked at me, not answering. He knew more than he was saying, that much was obvious.

"He didn't say anything about where he got his cash?"

"Look, Wally respected my family. He didn't want to get us in any sort of trouble. We were friends, but I didn't approve of his lifestyle."

"But you know where he got his money, don't you?" I could see that he did and that he really didn't want to tell me. "I'm not a cop. I'll forget I even talked to you." I smiled, maybe he would still tell me.

Henderson looked around. There was no one sitting near us this late in the game. "You didn't hear this from me."

I nodded.

"Wally sold drugs. Had been selling since high school."

"He went to QHS, right?"

Henderson nodded again.

"Who did he sell for?"

Henderson cocked his head at me with wide eyes like I was stupid to ask.

"Okay, who do you *think* he sold for?"

"Madeline Hessor until she got put in jail."

"And then Wally sold for who ever took over for her." I finished his thought. Henderson barely nodded this time.

"Wally was an okay guy," Henderson said quickly. "Just, he was lazy. Selling was easy enough money, when it came."

Henderson clearly didn't trust me and therefore was acting like he didn't like Wally. This was a puzzler. I knew that Henderson knew more than he was letting on. The problem was: how could I get him to trust me enough to tell me everything he knew?

We watched the game for a few minutes in silence. "Mr. Henderson, I've been told by other sources that Wally, Mouse, and Scott Hiccome were working on something that would set them up with a lot of money. Did he ever mention something like that to you?" I turned to watch his reaction.

Henderson hesitated. "Nope."

I stared into his eyes. He was the first person to confirm Beth's rumor. As I studied him, I realized that he was done talking. At least I had gotten more out of him than the cops. Mitch had told me that Henderson barely acknowledged knowing Wally when he spoke with him. "Okay. Look, if you should think of anything, give me a call." I began reaching into my pocket. "I'd like to find out who killed Wally and Eddie."

"Why? The police don't seem to care." Henderson's voice had a very strong, bitter note to it.

I turned to look out on the field. "I think Wally and Eddie were murdered by the same people. Eddie came to my brother for help. I was there. Before we could help him, Eddie was killed." I looked Henderson in the eye as I handed him a generic business card from the office. "My phone numbers are on the back. Call my home phone. My brother could lose his license if the cops found out that I'm still looking into this matter. Okay?"

Henderson slowly took the card. He looked at it, then back at me. "You haven't told me why you care."

I shrugged. "I guess I feel like we let Eddie down and in turn, Wally." I paused as I stood up from the bleachers. Holding out my hand to shake, I said, "I don't like that feeling. Thanks for your help."

I walked away feeling his stare lingering on me. I almost smiled. He'd call and he'd tell me everything. I just knew it.

***

Sunday evening the phone rang. I hopped up from the floor where I was once again going through boxes. I was currently working my way through some old photos. It was hard, and I was glad for the interruption. I took a deep breath to quell my sniffles. "Hello?"

"Melissa Addison?"

"Yes. Who is this?"

"Kerry Henderson. I think I might be able to help you out with some more information."

I smiled broadly. It felt good to know that I was right. "Okay, I appreciate the call, Mr. Henderson. When and where did you want to meet?"

"Tonight. Do you know where the Horse Shoe is at?"

"Uh, isn't that a tavern on Madison around 37th or so?"

"Yeah. Madison and 35th."

"When?"

"Soon. I have to be home in forty minutes."

I glanced at my watch. It was almost eight o'clock. "I can be there in about fifteen minutes."

"I'll be waiting." The phone line disconnected.

I stood stunned for a second, then I hurried to grab my purse and car keys. I ran down the stairs, stopping only briefly at the bar to let my brother Cam know where I was going. Just in case.

The Horse Shoe could only be described as another neighborhood bar, but more run-down. It had the same sort of family atmosphere as my dad's bar. I felt right at home. It was a lot smaller though. The bar itself extended the length of the place with only three tables. There was just one other patron inside, beside Henderson.

When he saw me, he rose from the bar and moved toward a table. He motioned for me to join him. I did after getting a soda.

"Thanks again for the call," I said as I sat.

Henderson was staring at the tabletop, nursing a beer. "Yeah. I want to know who killed Wally too. He may have been a loser, but he was still my friend."

I sipped the cold soda, waiting for him to continue.

"Wally had been seeing a lot of Mouse, before he died. He was recruiting her for his boss, I think." Henderson looked up. "She still had a big 'in' with the high school crowd, with her sisters and all. So, if he could work her, he'd make a lot of money. He told me that, before he died."

"I heard that Mouse was supposed to be some sort of spy for Hessor in Weedman's organization."

Henderson agreed. "Yeah. Mouse was feeding Wally all of Weedman's suppliers and any thing else she could come up with. Scott had started out the same way with Hessor, again through Wally." I took a drink, letting him collect his thoughts.

"A while ago, Wally found out something. He never told me what it was, but he was real excited about it. He said that with this information he could get his 'nest egg' and head to the Mexico. Wally always dreamed of retiring down there." Henderson took a small sip of his beer. "He brought Mouse in on it because she had connections."

"Connections?"

"That's what Wally called it. 'Great connections,' he said one time." The silence lengthened. "I saw him the day before he died. He was the happiest I'd ever seen him. He told me he had made contact with both his 'connections' and the 'opposition's connections', and both were going to pay royally for the information. Then he could pay me back the loan and retire in wealth." Henderson looked at me. "He was so happy."

"He owed you money?"

"A little. When he was short on cash, he'd come to me and I'd lend him some money. He always paid it with interest the next time he 'came into money'."

"You mean the next time he made a sale."

Henderson smiled coyly. "Exactly."

I frowned. "And you have no clue what this information was?"

A shake of the head was my answer.

"Anything at all? Even just a guess on your part?"

"It was big. Wally kept saying that. It was big."

It felt like Henderson was leaving something out, but I nodded, accepting his answer. Pushing was not something that seemed to go over too well with him. He was loyal to Wally, that was for sure. "Okay. Well, I know a little bit more. Thanks. It might help to find the people responsible."

"One more thing," Henderson said after he watched me for a few more seconds, moving his beer bottle in small circles.

He was struggling, so I waited.

"This arrived in the mail two days after Wally died." Henderson pulled out an envelope. "The letter asked me to deliver it to Eddie. I set it aside and forgot about it." He laid the envelope on the table and tapped it once, then pushed it toward me.

I could tell he felt bad about forgetting to fulfill his friend's last request. I reached out for the envelope. It was handwritten and sloppy. Wally must have been in a big hurry or something.

"I totally forgot about it until I read in the paper that Eddie got killed. I never did open what I was supposed to deliver to him, only the part Wally wrote to me. I wonder if, maybe if I had delivered it-that maybe Eddie wouldn't have..." His voice drifted off as he picked up his bottle and wiped at the condensation with his thumb.

"Mr. Henderson." I waited until he looked up at me. "I don't think it would have mattered one way or the other. Really. When it's our time to go, we go. Regardless of everything else." I tried to put as much conviction in my voice as I could. This was something I was still struggling with, and I didn't want to dwell on it myself.

Henderson stared into my eyes. "I still feel bad."

"I understand. May I keep it?" My hand was resting on the envelope.

"Yeah," Henderson said with a slight nod. "Maybe it will help find out who did this."

"Maybe." I reached out and patted his arm as my other hand slid the envelope into my pocket. "I think Wally would be happy that you're helping to find his killers."

Henderson looked sad. "That he would. Wally liked to finish what he started."

"I'll do my best, Mr. Henderson."

His eyes bored into mine. "I know you will; that's why I called."

CHAPTER 21

I hurried home, anxious to find out what was in the letter and why Wally had mailed it to Henderson. Once I got there though, I paused before opening the envelope. It felt sort of like dipping into someone's secrets. Dead people's secrets. I took a deep breath. If I was going to find out the reason Wally and Eddie were killed, I needed to get over my fear and guilty feelings.

I picked up the envelope and pulled out the contents. It was a hand written letter, obviously from Wally to Kerry Henderson. Along with it was another smaller envelope with Eddie's name on it. I laid the unopened envelope aside and read the letter.

From the look of it, Wally had written it in haste, just like the envelope. The handwriting was almost illegible. Many of the words were misspelled and it came to the point immediately. It read, "Kerry, I need you to deliver this to Eddie. Someone is after me and I want this in someone's hands who can do something about it. Thanks, buddy. Wally."

I laid it down and picked up the other envelope. With a knife from the drawer I slit it open. Out slid a small key and a note. This one was also in Wally's handwriting. It read, "Eddie-if I don't make it, use the information wisely. Give Mouse and Scott a cut. And watch yourself. Wall."

I sighed and looked at the key itself. It was a locker key, one of those things that you put fifty cents in and after you close it, you retain the key. I turned it over hoping to find the name of the place. No such luck. It looked well-worn. The only thing imprinted on it was a number, A345. I laid the key down next to the envelopes and stared at them.

So, Wally knew that someone was onto him for some reason. He sent Kerry the envelope to give to Eddie, in hopes that Eddie would use the information to get lots of money. Wally thought that the information was important enough that someone might kill him for it. That much was obvious. Then, Eddie was pursued by the same person, who assumed he knew where the information was. But he had no idea and ended up getting killed too. But before that, he found something he thought Rich would understand and sent it to Rich via Mouse.

Why Mouse? How well did Eddie know Mouse? I had never thought of that angle. *Were they lovers too, or just friends? Did they then go after Mouse and Scott thinking that they knew where the information was? And was this information concerning drugs? Hessor? Weedman?* The puzzle was getting bigger by the minute, and I was no closer to putting it together than I was the day Eddie pointed a gun at me.

Gathering up the new evidence, I carried it into the bedroom with me. Tomorrow, I'd talk with John and Rich. Eddie sent the disk to Rich because he would know what to do with it. Maybe Rich could figure this out.

I lay awake for a long time thinking. At least two people had been killed for the items in my room. I didn't quite feel like I was in over my head, but I was definitely treading water; water that was rising at a furious rate.
***

Gloria had already gone to work by the time I showed up at Rich's house. He moved very slowly. His arm in the cast was awkward, and I could tell that his ribs were still very painful. It turned out that his kidneys were bruised, but other then that there were no internal injuries. His face was still puffy and his black eyes shined in the morning sun.

"Sit Mel," Rich said as he settled into the lounge chair in the living room. He grunted once in pain, trying to get comfortable. Looking at me, he almost smiled. "You found something."

"Is it that obvious?"

"I just know you. John has been keeping me up to date on the progress of the various cases. You're doing really good. Thanks."

I nodded at the compliment. "It gets better."

Rich's smile turned into a chuckle. "I thought it would; you have a sparkle in your eye. Does John know any of this?"

"Not yet. I wanted to talk to you about it first, since Eddie came to you and assumed that you would understand what he meant."

"Tell me."

I proceeded to relate all the information that I had gathered up to this point. I gave him the two envelopes and he read the letters. The key he fingered for a minute, then handed back to me. I waited, letting his brain work. His body may have been in rough shape, but his mind was clear.

"Hmmm, I don't know. That's an interesting connection between Wally and Williams. You need to confirm that with Green Lawns." Rich paused. "Okay, so the key to this whole thing is Wally. What did he find out, and who was he blackmailing?"

"Blackmailing?"

"That is the most logical possibility. It sounds like he found something out and was going to use it to get money, lots of money. The million dollar questions are, what was the information, and who was he squeezing?"

"But what about the disk?"

"Forget the disk right now," Rich said. "Eddie had no idea what was happening. It sounds like he just got caught in the middle of something. That small key is the key to this and whatever information the locker contains." He paused and thought. "And what about those 'connections' of Mouse's? What is that about?"

"So far everything leads to drugs and Bart Hessor."

Rich glanced at me. "Yeah, I know. And I don't like that." We sat in silence for some time, each of us thinking our own private thoughts. Rich broke the silence. "Was Wally into computers too?"

I mentally reviewed all of my conversations. "Not anymore than the average guy, I think. Eddie was pretty good at them, from what Dan Kickery tells me, but I really don't know about Wally." I saw the look in Rich's eye. "I thought you said to forget the disk for now."

Rich smiled. "Just what did Eddie find out? What is on that disk that I'm supposed to know about?"

I shrugged.

"Okay, talk to John. Follow up on the Green Lawns trail anyway, just to cross all of our t's." Rich rubbed his chin in thought. "See if you can find out where the key goes. Take it to Miller's Hardware on Tenth and State. Ask for Milo. He's an old man that has worked there for years. See if he can ID it for you. He used to work for one of the old locker companies. Maybe he can point you in the right direction. At the very least, see if he'll copy it."

"Why?"

"If you don't find anything today, you'll have to turn that over Tom Hawkings, the lead Detective on Wally's murder. That's crucial evidence."

"But-"

"So, look hard today. Get going. You're wasting time, Mel."

***

I went to the hardware store, then in to work. John was already there, and I told him everything.

"Did he give you any indication of where the key might fit?"

"Maybe. He thinks it might be to the lockers at either the YMCA or the roller rink." I tapped my foot, anxious to get going. "But he said he was guessing."

"What are you doing here then?"

I shifted weight on my feet. "I don't know how I'll get into to the Y, especially the guy's side of it."

"Go hit up the roller-skating place first. If that isn't the place, call me on your cell phone and I'll meet you at the Y. I know someone who works there, and I'm pretty sure I can talk my way into the place. Do you know if Wally frequented either of these places?"

"No."

"Go." John made a motion with his hands to get going.

I stood. "One question. What if I find the locker? What do I do? I mean, it's evidence in a murder."

"Good point." John reached into a desk drawer and pulled out a set of latex gloves. He tossed them to me. "Use these as soon as you find the locker. Don't touch the locker at all without the gloves. Put them on and then open it. Look at the evidence and put it back. Call me. Go!"

The roller skating place was on the edge of town, and the twenty minutes it took for me to get there seemed like an eternity. I wondered if it would even be open, and was relieved to see the 'Open' sign. I walked into the very large and square brick building. It was ugly, even though they tried to hide that with a yellow paint job. In the lobby, I looked around to see if I could spot the lockers. There were none visible from the entrance. A brunette teenager who looked completely bored stared at me from the front counter. I smiled. "Hi."

She glanced at her watch. "Coming to pick someone up, ma'am?"

I bristled. I wasn't that old-looking. But I smiled at her instead. "No. I came to skate. How much?" I pulled my wallet out of my purse.

"Four-fifty for the open skate. The open session lasts until five tonight." The words were said in a monotone, like she was tired of repeating it. Absentmindedly, she tore off a small stub, and after getting my change she pointed to the desk where skates were hung from pegs in the ceiling. "Give the ticket to Brent at the skate rental desk." She went back to filing her nails.

"Thanks," I mumbled.

As I entered, I made note of the surroundings. There were lots of kids and families skating. *Why would Wally have picked here? Maybe he had accompanied Henderson one time and knew that there were lockers. Interesting. Maybe Eddie knew that Wally liked to skate. This is stupid. Just find the lockers.*

I spotted them in the corner, over where the benches were lining the walls. I sauntered over there, trying to contain my excitement. As an afterthought, I glanced around. It didn't seem like anyone was watching me. I scanned down the row of lockers looking for the number that was imprinted on the original key, A345. The lockers started at A325. My eyes swept ahead.

The locker marked A345 had the key missing. My heart stopped beating for just a moment. I had found it! I took a deep breath and looked around again. No one even seemed to care that I was there. I put the latex glove on my right hand, trying to hide it from view. I stuck the key in the lock and turned.

I opened the locker; an envelope was laying there. I cursed slightly. I was expecting a videotape. After all, that was what we had gotten beaten over. I let the door close and quickly put the other glove on. Then I pulled the envelope out and luckily it wasn't sealed.

With another glance around, I opened it. A single piece of paper was inside the envelope. I turned and sat down, once more looking around. Still no one cared about me. With another deep breath, I took it out and read it.

"Eddie-Sorry about the goose chase. This is really big stuff. This will blow everyone's mind. If you're reading this, then I'm dead and it's all in your hands, little brother. Use it in good health. Oh yeah, what is it and where? 'Romeo, Romeo... wherefore art thou, Romeo?' I'm laughing even in my grave. Wall."

I sighed and glanced around. Laying the note on the bench, I extracted a notebook from my purse and copied the note, word for word. Quickly, I put the note back, stuck fifty cents into the locker, and extracted the key again.

CHAPTER 22

"That's it? You're sure?" I nodded. "You touched nothing?" John's stared into my eyes.

"Only with the gloves on."

"Good." He leaned back. "But both Rich and you touched the other envelope and key." It was a statement, not a question.

I nodded again.

John reached out, picked up the phone, and dialed. "Rich, Mel found the locker… No, another riddle… Yeah, she took the proper precautions… Will do." John hung up and looked at me. "Call this Henderson guy. Get your story straight with him about why he came to you with the envelope. Then head to Rich's. When you get there, he'll call in Hawkings. Tom is a good cop and he'll understand to keep things quiet." John winked. "You're good at this. Way to show the cops up again."

All afternoon I tried to figure out what Wally's note meant. I had even spoken with Kerry Henderson about it again. He was not happy that I turned it over to the police, but after getting him calmed down, I explained my reasoning. He grudgingly agreed, and then felt better about it when I suggested that he go with the story that he had forgotten about the letter until yesterday. But he had no idea about the Romeo reference either.

Back to square one. *What is the information, and who is behind all of this?* My gut was telling me it was Bart Hessor, since everything pointed to drugs. He had the most reason to silence everyone and the seeming ability. Still, I couldn't picture Bart killing in cold blood. Maybe my perceptions were clouded due to the experiences of my youth, but that was how I saw things. The knock on the door brought me out of my reverie, and I scanned the porch through the peephole. I was still jumpy. My sore head kept reminding me that there were people out there not only capable of hurting me, but doing it with such ease.

Standing on my doorstep was Max Bauer. "Hey, Max," I said letting him in to escape the heat outside.

"Yeah. Just a quick question, if you have a minute." He stood at the counter, laying his motorcycle helmet down. He was dressed in tight jeans and a heavy denim shirt, open at the collar to show a white T-shirt underneath. He looked distracted for some reason.

"Sure. Can I get you a drink?"

"Thanks, no." Max tapped his finger on his helmet as he looked out my kitchen window.

He had never been this reserved before. *Now what's up?* "Yeah?"

"Oh." Max smiled, seemingly embarrassed. "Sorry, I've got a lot on my mind."

"It's good to exercise the old gray matter." I gave him a grin, trying to lighten his mood, but he didn't take the bait. "Have a seat and relax, Bauer." I motioned to the stool opposite me at the counter.

With a nod, he did. He gave a glance out the window again, then he gave me a serious look. "Your name was flying around the squad room today."

"Wally Baker's envelope and key."

"Yeah. I thought we agreed that you were done with this?" There was anger in his voice.

"No. You agreed. I merely let you deceive yourself." I gave him a big grin.

He sighed with a shake of his head. "What else did you find out? What was in the locker?"

I hesitated.

"Tom Hawkings is pretty suspicious that you know what's in the locker even though you said that you didn't look. I think we all know better than that." Max leaned closer to the counter. "Tom is being closemouthed about it. For some reason, he doesn't want any information to get out. Was the video in there?"

I gave Max a wry grin. "I can't tell you that."

"Come on, Mel. Was there a video in the locker?"

I said nothing but stared at him.

"You aren't going to tell me, are you?" Max asked, then he abruptly changed tactics. "Okay, fine. Don't tell me. Want to go for a bike ride?"

I bounced on my heels. That did sound like fun. "It's been awhile since I've driven a bike."

"I said ride, not drive. Besides, do you even have a license to drive a motorcycle?"

"I do. Do you want to see my license, Detective?"

Max shook his head. "I believe you. Maybe I'll let you drive. I even have a spare helmet for you."

I stood up. "Pretty confident I'd go, huh? Let me change into a pair of jeans and grab a long sleeve shirt."

Max's voice followed me into the next room. "Are there any fun places to ride to, here in the Midwest, that don't involve corn fields?"

***

We sat on some benches outside an ice cream parlor in a small town about forty miles away from Quincy. I remembered this place from when I used to cruise with friends in a car, bored out of our minds. I had often wondered if it was still in business. It served the best homemade ice cream in the area, in my opinion. But it was in a tiny town on a barely used highway, and I for one was glad it was still open.

"This is really good ice cream." Max smiled. "Who would've thought this gem would be so far out in Nowheresville?"

We sat in silence, eating the heavenly concoction. That was one thing I liked about Max; he didn't always feel the need to impress or keep up small talk. Finally, I glanced at him; he stared off into the distance with a troubled expression. "What?"

"What, what?"

"That look."

"Oh, nothing."

"Look Max, you had an ulterior motive for getting me go out on a ride. Do you want to talk about it?" He had seemed on the verge of saying something a couple of times.

Max looked down at his cone, but he wasn't really looking at it. "Do you know that you are probably the closest thing I have to a best friend here?"

"Really?"

Max nodded, finally looking at me.

I smiled. "I feel honored."

He smiled back. "Would you mind just listening, like a sounding board?"

"Not at all. Friends do that for friends. Go ahead."

"I got a call from a contact in California up the coast from Breakers Point." Max stopped for a few seconds. "They offered me a job on the force there."

I watched Max stare at his melting ice-cream cone, saddened by the news. I knew he missed the ocean and the 'better weather', as he called it. And I knew I'd miss him if he left. "And?"

Max looked at me. "I don't know what to do."

"You miss the ocean and California in general."

Max nodded.

"What is holding you here then?"

The blue eyes flashed to me quickly, then just as quickly turned back to the object he was holding. He didn't answer me.

I finished my cone and waited. His ice cream was running down the side of his hand. He looked lost, like a little boy, not knowing what to do. It touched my heart and I wanted to do something to change his mood.

I impulsively reached out and grabbed his hand, bringing it to my face. My other hand briefly touched his side. I licked his dripping cone. "It was melting," I said softly, almost in a whisper. I knew what he would think; a great distraction.

Max's eyes held mine, even as I released his hand, and they stayed locked, like an embrace. He bit into his cone still staring into my eyes. "Thanks."

"Can't have you with sticky hands as I drive your bike back to town. I hate sticky hands on my waist."

"And who says that you are driving back to town?"

I held up the keys that I had just taken out of his pocket, during our conversation.

His expression changed to surprise. "How did you-"

"Sticky fingers. My bad habits of the past strike again," I said, standing up and putting my helmet on. "Come on, Bauer, finish up. I haven't driven a cycle in a long time."

Max laughed as he pitched the rest of his ice cream cone in the trash. He stood and caught my eye, his voice deepened. "Then let's ride."

I pulled away slowly, getting a feel for the bike. It was a great ride. The BMW motorcycle accelerated easily and smoothly. I felt Max tighten up the distance between us as he tightened his grip on my waist.

It was a guilty pleasure. *I shouldn't be enjoying myself like this. I should be at home, working through the boxes of my life.* I accelerated faster, pushing the bike.

"There is a speed limit, Mel." Max yelled over the rush of air.

I didn't answer him, but as he again gripped my waist tighter, I grew anxious. *What am I doing?* I was happy, and at the same time, guilty and ashamed.

***

"Thanks for the ride, Max," I said, looking at the man poised on his bike. I handed him the spare helmet, shifting my weight on my feet as the tension built.

During the ride, I had been so aware of his body touching mine, his hands on my waist, his breath on my neck as he spoke to me. I was torn.

Slowly he took the helmet and hung it off the back holder under the seat; it stuck out from the side of the bike. His eyes met mine.

"You're not going to invite me in?" His voice was soft, and kind.

I shifted my weight again. "Sorry." I looked down at my feet, tears threatening. "Max, I like you. I really do, but I'm not ready yet. I shouldn't have flirted with you like that. I apologize for... I loved my husband and I can't do this. I took a vow."

Max didn't speak for a few seconds, just stared into my eyes. "Death has parted you, Mel," he said very gently.

"I know, but not yet." Tears swelled in my eyes.

Max nodded in understanding. "Grieving is important." He reached out and squeezed my hand. "But you've got to move on, in time. You've got to take the chance again, Mel. I don't know any of the details about what happened. And I don't know if I'm right or wrong, but it seems that your husband hurt you, even before the accident." He paused for a split second. "I also know that you are a beautiful woman, worthy of love. I hope I'm here when you're ready. I haven't decided about the other job yet."

"I know, but I-"

I thought I saw regret in his eyes, or maybe it was something else. Max gave my hand one last squeeze, then he winked at me. "I'll let you know."

I felt a bit of regret too as he drove away, but I had done the right thing. I knew I wasn't ready. I wasn't done grieving.

Slowly, I turned and with just a glance at the crowded bar, I headed upstairs. My place was dark as usual. I cautiously opened the door and stepped inside. I was still thinking about Max and Craig when an arm grabbed me around the waist and slammed me against the wall.

A whispered voice asked, "Where's the video?"

CHAPTER 23

"I don't know anything about a video," I managed to get out even though his hand held my neck against the wall. Luckily, the side of my head that he had banged against the wall was opposite from where the stitches had been.

My door was standing wide open.

The man banged my head on the wall again. "You lie. Where is the video? This is just a warning. Next time, I'll kill you," he whispered, then he slammed my head against the wall one last time and threw me to the ground. I was stunned. My head swam. I was disoriented. I lay there trying to collect my thoughts for a few moments, then I heard footsteps on the stairs. The lights flashed on.

"Mel, are you alright?"

I tried to move my head. Tom Bressler was bending down next to me.

"Lay still Mel, I'll call for an ambulance."

"No," I said with conviction. "Just help me up. I'm okay." I made it to a seated position. With Bressler's help, I was soon sitting on a stool at my counter.

"What happened?" Bressler asked concerned.

"Someone thinks I have something." I rubbed my head. There was a huge knot on the side of my head, but it wasn't bleeding. I stood up and got an ice pack, grimacing as I pressed it against my head. My anger simmered near the surface. "I don't have a clue what this person is looking for."

"What did he say?"

"'Where is the video?'"

"What video?" Bressler asked, looking baffled.

I shrugged. "I don't know. They asked Rich the same thing when we got beat up. A video."

"Let me call the cops, Mel."

I shook my head again. "It won't do any good. I couldn't ID the voice. He had latex gloves on. I could feel them in my hair and on my neck. So there would be no finger prints." I looked at Bressler. "He has accomplished one thing though."

"What's that?

"No." I shook my head again. "I'm mad. I'm more than mad. Who does he think he is? He's hurt me twice, and thinks he can get away with it! This is too much. I'm going to find this stupid videotape. I am."

Bressler smiled. "Oops, he made the wrong person mad."

I smiled back. "You bet he did. And I'm gonna nail his butt to the wall with it. Mark my words, Tom." I stood up and walked around my kitchen once, fuming. Suddenly it dawned on me, *Why is Bressler here?* "What are you doing here anyway?"

He shrugged. "I came looking for you. Seems it was a good thing I did." He motioned to the floor where he had found me. "I was going to ask you out on a date." Bressler blushed slightly. "I don't know that many single, non-crazy women and I just thought..." He drifted off, embarrassed. "Never mind. Are you sure you don't want to call the cops?"

***

Rich and John were both at work by the time I showed up the next morning. I described the incident from the night before. Both men were unhappy about it, but since there was nothing that could be done, we passed onto the subject of how to go about finding this videotape. Again, our thoughts ran in circles. We were out of ideas and places to look.

It was only about twenty minutes after the guys left my office that Mitch showed up wanting to talk to me. I lead him back to my office.

"Let me see the head, Mel," he said, still standing in front of my 'desk', hands on his hips.

"What? How did you know?"

"Rich called. He wants it on report. As he explained it, there is nothing that can be done about it, but he wants a report done anyway," Mitch explained. "It's a matter of having a record of it. If we ever find this person beating up my siblings, then I can charge him with this assault and battery too." Mitch's tone was serious. He wasn't going to take no for an answer, I knew from experience.

I sighed and moved over to his side of the table. Fingering aside my hair, I showed him the small lump and the big bruise there.

Mitch made a face and backed out of the office. "Rich, I need a camera," he called.

"Just a minute. I'm a little slow this morning." Rich's voice floated out of his office with a hint of humor. "Why don't you come and get it, Mitch. That way I don't have to face her anger yet for calling you."

Mitch left. Shortly, he was back with the camera and taking pictures of my bump. He extracted the film from the camera and sat down with notebook in hand. "Let's hear it."

I sighed and related, again, what happened.

"Bressler?" Mitch asked looking off in the distance. "Didn't he used to hang out near the Bottoms?"

"Yeah."

"What was he doing at your apartment?"

"Asking me out on a date."

His mouth twisted. "Did he see anything? You said it wasn't long after the attack that he appeared at your door."

"He said that he didn't see anything. Apparently he'd been at the bar waiting for me to come home. He said he had checked a number of times to see if there was a light on upstairs. When he saw the door open, he said he went to investigate." I shrugged my shoulders. I didn't tell any of them that Bressler mentioned that he noticed a green jag parked a block down. *Could Bart have been the one in my apartment?*

"Any idea who it might have been?"

"I don't know." I looked at my brother. "I can't place the voice."

"Okay. I'll do the paperwork and ask around about Bressler to confirm his story." Mitch stood and pointed a finger at me. "Be more careful, Mel."

He didn't need to tell me; this would not happen again.

"Mel?" Pam appeared at my door. She handed me a 'while you were out' slip. The message was from the owner of Green Lawns; I had called to confirm the connection between Williams and Wally.

After Pam left I picked up the phone and dialed. The owner answered immediately. "Sure, I remember Wally Baker. He worked for us last year during the spring and summer."

"Was he a good employee?" He didn't answer right away. "I know that you probably don't want to talk bad about him," I smiled as I said it, "but he's dead and I doubt he'll be offended. I'm just trying to get a feel for his personality."

"Well, okay. He was lazy. When he did work, he did a good job. But I caught him several times goofing off on the clock. He seemed to take a little more effort when he worked the houses in the north end."

"I heard he worked on Mr. Williams' property." I was guessing here, but a hunch is just that.

"Yes. And he did a great job on it. The property has several hedges and Wally did a really good job trimming them. Williams even commented on it once. Wally was good at times, when he wanted to be."

"Did you fire him or did he quit?"

The man hesitated again. "Let's just say it was a mutual parting."

"Thanks for all of your help." I hung up.

"Mel, let me know when you're off the phone." Rich called across the hallway.

"I'm off."

"Could you run an errand for me? Pam's busy."

"Sure." I grabbed my keys.

***

On my way back from the office supply store, a car accident made me detour a few blocks, and I found myself in traffic crawling past the Democratic headquarters.

I glanced into the adjacent alley and saw two men conversing. *Tom Bressler and Bart Hessor!* I jerked the Jeep into the nearest parking place, shut it down, and was out the door and running in one fluid movement.

As I neared the alley, I slowed. *What is Hessor doing in the alley with Bressler?* I crept forward to the corner and peeked around.

They were arguing; their voices were raised just enough to allow me to catch a few snippets. I heard Bressler laugh derisively.

"... don't play fair. You're dead, Tommy," Hessor was saying.

I strained to hear Bressler's reply. "... cost you more..." In response, Hessor handed over a bundle of something from his pocket. *It must be money, but what for?*

"... bring it next time..." Hessor threatened. Bressler's laugh echoed again. Hessor turned toward the other end of the alley and stalked out. Bressler watched him walk away, and then headed into his office.

I hurried back to my Jeep. *Could the thing Hessor wanted be what Mouse was to have delivered to him? And why would Bressler have it? Did Mouse give it to him the night they talked? Could Bressler have talked to Mouse the night she died? Or was it the videotape?* Yet Bressler had seemed confused by my statement that the guy in my apartment was asking about a video.

Confused, I headed back to work.

***

Later, I was heading out to deliver some papers for Rich when I passed Pam, she seemed really frustrated by the person she was talking to on the phone. "I can, but who may I say is calling?" With a finger, she motioned for me to wait. "I'll see." She put the person on hold and looked up at me, irritated. "A man is on the phone wanting to talk to you. He refuses to leave his name."

I furrowed my brow and reached for the phone, and Pam hit the hold button, releasing the call. "Hello. This is Melissa Addison."

"We need to talk, Mel."

I looked at Pam. Bart Hessor was on the phone. "Okay, I suppose. When and where? And more importantly, why?"

"The cops keep asking me about beating you up. We need to talk. Can you come to my house this morning?" His tone was very serious.

I glanced at my watch. "Sure. How about now?"

"Good." The phone line went dead.

I set it down. "This is getting interesting." I hurried to grab my stuff and left, ignoring her questions. I didn't tell anyone where I was going. Rich would have blown his top.

CHAPTER 24

Bart showed me to a chair in his living room. His expression told me that he was not at all happy. "I didn't beat you up or order it done, Mel. It's cowardly to do it like that."

"Like what?" I asked.

"I've asked around. I have contacts too. If I wanted to know something, I wouldn't hide behind Halloween masks." He smiled. "That's childish."

I said nothing.

"Twice now the cops have interrogated me about the incident with Rich and you. I wanted you to know that I had nothing to do with it." He sat still, watching me closely.

"Okay."

"You don't believe me."

"Honestly, I don't know what to believe."

"I would not beat up an unarmed lady. I would use other ways to get the information out of you." He smiled an arrogant grin.

"Like what?"

He merely cocked his head and lifted his eyebrows. His eyes took on a sexy look. A grin slowly curved the corners of his mouth.

"I don't think so."

"Maybe." His smile broadened. "Maybe not. Still, I didn't beat you up. An detective by the name of Bauer has cornered me twice to badger me about the incident." Bart paused. "Does he have a thing for you or what?"

"Or what," I said in a monotone. I was not going to discuss my relationship with Max. Besides, I had no idea about it either.

"I see."

"So what is the reason that you asked me here? That could have been said over the phone." I was relaxed, yet on guard.

Hessor shook his head. "Not over the phone. I wanted you to look into my eyes and know that I'm sincere when I say I would not want any harm to come to you."

Is he telling the truth? If not, he was a good actor and a much better liar than he had been as a kid. *Time to put him to the test.* "What is your connection with Bressler?"

"Bressler? Tommy Bressler?" Bart shook his head. "None. Besides ancient history."

"Hmmm," I said. He wasn't that good of a liar. "Where were you last night?"

"Why?"

"Because I asked, that's why."

"I was busy."

I watched Hessor closely. "I'll be honest with you, Bart. Someone broke into my apartment and roughed me up a little last night. A witness said that there was a green Jaguar parked down the block. You're the only one I know who drives a green Jag."

"I was occupied with business." His tone was cold.

"Not good enough. Did you come and visit me last night? I don't like having my head used as a hammer."

Bart sighed. "I'll deny saying this to you. I was entertaining suppliers last night at a club down in St. Louis. And my Jag has been in the shop for a week with some sort of computer problem. It hasn't run since last Friday." He paused looking me in the eye. "You can check at the shop if you don't believe me. I'm not lying to you, Mel. I did not hurt you or your brother, as much as I dislike Rich." His expression changed. "Should I be expecting another visit from your friendly cop boyfriend?"

I shook my head. "He's not my boyfriend, and I didn't report the green Jag." Bart concentrated on my face. I stood up and looked directly into his eyes. "I'm going to nail the guys that beat up on Rich. And I'm going to make them regret the two beatings I took, not to mention all the breaking and entering. I will not back off even if it is you, Bart, regardless of the feelings that I had for you as a kid." I stayed for just a heartbeat, then moved swiftly out of his house.

I drove away. Several blocks later I pulled over to think. *Mouse was carrying something. She must have given it to Bressler to hold. Now Bressler is blackmailing Hessor. But where does Wally fit into this? Eddie?* I shook my head in bewilderment.

Heading home to eat lunch, I decided that I'd take Bressler up on a date to milk him for information. He knew a lot more then he was telling, that much was for certain.

And Bart had been right about one thing, flirtation was a very good way to get information, and I knew I was up to the task. Bressler wasn't home when I called him, so I left a message on his voice mail.

My cell phone rang as I was just finishing up my can of soup. "Hello?"

"Mel, it's Kick."

"Hi, Kick. What's up?"

"I called the office, but Pam gave me your cell number. Do you have a minute? I'm at home and I have an idea."

"About the disk?"

"Yeah. Is there any way I can talk to you and Rich together? A couple of friends and I were working on the disk last night and in one of those serendipitous strokes of genius, one of them thought of something." Dan Kickery sounded excited.

"Uh, hold on. Let me call Rich at the office to see if he's still there. He's only supposed to work a half day." I grabbed my home phone. Sure enough, he was still there and would wait for us. I told Kick the news and we made plans to meet there as soon as possible.

In a short thirty minutes, the conference room I used as an office was crowded. Rich, John, Kick, Kick's friend, Buzz, and I were all there. I introduced everyone and nodded at Kick to start talking.

"Late last night, Buzz had one of those leaps in logic." Dan Kickery flashed a smile as he inclined his head to Buzz, sticking the copy of the disk into my computer. He turned the monitor so everyone could see the screen. "Mel told me that Eddie was a snitch of yours at one time. Right?"

"Yeah." Rich tried to get comfortable and winced in pain, his hand rubbing his side with the broken ribs. I watched my brother, worried about him.

"Bear with us," Kick said while bringing the accounting page up. "This is an accounting spreadsheet. We pretty much determined that early on; Mel even mentioned that when she gave me the disk. The questions remained, though: whose account and where was it located?" He pointed at the long number at the bottom. "We've determined that this is an account in People First Bank, assigned to a man by the name of Festis Mangrove."

"How did you-" John began.

Kick stopped him with a raised hand. "Don't ask." He smiled. "And don't reveal that to the police, please."

John gave him a knowing smile back. All of us knew that Kick's friend had hacked into the bank's computer. "Does the account show much activity?" John asked.

"It did." Kick smiled, this time at Buzz. "And we found something else of interest. This account never has more than $150,000 dollars in it at any point. When it reaches that amount, it automatically transfers to an offshore account."

"Whose?" Rich asked.

Kick's face fell at that point. Buzz shook his head in defeat too. Kick gave us a sad smile. "We're still chasing that one, but-"

"This has got to be rich," I said, seeing Kick's smile return.

"It stopped all activity the night Wally died. And better yet, for about three years the transfers out of the account were being picked at and sent to a third account."

"Picked at?" John asked for clarification.

"Just a tad siphoned off. Not enough for anyone to really notice, except this." He pointed to the screen. "Someone did a thorough search of the accounts. That's what we think this sheet is. We can show you how the sheet here matches up with the account in the bank and the third account, if you want."

The room fell silent.

I shook my head. "I don't understand. Someone was taking small, minute amounts of the huge sum and depositing it in a different account for what purpose?"

"Skimming money," Buzz spoke for the first time. "The person was skimming money from the other account into his own account, a lot of money over the three years. A lot."

"How much?" Rich leaned forward.

"To the tune of almost half a million dollars with interest, if the history of the account is accurate," Buzz said. "You see, the man was letting it build in that third account, then sending it to a different offshore account. The third account was under the name of W. Rekab. Same name as on the account offshore."

"W. Rekab?" Rich asked the two men.

"The last name is backward. Baker. W. Baker. Wally," I said.

John looked up sharply. Rich just shook his head.

"Wally was skimming money from Bart Hessor. I bet Mouse was going to give the information to Hessor but never completed the transaction." I looked down at the table. "And Bressler had gotten it from Mouse either the night that she died or the night before." *Did Mouse have sex with Hessor that night, before he killed her?*

"It gets better," Kick said. "Go on Buzz, you tell them."

Buzz smiled at the three of us. "We figured this out before we traced the third and fourth bank accounts with Wally's name. Eddie loved word scrambles so we played with the letters and numbers on the first page-" Rich nodded. "He used to work them with me. One time I got stuck baby-sitting him when Tom and I were working him for-" Rich stopped as a light went on in his head. "That's why Eddie thought I could figure it out." Rich reached out and grabbed the paper, and within one minute he had the words on the screen worked out.

"Remember 10th Street. Sex, drugs, and rock and roll." The message read.

"Eddie helped me bust a drug dealer when I was still on the Force," Rich informed us. "We barely missed nailing Hessor on that one. His lawyer got him off on a technicality." Rich looked at me. "Eddie must have found this on Mouse or something and sent a copy to me so I could get Hessor, as payment for helping him. He knew that Hessor killed Wally." Rich paused. "But why kill Scott and Mouse?" We were all stumped.

Rich leaned over and grabbed the phone. "Tom Hawkings please... No, have him call Rich Addison immediately. I've got news for him." Rich hung up the phone. He turned to the two computer guys. "Get out of here. You never saw this." He winked at them as they scrambled out of my office. "Thanks." He called down the hall at them. Rich looked at me. "Find out how we can pay them for their time, Mel."

I nodded.

"I'll give this information to Tom." Rich stood up painfully. "Good job, Mel. Again."

I smiled at him as he left the room. John was still sitting there thinking. "Is there a problem, John?"

"I don't know. Why use one caliber to kill two people and another caliber for the other two? Who did Mouse have sex with before she died? And the most nagging question, what's on the videotape?"

I stared into his eyes. True. What about the videotape? "Maybe it's not related."

John shook his head. "We don't know the full story yet. I'll bet you." He looked at me with his intense eyes. "Even if it were Hessor, why would he beat up on Rich and you? And why come back and ask for the video again?" He stood up and shook his head. "It's not over yet. Be extra careful now, Mel." With that, he walked out of my office.

My relief and excitement over solving the case vanished. John was right. It didn't all fit. There were too many loose ends. *Could I see Hessor killing in cold blood? Maybe. Someone was stealing his money. But, what did Bressler have to do with it? Did he just have the information that Hessor wanted? Or what? And why did Hessor still want it now that Wally was dead?*

I cursed softly to myself. *It's not over. It's only getting worse.*

CHAPTER 25

It was almost five o'clock by the time Tom Hawkings left the office after grilling Rich and me. We told him everything except where we had gotten the information on the bank accounts. Tom asked, but Rich told him that we couldn't divulge that information. He could get the same information with a court order, which was already in the works.

As Tom left, Pam handed me a couple of phone messages that had come in while he was interrogating me. I flipped through them fast. Two caught my eye. I dialed the first.

"Beth, it's Mel. Sorry it's taken me so long to return the call. It's been a different kind of day."

Beth laughed. "Yeah, Pam said you were being grilled by the cops."

I chuckled. "Again."

Beth hooted in laughter. "Feels like you're a teen again, huh? I got news for you."

"Oh really?"

"Yeah. I found out that Schnabel's mistress lives in Springfield. And that he almost never takes his wife to any meetings over there so that he can visit her."

"And the wife agrees to this?"

"I guess so. I hear she only wants the prestige that goes with being a mayor's wife. I wouldn't be surprised if she doesn't have a boy toy of her own," Beth said seriously.

"You don't by any chance have a name for this mysterious lady, do you?" I asked, hoping against hope.

"Sorry," Beth said disappointed.

"Still, you've found out a lot more than anyone else. Thanks." We quickly ended the conversation and I sat there thinking.

On a whim, I found my file on the case. I pulled out the sheet where I had detailed Wally's driving Schnabel to Springfield and the copies of the public filings. I dialed the number of the hotel, already formulating a story.

"Hi, I'm Trish Bellington in public accounting with Quincy City Hall. We're auditing the books. Is there someone who can look up some old accounts for me?" It was close to five and I was hoping that someone would still be able to help me. I figured everyone at City Hall had gone home for the day, so there wouldn't be anyone to corroborate my story, should the people in Springfield decide to call the mayor's office.

"Lucky for you, Mrs. Tellerman hasn't gone home yet. Let me put you on hold."

I waited with crossed fingers. I was good at lying, but even my acting could only go so far.

"Yes?" The lady was obviously annoyed.

"Sorry for calling so late. I'm Trish Bellington." I went through the spiel for her. "I'm swamped in this paperwork audit and the City Council is snapping at me to finish this before the meeting tonight. I really am sorry for calling so late in the day. I hate these old boy networks." I stopped, waiting for her reaction.

She actually chuckled. "I know the feeling. Like they care that we have a life, as long as they don't miss their golf games."

"Tell me about it. I just need one tiny bit of information from your records and I'll be done. Man, I need a break."

"What can I do for another overworked, underpaid fellow office worker?" Mrs. Tellerman sympathized with me.

I made a fist and brought it quickly back into my side. *Yes!* I wanted to shout, but instead I grabbed the paperwork in front of me. "Let's see. I show that Mayor Schnabel made a trip to Springfield with a stay over night at your hotel on June, uh, eighteenth of this year. Could you confirm that for me?"

"Just a minute. Let me boot the computer back up." I heard her moving in the background. "Good thing we have computers. I used to remember all of the paperwork involved in these sorts of transactions." She paused. "Okay, here we go. You said June eighteenth, hmmm, yes, usual suite assigned to him. One night only. Checked out at... Let's see, eight the next morning, but left his bags here for pick up by the limo service at five in the afternoon. They were picked up as scheduled."

"And that was-" I paused to make it sound like I was looking for something. I even shuffled some papers around. "Top Hat Limo that picked up and delivered the mayor?"

"Uh, the notation says... Yes. Top Hat Limo. The guy that signed for the bags was....What a signature! I'm pretty sure it says Wallace Danker, or maybe Banker."

I frowned. "Okay, just to make sure I've got all the information correct, like computers would be wrong-."

"You'd be surprised," Tellerman interrupted.

"True. I guess that's why they make us do these audits. Mayor Schnabel checked in on the eighteenth. Stayed the night in his usual suite. What about room service?" I paused again. "I know I've got that paper here somewhere." I shuffled some more papers around.

"Says he had dinner for two in the room along with breakfast. Also for two."

"Two?" I let slip before closing my mouth. I cursed at myself silently.

"Yes. Two. From the records here, he usually brought his wife."

I smiled. Beth did say that the mistress was in Springfield. "Oh yes, here it is. Yes, two. Okay." I paused. "Do you see anything else odd in the records? I have some sort of scribble here that I just can't read. I don't know why people can't learn to type."

Tellerman chuckled again. "Nothing else. Wait. There was a note about luggage. Let me get back to that screen. Here it is. The note says to place the luggage in a secure area. There were several important and expensive items in the luggage."

Expensive items? It was a one-day trip. Overnight. Just how much luggage did the mayor need for an overnight trip? "Hmmm, does it say how many pieces of luggage? My paperwork seems to indicate, uh, two pieces." I took a guess.

"Yes, one regular suitcase and a camera case. The camera case was to be put into the safe. The note says that it contained a video camera."

I was stunned into silence. *A video camera. Could it be?* I quickly got myself back together. "Exactly matches what I have here. Thank heaven. I'd hate to have to track more stuff down. I really appreciate your help, Mrs. Tellerman. Thank you."

"You're welcome. Call anytime. It's fun helping out another in need."

A video camera. Could that be where this video came from? But that made no sense. Wally had been killed because he was skimming money from Hessor. Yet, someone was determined to find that videotape.

I stared at my papers for a few more minutes before flipping to the note that I had made of the contents of the locker. *The Romeo reference. Could Wally have had the video and been trying to give it to Eddie?* That made more sense than his giving Eddie information to incriminate himself. *Could Mouse have been spying on Wally instead of Weedman? Where and what was this video?*

I glanced once more at the other phone message, but waited on calling Max back. Since my thoughts were working overtime, I needed to concentrate on the problem at hand. My eyes wondered back to Wally's note.

Romeo. A former lover? Mouse? I shook my head. No one had ever indicated that Wally had loved Mouse. I doubted that the message was referring to her. *What else could be implied by the Romeo reference?*

I closed my eyes and tried to remember the story from high school. Maybe it would have been easier had I paid more attention in Mrs. Leadbotler's English class. If memory served me right, that particular passage from the

Shakespeare play was spoken by Juliet on the balcony. But it would also have to be something Eddie would immediately recognize, too. I thought about both men and the information that I had gotten from all of their friends.

A balcony? Wally's room at his parent's house had a balcony. If he'd been selling drugs since his high school years, he would have needed some place to keep them. Some place secure from his parents. *Could there be some sort of place on the balcony to hide things?* Wally's mom had said that he had a key to the house and regularly checked on her.

I shook my head, what a long shot. *Was it worth invading her privacy to ask to see the balcony?* I rubbed my sore head and made a decision. As I stood up the phone rang. Without really thinking, I picked it up, since the office was empty. "Security Investigations."

"Mel, glad I caught you," Bressler said with a silky tone in his voice. "I got your message. I was hoping to find out how you are, and if you are up for a date tonight?"

I hesitated. I still needed to find out what Bressler knew. I tried to relax. "I'm fine and yes, I'd like a date tonight. Where do you want to meet at?"

"Well, I was thinking that I'd come and pick you up. I have a meeting with the mayor here in a couple of minutes. How about an hour or two?"

"Okay. I have an errand to run, then I'll be home. See you there, Tom." I hung up and quickly locked up the office. My jeep was parked close, so it wasn't long before I was on my way to check on the balcony theory.

***

"I really am sorry for the intrusion Mrs. Baker, but thank you for letting me see Wally's old room," I said as the lady showed me to the small bedroom that overlooked the garage roof. *This would be a great room to sneak out of at night. And I bet that's what Wally did all the time in high school. A quick jump to the garage roof, climb off the woodpile on the far side of the garage, and away you go.*

"It's my sewing room now," Mrs. Baker said. "I don't see why you want to see it. I don't understand."

I smiled. "It's just a theory of mine. Do you mind if I step out on the balcony? I want to know what it might have felt like to be here when Wally was a kid."

The lady motioned to the door and watched me with curious eyes.

I stepped out onto the small wooden structure. It was only about three feet wide and about four feet long. A wooden planter was nailed to the side of the railing off to the right. "Has this planter always been here?" It looked rather weathered.

"Oh, yes. Wally liked to grow flowers up here." She smiled. "He always brought me a couple when they were in bloom." Her eyes got misty. "I do miss my boys."

I gave her the usual platitudes as I checked out the planter box. As I was talking, sure enough, one side of the box opened up. I glanced in quickly to see her looking down at her sewing table. I looked inside the box and sitting there was a plastic box, the size of a videotape. I quickly took the tape and stuck it in the top of my pants over my hip. I entered the room and to distract her, I patted her shoulder as I closed the balcony door, keeping the side with the video away from her view. "Thank you for the look."

"I hope it helped," Mrs. Baker said wiping her tears. "I sure would like to know who killed my sons."

"I'm working on it, Mrs. Baker."

CHAPTER 26

As I pulled away, I dialed Rich's cell. I got his voice mail and left a message. He wasn't at home either. I left a message there too. Next I called up John. His cell phone immediately transferred me to his voice mail, which meant he had turned his cell off. He was probably tracking someone. Then I called Max. Another message.

By this time, I was almost home. I pulled into the parking lot and out of the corner of my eye, I caught sight of another car, black, pulling up to the curb down the block. I put it out of my head; probably just a patron of the bar. I hurried up to my apartment, desperately wanting to know what was on the tape.

I unlocked the door and took a quick look around as a precaution. I made sure the lock and the dead bolt were on before I moved into the living room to view the video. It looked innocent enough. There was no writing on the case.

At first the picture was grainy, as though someone had taped static off of a TV station, but in less than a minute, the picture cleared. I gasped in surprise, although I had already suspected what I was going to see. *If nothing else, I have verification that Schnabel has a mistress.* I snorted in laughter, but grew more sober when I realized that Rich and I had gotten beaten up because of this particular tape, and people had been killed because of it. I turned the sound down and sat watching it without really looking.

What did it all mean? I shook my head trying to put it together. Wally had rifled through the mayor's belongs apparently, and come across the video. Something didn't make sense. *Wally was embezzling money from Hessor. And now he was also blackmailing Schnabel? Was this the money that was to set them up for life?* I shook my head. *What significance did this tape have? Bressler didn't appear to know about it. If he was Schnabel's right-hand man, then he would have to know, right? He isn't that good of a liar. The tape is important, but why?*

A knock rattled my door. I jumped up and shut off the VCR. Looking around, I shoved the tape into a large manila envelope sitting on my coffee table. It had Craig's law firm's address on it and I quickly sealed it. I glanced at the door. This had to be Bressler. *Does he know about the tape?* I took a breath to calm myself and then opened the door. "Hey, Tom."

"Hi Mel," he said. His eyes panned across the room. "Ready to go?"

"Sure." I picked up my purse and the envelope. "I just need to drop this down at the bar. Max Bauer wanted some information from a law firm." We tromped down the steps. "I'll just be a minute." I found Cam on duty in the bar. With a quick look, I also noticed that Bressler followed me into the tavern. "Hey Cam. Can I ask you do to me a favor?"

"Sure, Sis. What?" Cam asked, leaning on the bar and giving Bressler a quick glance.

"Max Bauer wanted this information. ASAP. I'm heading out on a date with Tommy and I thought that I could leave this with you. Could you call Max and have him pick it up here?" I handed Max's card to Cam. I wanted to get the stupid videotape into the hands of the police as fast as possible so no one else, namely me, died because of it.

"Sure. Have fun. Don't do anything I wouldn't do!" Cam winked in a brotherly way.

"Shut up!" I said and smiled. I turned to see Bressler staring at me. "Ready?" We left, and as he opened his car door for me, I asked, "Where are we going?"

"I thought we'd visit a couple of old haunts of ours."

"Are you wanting to reminisce or trying to recapture some of your youth, Tom?" I asked with a laugh, but something was eating at me. Something I should have been able to pinpoint. My gut was in knots, my sixth sense screaming at me about something.

"Maybe a little of both," Bressler said, then closed the door and rounded the car. He got in, saying, "I thought we'd start off with a nice meal at one of the last places we would have been seen in as kids. Can you guess where?"

I noticed that we were headed toward the richer side of town. I chuckled at Bressler's glance. "We must be going to the country club."

"Yep. The Brookside Golf Club Restaurant. I called there after I talked to you on the phone."

"Tom, two things. One, aren't I slightly under dressed?" I was in my usual uniform of jeans and a baggy T-shirt. "And two, I thought that you needed reservations far in advance to eat there."

"Let me address your concerns in reverse order. I'm with the mayor's staff. I can get a table any time I want. The mayor holds a lot of working meals there and I'm well known. They wouldn't dare turn me away for fear that I'd tell Schnabel." Bressler smiled a big smile at me. "I find that incredibly funny, don't you?"

"Considering your past, yeah." Bressler's family had been one of the less-than-privileged families in town. I knew that Bressler's mom had been a maid in many of the houses in the golf club community. He always used to complain about how they treated her and how he hated all the rich people. "A little bit of payback?"

"Let's just say it's fun seeing some of the old timers' faces when I get introduced, and I let it be known that my mom used to work in the area. One old lady about spilled her drink when she realized that my mom used to pick up her used condoms and clean her toilets." He paused. "Funny thing about that, I know a lot of dirty little secrets about many of the elite at the club. I get treated with respect now."

I shook my head. Funny how life takes mysterious turns. I would've thought for sure that Tommy Bressler would have ended up in jail.

"I even took my mom there for a lunch with the mayor one time."

"No kidding! I bet that was fun."

"Mom got a big kick out of it. All those old ladies were hurrying over to say hi to us."

I was sure that he had arranged it just to make his mom feel good and to show up the Quincy elite. "And my first concern?"

"I figured that you'd be wearing a T-shirt, so I stopped by a friend's house and picked up a nice jacket for you to wear. Nice jeans are accepted most of the time, unless it's a formal affair. Besides, they won't say anything about your clothes while you're with me." Bressler smiled that old familiar 'I've put one over on them' grin.

I glanced at the backseat; the pretty linen jacket was hanging from a hook above the rear window. As I turned back to face the front, I caught sight of a black car following us. *Is that the same car that was parked at Dad's bar?* My gut told me it was. I was being followed. *But by who? Could it be Hessor?*

I thought about that even as I made small talk with Bressler the rest of the trip. I was still missing something. Maybe when I spoke with Rich and John, it would make sense. After all, they were the professionals here; I still felt like I was playing in waters too deep for me. Deep and more than dangerous, but I was going to tread that water until I found out what had happened.

I made a mental note that the black car followed us until we turned into the restaurant parking lot, then it swung around and left; anyone loitering around the club would be immediately apprehended. I was interested to see if we would pick up the tail again when we left the golf course.

The meal was as good as I expected, but all the way through it, I was hardly listening to Bressler. I was thinking about the video. Nothing seemed to fit. *Could all of this still be drug-related?*

I studied Bressler as he ate. He tried to seem relaxed and content, but his body language was wary somehow. His conversation was too forced, too polished. I knew he knew something. *The video?*

"Uh, Mel?" He shook me from my reverie. "I asked if you wanted some more wine."

"Sorry. I was just thinking. No thanks."

"You've been distracted all night. Still worried about that intruder?"

"I've been thinking about it," I admitted. "You don't remember anything else?"

Bressler shook his head. "I really don't think you have anything to worry about, Mel. Speaking of the incident, Mitch talked to me about it."

"Yeah?"

"I'm glad you decided to go to the cops."

I noticed that his last statement was more than a little forced. *What is that about?* He had volunteered to call the police at my place. I nodded as I finished off my food. "Yeah. I decided to at least get it on report. I doubt anything comes of it."

Bressler's eyes had drifted to the door. He made a disgusted face.

"What?" I had my back to the door and didn't want to turn around.

"Marion Williams just walked in and is talking with several of the waiters. He thinks that he can appeal to the workers here so they will vote for him. This is our turf. He should know that the mayor owns these people." His tone was tough and hard.

I watched his face. He was suddenly a different person. His eyes took on a controlled look that made me shiver. And his tone left no doubt in my mind; he would do anything to defend the mayor's territorial rights.

Turning slightly, I saw Williams making his way around the room, joking and shaking hands, a typical politician trying to garner votes. Slowly, he made his way over to us. If I didn't know better, I would have thought he was heading our way from the beginning.

"Good evening, Mr. Bressler. Ms. Addison." He smiled a Cheshire Cat's smile.

Bressler nodded back, adopting the same smile. "Mr. Williams."

I watched the interplay between them. There was a lot of animosity. The atmosphere was thick and heavy.

"What brings you into the clubhouse?" Bressler asked. "I don't recall seeing your name on the membership list." It was an obvious jab.

"I've been looking at a house here in the subdivision," Williams replied. "The manager of the club invited me to look around the facility anytime." Williams smiled and waved at another person across the room, then turned his attention back to Bressler. "I like it here. After I win the mayor's race, I think I'll move out here. It looks like a lot of influential people come here, but they'll have to get rid of the, uh, riffraff." Williams jabbed back.

Bressler's eyes hardened, but he said nothing. His smile stayed frozen in place.

"Well, have a good evening folks. Perhaps we'll meet again." Williams gave a nod and headed off to greet another table, slowly making his way out of the dining room.

"I'd like to give him a piece of my mind," Bressler said softly, his eyes never leaving the opposing candidate.

I was fascinated by the change in my old friend. Something about it scared me, to be honest.

Bressler finally turned his attention back to me as Williams left the room. His smile became more relaxed, yet there remained a strange, hard look in his eye. "When you're done, I have a special place I'd like to take you. I want to see if you remember some things."

"I forget very little."

His eyes changed just a bit, the wariness growing. "I remember."

***

The scene that greeted me made me laugh. Bressler had driven us to a park that overlooked the river from a bluff. Many times when I was hanging out with the group at Eleven Bottoms, Bressler would take me to this park where we'd sit and watch the river.

River View Park had changed little since then. The statue of some military guy, the basketball courts, tennis courts, and playground equipment hadn't changed; even the brick wall guarding the edge of the bluff was the same. As kids we had found a path down the steep incline to a place where we could sit unobserved from the top.

I turned to Bressler. "I thought for sure that you were taking me to Washington Park, the site of your biggest defeat." I winked .

"Yeah, I really wanted to win that bet with Bart. But there are too many people downtown." He looked out over the edge. "Besides, we had some good times down there." He pointed down the steep side.

I nodded. "You were a good kisser."

Bressler's eyes softened a bit when he looked at me. "And you were good too." He started to move toward me when his phone rang.

Saved by the proverbial bell. *Thank goodness!* I took a deep breath. I certainly didn't want to kiss him. If I had to kiss anyone, it would be Max.

"I need to take this," Bressler whispered to me. "I'll be right back."

I nodded as he walked a short distance away. He apparently didn't want me to hear whatever he was saying. He was visibly angry. "I thought I..." I strained to overhear, but he kept glancing at me then turned his back.

I didn't hear the man walk up behind me. "Don't move or say anything." The same whisperer from my apartment stuck something into my side. Without looking, I knew it was a gun. I swallowed my anger; I should have been paying more attention to my surroundings.

"Isn't that a tired, worn-out phrase?"

"Maybe, but nevertheless it's true. I will kill you, but first we need to talk." The man paused. "Not here. Move."

The gun put pressure on my side, and I moved around the slight curve and bushes as told. As I did, I glanced back at my captor. "You?"

CHAPTER 27

I was shocked into silence as Marion Williams pushed the gun harder into my side. "Just walk and don't make anyone suspicious."

I glanced around to see that there were two other couples in the area. One was playing basketball on the courts, and the other had just driven up in a car. I looked down at the gun. It was a semi-automatic nine millimeter. I looked back at Williams. "Why?"

Williams didn't answer me, but led me to his car parked at the very end of the wall. With a quick move, he pressed me against the car, quickly cuffed my hands behind my back, and opened the passenger door. "Now, you're going to get in the car, and you will do it quietly."

I shook my head. I knew better then to leave the scene. Dad had drilled that into us. *Stay where you were taken and make lots of noise, because you can bet that the next place will be much more secure for the perpetrator.* "No way, Mr. Williams. You can shoot me, but I'm not getting into your car." I started to move away from him, opening my mouth to yell when an electrical shock hit me, like I was struck by lightning. I felt as though my insides were on fire, and my legs collapsed under me. I heard Williams chuckle; he caught me as I fell.

"Yes, you will." Williams pushed me into his car. He locked the door and moved to the driver's side. "He saw," he said looking over his shoulder toward Bressler as he backed up. Williams accelerated away, barely in control of the car. "He saw me. You-" He turned his anger on me. "You took way too long to get in the car. Now Bressler is following me."

I struggled to regain some sort of coherent thought other than rage.

Williams smirked. "The stun gun's effects will wear off soon. You'll be fine. Now tell me, where's the videotape? I'll kill you this time if you don't tell me."

"I don't know what-" I slurred out.

"Wrong. I followed you to Baker's old house. There is only one reason for you to have gone there. You found the tape. I saw that you had something under your shirt when you came out. Where is it? I had your apartment checked after you left. Where is the video?"

I tried moving my legs around to get into a more upright position. It was hard with the car's swerving; he was trying to lose Bressler. But Bressler was a great driver. At one point he had wanted to race for NASCAR.

"Where is it?"

"The cops have it."

"That was my election! All this and now nothing!" He scowled. "Now you will die. I promise you."

I had a revelation. "You killed Wally and Eddie!" Both of them had been shot by a nine millimeter.

Williams struggled to keep control as we went around a corner. "Wally promised me the tape. He called and said that for the right amount of money, I could win the election. But he kept raising the price. He said the other side was going to pay for it too. He had contacted Schnabel. Wally was having us bid against each other. So I tried to convince him otherwise."

"Then why hire John and Rich?"

Williams grunted as he struggled to stay in front of Bressler. His eyes were riveted to the road. He accelerated with a sinister chuckle. "I knew Eddie knew about the tape. Wally said that someone else would take up where he left off. I knew about Eddie. But he was dumber than anything. Said he didn't know anything about the video. I found out he tried to hire Rich. I wanted to keep a close eye on the three of you. I was hoping that you'd find the tape or at least give me a good idea of where it was. But John wasn't real talkative. I was hoping he would spill about the murder case. He wouldn't. After talking with a bunch of people, they said that you were like a bulldog. That you never give up." Williams smiled. "And you didn't. Now, WHERE IS THE VIDEOTAPE?"

"I told you, I gave it to-" I began, but the car swerved sharply.

Once more he tried to regain control, but this time he couldn't straighten the wheel and the car flipped. I felt like I was in a dryer tumbling around inside the car. The car skidded to a stop, upside-down against a tree, and I lay there stunned for a second.

I looked over at Williams and he appeared to be unconscious. He was breathing, but he had a steady stream of blood running up his forehead. He was hanging upside down, strapped into his seat belt. I took stock of my body and realized that I was mostly okay. Nothing appeared to be broken.

The door groaned open and Bressler stuck his head into the car. "Are you okay, Mel?"

I nodded. "Yeah, I think. Can you get help for Williams? I think he's hurt, bad. And call the cops."

Bressler reached in and grabbed my arm. "I'll take care of it. Come on. Let's get you out of there."

With Bressler's help, I made it out of the car and onto the road. The night was already darkening, and I took several deep breaths to calm my nerves. Then I looked around. We were on the road not far from the turnoff to the levies and Eleven Bottoms. I gave out a big sigh and turned to Bressler who was staring at the overturned car. "Tom, can you get the keys to these cuffs out of Williams' pocket?"

Bressler merely looked closer at the car, his eyes narrowing.

"Tom!" I called to him. He appeared to be thinking really hard. "Looks like the election is a wrap now. Williams admitted to me that he killed Wally Baker. And I'm pretty sure he killed Eddie, too. The gun he used is probably the one in the car with him. I guess the mayor just got reelected. We need to tell the cops this-"

Bressler turned to me, his eyes vacant and blank. "Not quite, but close." He grabbed my arm and began pulling me toward his car.

"Um, Tom, the handcuff keys," I reminded him.

Bressler shook his head. "You won't need them." Bressler shoved me into his car and shut the door. He jumped into the driver's seat.

"Tom?"

"Where is the video, Mel? I need to know," Bressler said in the same low, scary tone he'd used in the restaurant. "Williams knew that you found it. Where is it, Mel?"

It all made sense when I caught a glimpse of the gun that slid out from under his car seat. It was a thirty-eight. I looked at it, then back to him. He was watching me as he turned and headed to the old campsite, the scene of Mouse and Scott Hiccome's murders. I swallowed. I was in big trouble. Big Trouble.

"Where is it, Mel?"

"I uh, I uh…"

"You found it, didn't you? I knew you would," Bressler said with a slight shake of his head. "Where is it?"

I swallowed again. "Even if I tell you, you're still going to kill me." I paused. "You didn't call for help, did you? You didn't call for an ambulance or the cops." Bressler just stared at the road ahead. "I think I'll take the video's location to the grave with me then." I took another deep breath. I guess I would soon be seeing Robbie again after all. "Rich and John will find it."

Bressler sighed, then as he crossed the first levy, he turned to me. "It doesn't have to be this way, Mel. Tell me, and the mayor will pay you to keep your mouth shut. He says he just wants the video back. He doesn't want any more killings. He says it's ruining the image of the city."

"No, he won't. You'll still kill me. Like you killed Mouse and Scott, because they knew."

Again Bressler didn't answer, he just drove.

The silence was creepy. I could feel the hairs on my neck rise as my thoughts jumped around. I couldn't seem to focus on any one in particular. Robbie and Craig kept intruding. I thought about Max and how I would miss him. Then I started getting mad. Not my usual volcano mad, but a too calm mad.

Bressler pulled into the campsite, then eased his way out of view of the road. He shut off the engine and looked at me with those hard eyes. "Yep. I had to kill them. Mouse contacted me with the offer to sell it back to the mayor. It would have ended at that, had they not already spoke to Williams. They got greedy. Scott saw the tape, so he had to go."

"And Schnabel knows all this?"

Bressler nodded. "He didn't like the way I handled it initially, but he finally approved. He was the one who said to stay on top of Williams. If I kept my eyes on everyone, then when someone found the tape, I could get it. But I knew you'd find it." He smiled a satisfied grin.

"What about Hessor? What was he buying from you?"

"You knew about that?" Bressler seemed surprised. "It doesn't matter. I got a disk off Mouse the night she died. I figured it tied in with Hessor and his drugs. I was selling it back to him. I planted the coke on her and Scott. The cops are trying their hardest to pin the deaths on Hessor." Bressler laughed at that, seemingly pleased with himself.

It all makes sense. I glanced around desperately. *I've gotta figure some way out of this.*

Bressler turned and looked off into the woods toward the river. "Mouse was always sweet. She always was, even that night."

"So you had sex with her before you killed her."

Bressler nodded. "One last time." He turned. "And I intend to do you too, before I kill you that is. But first, where is the video?"

"So, you're finally going be the big man at Eleven Bottoms, huh? Are you going to brag to Hessor about it?"

"I wasn't going to. But that is a good idea. Maybe I will. Bart has always had a thing for you. Still does. This past week he's been hitting up all of his people to find out who was behind your beating."

"So Bart had nothing to do this any of this?"

Bressler shook his head.

Suddenly it dawned on me. "You were the man in the skeleton mask."

"Yep. I really didn't want them to hurt you."

"And the break-ins?" I watched Bressler nod with a smile. "The other night in my apartment?"

"Williams. I saw him leaving. I knew since he had left, you hadn't told him. But I also knew that you were probably getting close." Bressler reached out and stroked my face with his fingertips. "Where's the tape, Mel?"

I shook my head at him. "What about the green Jag you said you saw?"

"I made that up. I thought that with a little bit of pushing, I'd get you on Bart's track, then he would be arrested for drugs and that would create more evidence that he killed Mouse and Scott." Bressler smiled. "I have to get the mayor re-elected. I'm needed by the next governor. It's a matter of ethics, don't you see."

"Ethics?" I shook my head. "No ethics at all, Tom. None. It's murder, plain and simple."

"Okay. I'll concede. Let's call it questionable ethics. Every politician has his skeletons. I'm burying another one with you. Where is the tape?"

I merely shook my head.

"Too bad." He grabbed the thirty-eight off the floor and stuck it in his waistband. As he exited the car, he looked around. Opening my door, he pulled me out and leaned me on the car using his weight to hold me there. Smiling, he began kissing me.

I tried to get away, but realized that my struggles were just making him more excited. So I stopped. And waited.

Bressler reached up and ripped my T-shirt so that it hung off my shoulders. His eyes came to rest on the very visible scar poking out of my bra. Bressler reached out and touched it, then he stroked it with his palm. His eyes met mine. "You'll soon be joining your son and husband."

I swallowed. *Hold on to the anger. Don't give in to the fear.* I looked at him, but said nothing.

Bressler stood up straight. He looked down at me, his eyes raking across my chest. "Nice. Tell me where the video is Mel, and I'll make your last minutes unforgettable."

"Like Mouse?"

"She didn't realize she was dying until she was almost dead," Bressler said excitedly. He reached for my jean snap but he made a mistake. As he bent down, I head-butted him. Bressler fell to the ground and I took off running. My head was swimming from the impact, but I was still alive. Alive enough to hear laughter behind me. It was hard, running with my hands cuffed behind my back.

"Okay, Mel. Let's make it a game. I've always liked that about you. I'll even give you a head start."

I skidded into the woods and kept moving, zigging and zagging between the trees as best I could. I felt something running down my face. I must have busted my head open when I head-butted Bressler. I wiped the blood out of my eyes with my shoulder and looked around, trying to get my bearings. *Okay. The main road is only five miles from here. I can do this, as long as I stay ahead of Bressler.*

There were crashing noises behind me in the woods. Bressler, making no attempt to be quiet, was getting closer, and I could hear him talking to me; he was telling me what he was planning on doing to me when he caught me. I swallowed a deep breath and as quietly as I could, moved further into the woods, dodging trees and hopping over snags.

A couple of minutes later, I paused to take another look at the area. I was currently heading more or less parallel with the river. I needed to head off to my right, more toward the road. If I could back track, I knew that I could then parallel the road and get help from a passing car. Not that there would be a lot of traffic on Bottoms Road that late at night, but at least I had a chance.

Noticing a large hollowed out tree still standing upright, I slipped inside of it to wait. It may have been a very good decision, or maybe it was a really dumb one. I needed help, though, soon. The pain in my head made it hard to organize my thoughts. And my right leg was beyond throbbing; it was shaking visibly. I consciously tried to slow my breathing and do it silently.

I heard movement coming my way.

"Oh Mel, you can go see Robbie again," he taunted me. "You can hold him in your arms. Do you remember what he felt like in your arms? What about your husband? Did you love him? How was he in bed? I bet I'm better. Come on, Mel. I'll make you feel like a woman again."

I squeezed shut my tearing eyes. As much as I loved my son, and as much as I wanted to be with him again, I did not want to die. Especially like this, at the hands of a maniac. I wanted to live. I wanted to go on with life. I just wanted to be out of the woods, to take the handcuffs off. And I wanted it more than anything else in the world. I mentally apologized to my husband and son. I wanted to live.

Bressler was getting closer. Any noise I made would instantly alert him to my presence. I stood stone-still and tried to slow my breathing even more. I could see him looking around and walking slowly, listening.

"I don't hear you anymore, Mel. Where are you?" He paused to listen. "Come out, Mel. I really want you." Bressler chuckled. "You wouldn't try to swim out of here, would you? I'd still get you in the water." Bressler turned toward the river, bringing him right past my hiding place.

I cursed mentally and tried to make myself as small as possible, tried to become part of the wood itself. If he even looked the wrong way, he might see me.

Bressler continued toward the river without looking back. He continued to taunt me. I could see the gun in his hand. The Tommy of old was long gone, replaced by this lunatic I didn't know.

When I heard him down by the river, I slipped out of the stump and headed back toward the main camp. It was my only hope.

The moon was full, which was both good and bad. Good, because it allowed me to negotiate my way in the woods making less sound, but it was bad because it also allowed Bressler to see me. And he had all the advantages.

I stopped to wipe the blood from my head again when I heard crashing through the woods behind me. I could tell he was now heading my way.

"Hi, Mel. I hear you." Bressler was almost yelling. "Thought you could backtrack on me? You're good, Mel. But I'm better. Give up and surrender to me."

I ran faster. I didn't care about making noise or crashing into branches or shrubs. I hit a path leading back to the camp area and took off even faster. My breath was coming in gasps. I was hobbling on my injured leg and I knew it would give out on me soon. I could hear the crashing getting closer behind me. I was losing ground fast.

My brain started to accept that fact that I was going to die. Die a horrible and tragic death. I almost whimpered, but then I remembered Wally, Mouse, Scott, and lastly, Eddie. His face flashed in front of my eyes. I was not going to die without a fight. *Leave enough evidence at the crime scene. Max will figure it out.*

Max.

I turned a corner in the path, hoping I would be blocked from Bressler's line of sight by the thick vegetation, giving me a few seconds of precious time to get a bigger lead. It wasn't much, but hope was all I had. It would have to be enough, because there was no way I was going to let Bressler and Williams win.

As I moved past a tree by the edge of the path, a strong arm swiped at me, stopping my progress instantly. A hand clamped down on my mouth. I instantly struggled against this new, unexpected threat.

"Calm," someone murmured into my ear as I was dragged behind the tree. The voice seemed familiar. I stopped fighting, and turned to see John smiling down at me.

John inclined his head to my ear again. "Call to him." He looked over his shoulder and nodded, then murmured, "Bring him closer."

I followed his gaze and saw Max standing behind a tree. His eyes locked with mine and I could see him let out a breath. Behind him, I saw two more cops, also hiding. I smiled up at John as he released me from his arms.

I stepped back out onto the path in plain view, taking a deep breath to calm myself. Bressler paused on the path in front of me, about fifty yards away. "Okay, Tom. I give up. I'm over here." He looked surprised, and I teased, "Come and get me, if you think you can handle me." I smiled at him in the moonlight. I shifted my weight, barely standing on my right leg, which throbbed and shook.

I heard Bressler stop, take a deep breath, and laugh. "Oh good, you decided to join in the game. This is going to be great. I'll be the best you've ever had, or at least your last." He strode toward me, and toward the group of waiting cops.

I turned my head slightly to see Max still standing behind a tree, waiting. He whispered something into a portable radio, then glanced at me, but quickly turned his attention back to Bressler hurrying up the path.

Suddenly Bressler stopped. He was only about ten yards from me. His eyes narrowed in the moonlight as he looked around the woods. "What dirty trick do you have up your sleeve this time, Mel?"

I smiled. "I decided to face you. Besides, I told you I'd nail you to the wall, didn't I?"

At that instant, John appeared from out of nowhere and stuck his gun to Bressler's temple. Bressler moved just a fraction of an inch, then froze. His eyes panned across the trees near me as the cops all stepped out with their guns pointed at him. Bressler's eyes came back to me as he dropped his gun to the ground. He scowled.

"You pushed the envelope too far this time, Tommy. I guess you never did learn." I sneered.

Bressler cursed several times and took a slight step forward, but at that point the police officers were already handcuffing him. He gave me a hard glare, but said nothing more.

I felt Max move in next to me and I turned to face him. With a smile, he reached out and used his hand to wipe the blood from my cheek.

"You need to get looked at, Mel. We have an ambulance waiting on the hard top." Max's eyes were smiling in the moonlight. He quickly took off the cuffs.

The cops escorted Bressler past us. He scowled at me, but said nothing.

Max stripped off his outer shirt, then held it out for me to slip into. After I had put my arms into the sleeves, he buttoned several of the buttons for me, covering me up, all the while staring into my eyes.

I looked around; everyone was gone. Max took me by the arm and we walked slowly toward the camp, very slowly. As I hobbled, I rubbed my sore wrists. I began to shake all over.

Max put his arm around and said with a smile, "Adrenaline. Gotta love it."

I chuckled. "Yeah, and I'll sleep like the dead tonight."

Max's expression sobered. "Don't say dead. It was almost a reality."

My hobble turned into a mostly one-legged hop. We were almost to the clearing when I stepped and my leg gave out. I grabbed at Max, but he already had a hold on me. "Thanks." Max just smiled and kept his arm around me. I put my arm around his waist for support.

I stopped before leaving the woods. We could see and hear the others, but we were still hidden by the shrubbery. Max looked at me and I looked around, then at him. "I wanted to let you know, as one of my best friends said a short time ago-" I smiled. "It's time to be moving on. I need, no I want-" I stopped as a strange look appeared on his face, one of maybe regret and sadness.

"For me, too."

I couldn't speak for a second. "So, you're heading back to the west coast?" My heart suddenly felt very heavy.

"I leave in three days. I've already resigned." He gave my shoulder a squeeze. With his head, he nodded to the ambulance waiting near the cars; apparently someone had called it down to the camp area. "You need medical help. I'll come see you at the hospital. They'll need to take your statement there."

His news had hit like a hard punch to my solar plexus. *Don't cry. Think about the case.* "Did you find Williams? He kidnapped me from River View Park."

"Yeah. He's in serious condition, but the EMTs were optimistic."

"How did you find me here?"

"You're going to the hospital. We'll talk later." He gave me a light kiss on the lips and then started us walking again, letting me use him as a crutch. "Her right leg is injured from a previous accident, and it gave out. Take care of her, guys." He let go of me as the two paramedics each took a side.

I watched as he walked over to the group of police officers gathered around the cars, talking with John. With a sigh, I went with the paramedics. Now I hurt. All over. Again. And more than just physically.

"Ma'am?"

"Yeah?" I turned my attention to the paramedics as they strapped me down and loaded me into the ambulance. One of them began asking me questions. I'm sure I answered them, but my mind was completely occupied. I began to cry. Not sobbing, but just a soft, gentle weeping.

CHAPTER 28

The hospital was holding me overnight for observation. I had a significant concussion, from the car accident and head-butting Bressler. Coupled with the other two previous injuries, they apparently warranted the stay. I hate hospitals.

After getting settled into my room, I was interviewed for a long time by Tom Hawkings. He was extremely happy with how the cases had worked out, although I did get a slight reprimand for tampering with the evidence in the locker.

I was starting to relax, trying not to dwell on the new turn in my life. The painkiller was making it easy to do; my brain felt like mush. I sighed, remembering this feeling from my other accident, and for once I was grateful for it. I closed my eyes and saw Eddie Baker again.

"Well, at least we helped you," I whispered to myself. I thought about my life. *Craig, the rat bastard. Robbie. My baby. My only child.* I squeezed my eyes tighter. I didn't want to cry again, but the painkillers were making it hard not to. My heart twisted.

Max. I would miss him. Just as I thought my heart might be on the path to healing, I had sprung another hemorrhage. The tears flowed down my cheeks.

The door opened. Max hovered in the doorway. "You might as well come in. When I do go to sleep, I won't wake up for a long time." I tried for a light tone in my voice.

Max walked to my bedside and took my hand in his. His eyes radiated worry, like a deep blue churning river. "Are you okay? How do you feel?"

"Like I got run over."

"You did good."

I smiled at him, trying to keep the mood light. I didn't want him to see how much his leaving was affecting me. "So tell me, how did you find me?"

"Well, actually, we had help from an unexpected source."

"Yeah?"

Max nodded. "I got Cam's call and hurried over to the bar. After getting the video, I viewed it, then I headed into the office. Hawkings had arrested Hessor on murder charges, but Hessor was, of course, denying that he did it. I spoke with Hawkings at length. We called in Rich and John. Between the four of us, we began to suspect that Hessor might not be guilty of murder. We confronted him with this and as soon as he heard that Bressler had taken you out on a date, he suggested we check the Bottoms campsite. He apparently had been working on getting information on your beating and said he suspected Bressler. From past experience, Hessor said that Bressler would probably take you someplace familiar."

I shook my head. I had been saved by a drug dealer.

"John and I came upon Williams' car. He was conscious and we, uh, *convinced* him to tell us about Wally and Eddie. Williams freely told us about kidnapping you and being chased by Bressler.

When we got to the camp, the car was there, but no one was around. To be honest with you, I was very-" Max stopped with an almost embarrassed look. He cleared his throat. "Anyway, John tracked the two of you to the woods." Max shook his head. "He's really good at it."

"John was in Special Forces, the Army Rangers."

"Yeah, he said that. And you know the rest."

I nodded and yawned. "What about Schnabel?"

Max shrugged. "The tape will probably break up his marriage, to say the least."

"No criminal charges?"

"We can't prove he knew about the murders."

"He did. Bressler told me he approved of the killings."

"Bressler claims he acted alone. The mayor denies all knowledge."

"So he'll skate?"

"Maybe. Maybe not. All the evidence isn't in yet. Besides, I doubt the public will stand for a lying, cheating mayor."

"You don't know much about politics, do you?" I yawned again.

Max stood up and kissed me on the cheek. "Go to sleep. I'll see you later." He walked to the door as I settled into the bed further. Glancing back, he smiled. "You did good, Mel. You're still a snooping sneak, but you did good."

"Thanks," I mumbled as my eyes closed. I was suddenly very tired, but happy. Max's smiling face floated in front of me as I fell asleep.

***

I walked up the sidewalk to the open door of Max's apartment building. His dark green Trooper was at the curb, and it looked like it was packed for travel. I had been kept in the hospital for two days and finally convinced them to let me go if I promised to take it easy for several days.

I tapped lightly on the open door. "Max?" I walked into the apartment.

He appeared from the back bedroom with a surprised look, then a smile. "Convinced them to let you out, huh? How are you feeling today?"

"Much better, now. I was hoping I hadn't missed you." I tried to keep the smile on my face, but I was sad.

"I was going to stop by the hospital on the way out of town." His eyes narrowed and his mouth turned down. "Well, I guess this is good-bye."

I nodded, glancing down at the floor, trying to stay composed. My heart felt heavy, as though it was working hard to beat. Finally I looked up at him. "Yeah. Good luck in the new job." I tried to put some enthusiasm into my tone, but it sounded flat, even to me.

Max said nothing for a few minutes. He just stared into my eyes. "You know, California's not *that* far away. You can come out and visit me anytime."

"Yeah." I hesitated. "Well, I'd better get going. Mitch is waiting to take me to the office to fill out some insurance forms, then it's home for me to rest." I lifted my arm and showed him that I still had my hospital wrist-tags on.

"Really Mel, come out and visit. Or maybe I'll come back here-" He smiled and looked around. "Nah!"

"I'll think about it." I hesitated again. Then on a sudden impulse, I stepped toward him and kissed him.

He was tentative, his kiss gentle, until I pressed for more.

His hands pulled me into him, snuggling up close as he started massaging my lips with his. Warm. Succulent. He moved his hands up my back and into my hair, holding me captive between firm hands and honey-smooth lips.

I moaned softly at his aggressive, yet gentle touch. I brought my hands to his waist, and with regret, gave him a slight push.

He pressed his lips harder against mine again, then slowly, ever so slowly, pulled them away. His hands were still entwined in my hair, holding me. Our eyes locked as his fingers slowly traced down my jawline. I shivered.

A smile grew on his face. He knew the reaction he was causing in me. Still only inches apart, he leaned in and gave me another sweet, tender, but short kiss. We parted, both of our hands lingering as long as possible.

I took a deep breath. "I wanted to know if you were a good kisser. No disappointment there." I took my hands off his waist and let them drop to my sides.

Max smiled, his one hand cupping my jaw. With the other he wiped his lips with his finger. "Hmmm. I knew you would be but... That was-" He slowly ran his fingers across my lips, then down my face.

I chuckled.

"Now you have to come out and visit. If I wasn't due on duty soon, I'd stay and just fly out later." He actually seemed to be considering it.

I leaned in and gave him a kiss on the cheek. "I'm not ready for the whole 'shooting match' yet. Soon, but not now. I still need to work out some things, but thanks for helping me this far."

"Okay. If that's how you want it, but I think it would have been nice."

"Bauer, you will never change. I hope." I held out my hand and we shook. I turned and headed out of the apartment. I needed to move fast, or I might change my mind and ask him to stay.

"Mel?"

I turned back to look up the sidewalk.

"Can I call you? You know, can we still be friends?"

"Yeah. I'd like that." My eyes met his, and he didn't need to say anything else. I smiled and turned away. Slowly, I walked down to the waiting car. As Mitch drove away, I waved at Max who had walked out to the curb.

I was sad, but I knew that it was the right thing to do. Although I was starting to finally accept the hand that life had dealt me, I wasn't ready for another relationship. Not yet.

"Are you okay, WT?" Mitch asked me quietly after a few minutes.

"Yeah. He's a good guy."

Mitch chuckled. "He fell hard for you. We talked about it one time. I told him that it would take time for you to get over Craig. He said he understood."

"Yeah." The rest of the trip passed in silence.

When we got to the office Pam greeted me with a smile. "Looking good, Mel."

"Yeah, thanks." I smiled back, but it was a forced smile. I was still sad from the parting with Max.

"Back here, Mel." I heard Rich call to me from his office. I appeared at the door to see Rich still sporting a nice shiner.

"So, what sort of stupid forms do I need to fill out this time?" I asked my brother as I sat in the nearest chair.

Rich smiled. "Just one, then John will run you home." He pushed the paper to the edge of the desk. "But first, we have a question for you."

I merely looked at him expectantly.

John cleared his throat. "We were wondering if you would like to apprentice with us as a detective?"

I turned my stunned look from Rich to John and back again. "What?"

John chuckled. "You're good at this, Mel. We picked up several new cases and we could use the help. Do you want to stay on with us?"

I looked at Rich. "Well, I don't know. I'll need to think about it."

Rich laughed. "She's hooked, John. She's hooked."

I smiled. Rich was right. I was hooked.

Dedication

This book is dedicated to many people. First, to the doctors and nurses who saved my life during my cancer treatment. Without you, I wouldn't be alive. Thank you so very much. For my writing buddies, Mary, Cheryl, and Ray, you guys helped me get to where I am today. Without you, I wouldn't be writing this dedication page. Also to my family, who supported me and encouraged me every step of the way.

Thanks to the former Chief of Police in Quincy for answering my questions. And a big thanks to the people of Quincy, Illinois. It really was and is a great place to grow up. It's not nearly as dangerous as the book makes it out to be. Hey, this is fiction after all.

But mostly, I'd like to dedicate this book to my mother who passed away in 2007. She died before my dream was fully realized. She totally believed in me from when I started writing at the age of nine. I did it, Mom! This book is for you.